The Assassin Johannesburg

JIM WEST

Other Books by Jim West

DNAlien

DNAlien II

DNAlien III

Genocide by GMO

Living Within a Strange Mind Vol I

Living Within a Strange Mind Vol II

The Making of an Assassin Atlanta

The Assassin Baltimore

The Assassin Chicago

The Assassin Denver

The Assassin El Paso

The Assassin Fort Worth

The Assassin Galveston

The Assassin Honolulu

The Assassin Indianapolis

Many thanks to my long-time friend John Fleenor for his ever-ready wit and sarcastic comments as I muddled my way through this most recent attempt at writing. Forever grateful.

Chapter 1

Jim Lashley followed the rest of the flight crew into the hotel for the 12-hour layover before heading to Los Angeles the next morning. As the First Officer (FO) of American Airlines flight 2475, it had been his leg to fly from Dallas Fort Worth Airport (DFW) to Chicago O'Hare International Airport (ORD), and it had been as boring and routine as ninety percent of the flights always were.

"Still want to meet for dinner?" Captain Mike Rhine asked as he signed in for his room.

"Sure, as long as you're paying," Jim said, as they watched the Flight Attendants head for the elevator.

"Just when did I agree to buy your dinner?" Mike asked as Jim signed in.

"When you asked, 'Want to go have dinner when we get in?'," Jim replied. "When someone asks me out to eat, I consider it an offer to pay. But I must warn you, I don't go all the way on the first date."

"Excuse me, sir," the hotel clerk said, looking at Jim. "I believe I have a message for you, if you are Jim Lashley."

"I am Jim Lashley," Jim acknowledged. "Unless there are more Jim Lashley's coming here today, I'm going to hazard a guess and say the message is meant for me."

The clerk handed Jim an envelope and agreed that he was the only Lashley registered at the hotel for that day. "Enjoy your stay, gentlemen," the clerk said, as they took their keys.

"What do you think the message is?" Mike asked as he hit the elevator button for the fifth floor, where their rooms were located.

"Probably a contract for a new reality show I've been asked to star in," Jim said, as the elevator doors slid open.

"And what the hell kind of reality show would you be starring in?" Mike asked, shaking his head, knowing that there was no such show.

"The show is going to be called 'True Lives of Trophy Husbands,'" Jim said with a straight face. "I suffered the traumatic life of being a trophy husband for years.

"This show is going to expose the horrifying effects of being just arm-candy for an uncaring woman," Jim continued, as they reached their floor.

"Good lord," Mike replied, shaking his head as they headed down the hall to their rooms. "Where do you come up with this shit?"

"It's a gift," Jim answered as he used his key to unlock the door to his room. "Thirty minutes?"

"Sounds good," Mike said, opening his door. "See you there."

Jim tossed his suitcase on the bed, tore open the envelope, and read the simple statement, *Call room 345 as soon as you get in.*

Hanging his jacket in the closet and removing his shaving kit from the suitcase, Jim set it in the bathroom and picked up the phone from the desk beside the bed.

"Hello, Jim," came the voice as soon as the phone was answered. "How was the flight?"

"Good evening, General," Jim said, shaking his head. "To what do I owe the pleasure?"

"Just thought I'd see if I could have a nice dinner with you since I'm stuck in Chicago for the night," Gene told him. "Do you think you can spare a couple of hours for an old friend?"

"I agreed to meet the Captain for dinner," Jim replied. "But I'm sure he wouldn't mind having you join us."

"That sounds good to me," Gene told him. "I'll head down to the restaurant and get us a table. Are any of the flight attendants going to join us?"

"No," Jim answered, as he removed his starched white shirt with the three stripes on the epaulets and hung it in the closet. "Just the three of us."

"Excellent," Gene replied. "I'll see you in a few minutes."

Jim finished undressing and took out a pair of starched Wrangler jeans and a clean, knit short-sleeved shirt. Taking a moment to call Marie before heading downstairs, he told her he was having dinner with Gene.

"What's the General doing in Chicago?" she asked.

"I don't know," Jim answered. "Black Water keeps him moving all over the world. It never surprises me when he shows up wherever I am."

"What do you think he wants with you this time?" Marie asked.

"Possibly just dinner," Jim answered. "I haven't heard from him in a month or so, and this just might be a coincidence."

"Oh, I don't think Gene has coincidences," Marie replied. "There's always a reason for everything that man does."

"Let's not get into that," Jim said, as he finished dressing. "If there's something he wants, I'll let you know when I find out. Until then, let's just assume Gene and I will have a nice dinner and catch up on what's been going on in his world."

"Okay," she said. "Tell him I said hello and hope he can find time to swing by for dinner at Dad's place soon. And I'll try not to see something ominous every time he just shows up unexpectedly."

Chapter 2

When Jim walked into the restaurant, he spotted Gene at a table against the far wall, as was his usual habit. Walking over, he waved to the maître d signaling he had a table and didn't require any assistance.

"General," Jim said, as he approached the table and Gene stood to shake hands. "It's good to see you."

"And you as well," Gene said, motioning for Jim to have a seat. "How's the trip going?"

"Pretty mundane," Jim answered as a waiter appeared at his side. "Everything went smoothly. Clear skies. Very few traffic delays. And I'll have Cinnabon's for breakfast in the morning."

"How do you know that?" Gene asked as Jim told the waiter he wanted a glass of unsweetened tea.

"The Captain let me pick the legs I wanted to fly," Jim said, smiling. "I said that would be great, but I wanted whoever flew the first leg of the day to get Cinnabon's for the crew if the airport had them.

"So, the flight sequence today was Dallas to Chicago, my leg," Jim explained. "Then tomorrow we fly from

5

Chicago to Los Angeles, the Captain's leg, and back to Chicago, my leg.

"Then we just fly from Chicago back to Dallas on the third day," he continued.

"Let me guess," Gene said. "The Captain will fly every leg from Chicago, the first flight of the day, other than Dallas, and the only airport with a Cinnabon is Chicago. Mighty smooth, making sure the Captain flies each leg from Chicago."

"I'm just a poor little First Officer," Jim told him. "The Captain makes all the money and can afford to buy a couple of treats for the crew at the start of the day. And it's only twice."

"What would you have done if you weren't flying out of an airport with a Cinnabon?" Gene asked, as Jim waved to Mike as he came into the restaurant.

"Well, then I chose the leg with the best meal," Jim answered, standing to introduce Mike to Gene.

"Mike, this is an old friend of mine, General Gene Barker," Jim said, as Gene stood. "He was the Commander of Marine Aviation in Vietnam when I was there.

"Gene, this is Mike Rhine, currently babysitting me as I fumble my way across the skies of America," Jim finished.

"Nice to meet you, General," Mike said, shaking Gene's hand.

"Please, it's just Gene. I'm retired now and have hung up all my uniforms," Gene said, returning the handshake. "Please have a seat and join us for dinner."

"Thanks," Mike said, taking the seat across from Gene. "I guess you two have known each other for several years now."

"More than I'd like to remember," Gene replied, signaling for the waiter. "While we're waiting for our meals, would either of you like an adult beverage?"

"That's nice of you to ask," Jim answered. "However, American Airlines does not allow drinking on layovers."

"What Jim is referring to is a long-standing tradition of no alcoholic beverages when the layover is less than eight hours, the FAA's guideline for time from a beverage to flying," Mike explained. "Since we have a full twelve hours, we are well outside of the minimum time.

"So, to put it into language that even Jim can understand, I'd enjoy a pre-dinner martini," Mike said, as the waiter nodded his understanding.

"I'd love a Glenlivet, fourteen-year-old, single malt," Gene told the waiter. "Neat."

"Yes, sir," the waiter said, and looked at Jim, asking, "And for you, sir?"

"Jack and Coke," Jim replied. "In a tall glass with ice, please."

"I'll have your drinks right out," the waiter told them. "Will you be ready to place your dinner orders when I return?"

"Definitely," Gene answered for them. "And please put it on my room bill, if you don't mind."

"It'll be taken care of, sir," the waiter said as he turned to walk away.

"Thank you very much," Mike said, glancing at Gene as he picked up a menu. "I certainly didn't mean for you to buy my dinner tonight."

"Not a problem," Gene replied. "I heard Jim say you were going to be buying the Cinnabons for the crew in the morning, so I thought I'd chip in."

Mike looked at Jim and asked, "Does O'Hare have a Cinnabon's?"

"Not sure," Jim answered, with a questioning look on his face. "Guess we'll see in the morning."

"I'm guessing you picked the legs you're flying so I would have each flight out of here," Mike said, laying down his menu. "And twice. You knew Chicago had a Cinnabon's and made sure I flew the first leg of the day from here."

"I'd keep a close eye on him, if I were you," Gene said, laughing. "I've known him for several years, as you mentioned. And you'll find out that he always has an ulterior motive when given too many choices. Just beware in the future."

Chapter 3

As their drinks arrived, Gene turned to Mike and asked, "What did you do before American?"

"Marines," Mike answered. "I did two tours in 'Nam in F4s."

"Small world," Gene added. "I guess you know Jim had a tour in F4s."

"He said he flew F4s in Vietnam," Mike replied. "Is that how you met?"

"Sort of," Gene replied, glancing at Jim. "I met him when he was just a regular mud grunt living the life of adventure. But I'll let him tell you that story."

As the waiter returned to take their orders, Mike asked, "You said you were retired, what brings you to Chicago?"

"I work for a little company called Black Water," Gene answered, after placing his order and handing the waiter his menu.

"I've heard of them," Mike replied, handing back his menu after ordering. "Some connection with the CIA, isn't there?"

"Sometimes," Gene clarified. "Just as there is an occasional connection to various international companies or organizations that need our expertise.

We basically provide security services or design security systems for private companies or foreign governmental entities."

"I believe I heard something involving Black Water in connection with a prison in Iraq," Mike said, taking a sip of his martini. "Some sort of tie to the CIA who ran the prison."

"There's always some conspiracy theory out there," Gene replied. "I'm sure you're referring to Abu Ghraib, and I know of no actual involvement. The company did contract for some guard operations at an American governmental station in Afghanistan, and did some security work in Iraq accompanying CIA officers.

"No, most of our contracts deal with security systems design or implementation. Occasionally, we provide security for visiting dignitaries, both US and foreign, when traveling around the world," Gene finished by taking a sip of his scotch and looking at Jim.

"I neglected to ask, but how's Marie?" Gene asked, changing the subject.

"She's fine," Jim said, smiling at Gene's smooth transition. "I told her I was meeting you for dinner, and she wants to know when you're coming back to Texas."

"Actually, I have to be down there this weekend," Gene replied. "How about if we have some steaks at your house? I'll pick up some Wagyu steaks, and you guys can add whatever else you want."

"That sounds good to me," Jim answered. "But I think Marie wants to take you to Siciliano's. Her dad must have said something about you avoiding his restaurant."

"How about a compromise?" Gene said. "I'll get enough steaks for everyone, and Tony can cook them for us."

"I'll ask," Jim told him, as their meals arrived. "Maybe Tony will toss in a couple of lobsters and some of that Italian roasted asparagus with Parmesan that he likes to make."

"That sounds great," Gene replied, as the last dish was delivered. Lifting his glass, he said, "Here's to good friends and good food."

"Amen," Mike said, lifting his glass.

"I'll drink to that," Jim said, lifting his. "Not to plagiarize, I have to say that line is from the movie *Arthur* with Dudley Moore."

"At least you didn't use that old Popeye line about drinking to swimming with baldheaded women," Gene said, laughing.

"It was originally about swimming with bowlegged women," Jim corrected him. "But that was changed due to some social stigma. I believe at one time it was common to refer to ladies of the evening as bowlegged women, or something like that."

Gene looked at Mike and said, "You have to be very careful around Jim. He comes up with some of the most obscure things during an otherwise normal conversation."

"I've noticed that," Mike agreed. "Half the time, I don't know if his story is factual or some long-winded means of telling a joke."

"Just because I try to interject a little humor as I pass along some worthwhile information is no reason to belittle me," Jim said, shaking his head. "And you know I'd never knowingly spread a falsehood."

"Well, Mike, since I believe you two will be flying together for the month, I suggest you brief all of the flight attendants on Jim's particular brand of humor," Gene said, setting his glass back on the table. "At least he has enough intelligence to stay away from most of his slightly off-color stuff around the gentler sex."

"I don't think you can refer to most of the flight attendants as the *gentler sex*," Jim countered. "Some of those ladies are as rough as bark on a mesquite tree. Too many years of putting up with some of the rudest people I've ever met."

After finishing their meals, Gene said, "Mike, it was nice to meet you, and I hope you can keep Jim in line for the remainder of your trip."

"Not a problem," Mike said, shaking Gene's hand. "I set low standards, and Jim seems to struggle but usually meets them. It's been a pleasure meeting you and thank you for the most enjoyable dinner I've had in a long time."

"I'll see you in the morning, Mike," Jim said, standing, knowing that Gene wanted to discuss something and it wasn't for public knowledge.

As Mike headed out of the restaurant, Gene said, "Why don't we head to my room, and I'll give you a little light reading material that might interest you?"

Chapter 4

When they got to Gene's room, he asked, "What do you know about Johannesburg?"

"Not much," Jim admitted. "Some big city down in South Africa."

"Yeah, that it is," Gene replied, pulling a file from within his briefcase, which was lying on the small desk in the room. "The largest city in the Republic of South Africa. The current population is over five million people.

"When you throw in the surrounding urban areas of almost fifteen million people, you have a monster megacity," Gene added as he handed Jim the file.

"I've included much of the history of South Africa in the file," he continued. "You don't really need to know much about the people who lived there over one hundred thousand years ago but look at the group known as Boers.

"There is quite a bit of information in the file that you can read if you care to," Gene informed him. "But for now, I'll give you a quick history lesson on how South Africa came to be so important.

"In the early days of the silk trade, traders had to cross most of Europe, Persia, India, Mongolia, and other countries of Asia in order to get to China," Gene continued.

"Then the Portuguese sought a route around the bottom of Africa," he told Jim. "Much as the Europeans sailed west from Europe looking for a trade route to Asia. You'll see numerous parallels with our own founding as you read the information.

"Anyway, Portuguese explorers had already traveled down the west coast of Africa and had detailed maps of the area," Gene explained. "In 1488, they rounded the Cape of Good Hope. In 1652, the Dutch East India Trading Company established a trading post in Cape Town.

"This post was to supply the ships now traveling the ocean route to replace the arduous Silk Road," he further explained. "They brought in farmers who would supply the ships as well as the growing population.

"These farmers, mostly Dutch and known as Free Burghers, established farms in what became the Dutch Cape Colony," Gene said. "Not to show the parallel, but we established colonies before we became a nation.

"To continue, the British invaded around 1795 and again in 1806. Causing many of the farmers, or Boers, to migrate to the interior of South Africa and establishing Boer Republics," he added.

"Then diamonds and gold were discovered in South Africa, which led to conflict with Britain, and open warfare broke out," Gene continued. "Again, some semblance with our original colonies, ongoing issues with Mother Britain.

"The British defeated the Boers in 1910, and the Union of South Africa was created as a self-governing dominion of the British Empire," he explained. "It was comprised of four separate colonies and finally became a nation state in 1934 and a Republic in 1960.

"During this period, 1948-1994, a system of racial segregation and white minority rule, known as apartheid, was imposed," Gene said. "Much like our history dealing with our slaves.

"In 1994, the African National Congress, or ANC, gained a majority in a democratic election and ruled until recently losing Parliament," Gene finished. "This was the beginning of the problem we have today."

"And just what is our problem today?" Jim asked. "I see the parallels you've described. I see where a country, such as ours and theirs, wanted freedom from Britain.

"What I don't see is why we want to get involved in the internal politics of a country half a world away," he said. "And even if you explain why we're getting involved, I'm under the impression that international contracts, assuming that's what we're discussing, are the responsibility of Dark Water.

"Not to remind you of my status, but I work for Muddy Water, which is concerned with domestic issues only," he finished.

"Let's see if I can't clear this up for you," Gene replied. "First, you work for Black Water, and they assign you where they determine they need you. If you'll remember, your first assignment with Black Water was a Dark Water contract.

"As to why it's our problem?" Gene lectured, "Because Black Water made it our problem. And they were handed the problem by our government.

"I'll see if I can't explain why our government handed us the problem, also," Gene continued. "There is currently a system of ethnic cleansing and racial genocide in South Africa.

"There have been thousands of white farmers, or Boers, who have been killed, had their families killed, and had their land expropriated by the government," he explained. "Now this land belonged to over thirty thousand farmers. It was never occupied prior to the original Burghers creating the farms that have been passed down from generation to generation.

"The expropriated land has been given to supporters of the current President, and it mostly sits vacant since the recipients have no clue as to how to manage a farm," he continued. "As this land sits vacant, the crops it formerly produced and fed their nation are no longer being produced. There is a self-induced famine coming if this continues.

"Additionally, over a hundred and thirty laws have been enacted against the white South African," Gene informed him. "Our government can't be seen as forcing changes to the laws another country passes. We'd raise holy hell if some country tried that with us.

"When I say the families have been killed, they have also been tortured, raped, burned, any number of heinous acts," Gene told him. "These people are savages. They rival even the most brutal gangs we've had in our country.

"They are on a level with MS 13 and Tren de Aragua," Gene finished. "Back to why it's Black Water's problem. Our government doesn't want to be seen as meddling in the internal affairs of another sovereign nation.

"Nor can we sit back and allow what we consider a terrorist organization to destroy a democratic nation," he explained. "That means that our government can't be tied to the solution. It can't even be involved with the funding."

"Our government has been involved with Black Water's funding since they were started," Jim argued. "I'm not certain of the exact method, but I'm sure it involves moving funds from some obscure project, let's say monitoring the mating habits of the long-tailed kangaroo rat, to some other worthy project, such as a comprehensive study of the effects of volcanic ash on the fertility of the cottontail bunny.

"So, how is this contract being funded if the current administration can't find the honey pots that reside in every corner of the White House?" Jim asked.

"Let's just say it's from a private individual who has ties to South Africa and is determined to reverse its rapid decline into a third world country," Gene answered. "Now, as with all your assignments, you have the option of refusing.

"Unfortunately, I can't provide more detail than is in those files you're holding, but I will give you time to review them and make your decision," Gene told him.

"I'll give you my decision now," Jim said, looking directly into Gene's eyes. "I've never refused an assignment because I trust you. You've been the reason why I'm here today, and I'll never let you down."

"Good," Gene said, putting his hand on Jim's shoulder. "Just take the folder and study it. I'll be in contact with you sometime in the next few days and let you know when we'll be pulling the team together.

"Needless to say, this is going to be one of the largest and most complex operations Black Water has ever gotten involved with," Gene told Jim as he walked with him to the door. "And I think you'll be glad you were a part of it."

Chapter 5

Two days later, when Jim arrived home in Mesquite, he quickly removed his uniform, replaced all the soiled clothes in his suitcase, and made sure he had starched shirts and clean uniform pants for the next trip, four days in the future.

Taking a bottle of cold Ziegen Bock from the refrigerator, he turned on the television and sat back to check the local news. Seeing nothing but the usual traffic issues on the always under-construction I-35E that ran from Laredo, Texas, to Duluth, Minnesota, he opened the file Gene had given him in Chicago and flipped to the portion dealing with the history of South Africa.

Still thinking about the similarities between South Africa and the United States, both from how they were discovered by Portuguese sailors looking for a route to China, and racial issues plaguing the nations long after efforts to resolve them had been enacted, Jim was slightly startled when his phone rang.

Seeing Marie's number, he answered, "Hello, pretty lady. Interested in an evening of romance or just a quick bout of nude mattress wrestling?"

"You're always such a romantic," she said, laughing. "How about if I come over for a quiet dinner and maybe, just maybe, an evening of snuggles?"

"You always seem to know exactly what's on my mind," Jim replied. "The biggest problem with my desire for a quiet dinner and snuggles is that I don't have anything here. And I'm referring to dinner.

"How about if I meet you at your dad's for dinner and we can decide where to snuggle afterwards?" Jim suggested.

"How about I call Dad and get a to-go order and come to your house?" Marie countered.

"I'd rather go there," Jim told her. "Your Dad hasn't seen me in weeks, and I think lasagna would be just fine this evening. Are the girls at home?"

Marie laughed and said, "Okay, we can meet there. And I'll tell Dad you have been looking forward to his *just fine* lasagna. And no, the girls are still in Denton. I think they have mid-term exams or something next week. Or they could have dates. I never know what they are up to these days."

"By the way, Gene has offered to bring some Wagyu steaks for us, meaning you, me, the girls, your mom, and your dad," Jim told her. "He asked if Tony would provide a lobster for each and some Italian Parmesan asparagus. Maybe you can find out when the girls will be available and ask Tony about the lobsters and stuff tonight when we get there."

"Speaking of Gene, what was he doing in Chicago?" Marie asked.

"I get the impression he was there to see me," Jim admitted. "But you know Gene. If you start thinking you've got him figured out, he'll surprise you."

"Maybe he surprises you," Marie countered. "But he doesn't me. If he's here in the Dallas area, he's here to see you. If he shows up where you are laying over, he's there to see you.

"What I'm asking is what is he asking you to do this time?" Marie demanded.

"I'm not exactly sure," Jim answered. "We discussed an issue regarding a foreign nation, but other than giving me some history lessons and a little about the current problems, I don't know what he, or the company, have contracted.

"It could be something to do with security issues," Jim offered. "There's been a marked increase in crime in that area. But I'm only guessing. Gene will probably have more to tell me when he comes down in a few days."

"I just don't want you to tell me all you're doing is designing roadblocks for a Presidential parade," Marie said sarcastically. "Sort of like you did when you guys were in Indianapolis. Or like when the guy who killed my husband was finally identified and died mysteriously."

"We've had this discussion enough times," Jim reminded her. "I'll try to be as open and honest as I can about my operations with Gene and the company, but there's a limit as to what I can tell you.

"And believe it or not, there's a limit as to what Gene can tell me sometimes," Jim argued. "And I'm pretty sure there's a limit of what Black Water can divulge to Gene. I hope we don't have to have this discussion every time I meet with Gene. And I've given you my word that I'll tell you as much as I can without possibly compromising an operation."

"I guess there's no use in continuing this conversation then," Marie announced. "Maybe once Gene tells you more, you can at least let me know where you're going, when you're going, and how long you'll be gone."

"That is the best approach," Jim agreed. "Now, what time do you want to meet at Siciliano's?"

"How about six thirty?" Marie asked. "I just need to take a quick shower and grab a few things if you still want me to come over after dinner."

"Of course I want you to come over," Jim told her. "Six thirty seems good. I've got to toss a few things in the washer, take a shower, and make sure the mattress wrestling arena is prepared for this evening's bout."

Marie laughed and said, "I think you've misread tonight's venue, mister. I believe there's a snuggling contest, and it doesn't include any nudity. Don't make me send you to your corner for a ten count and make you stay there!"

"I'm going to look into the official rulebook," Jim countered. "I'm pretty sure there's regulation apparel required for any official wrestling contest. Sometimes, no apparel is allowed. I'll explain it to you later this evening."

"You do just that," Marie said. "Maybe you should bring a copy of the *official rulebook* to dinner this evening and let my mother verify your interpretation."

"I'll see if I can find it by then," Jim replied. "I'll see you in a couple of hours. Love you."

"Love you, too," Marie said before hanging up.

Chapter 6

Marie was already at Siciliano's when Jim walked in. When her mother, Aurora, met him coming in, she said, "Hello, Jim. Marie said you were on your way, and Tony has reserved you two a table in the rear."

Giving her a quick hug, Jim replied, "That's great. What's Tony up to this evening?"

"Oh, you know Tony," Aurora said, leading Jim to the separate dining area he preferred. "He's got to complain about something. Tonight, it's too many orders of shrimp scampi and the basil isn't as fresh as he likes it. It's always something."

"Just go tell him I said the basil he's using will be *just fine*," Jim joked as Marie came in with a bottle of her favorite red wine.

Aurora gave a short laugh and said, "He'll never forgive you for the first time you said his lasagna was *just fine*. But you're still his favorite man, and he knows you'll always tease him about it."

"Did you tell your dad I wanted lasagna?" Jim asked as Marie set the wine and four glasses on the table.

"I did, and he said you'll eat what he decides he wants to cook," Marie answered. "But it wouldn't surprise me if you get lasagna. I think dad just likes to screw with you, sometimes."

"You two have a seat, and I'll go check on what's happening in the kitchen," Aurora said, as Marie took her seat. "Maybe Tony can stop by for a quick visit and a sip of wine before more customers get here."

Marie poured two glasses and handed one to Jim, saying, "To a pleasant evening with a handsome gentleman."

As she raised her glass, Jim replied, "To a pleasant evening with a beautiful lady. And a three-round bout of … snuggling."

"You're learning, Jim Lashley," Marie said, leaning over to kiss him. "You're learning. Slow, but learning."

"What do you mean, slow?" Jim asked, smiling at her.

"Slow. As in the speed of smell," Marie replied. "Possibly continental drift slow. Slow."

"Haven't you heard about haste making waste?" Jim asked, as Tony got to their table.

"Jim, so good to see you," he said, as Jim stood for the hug he knew was coming.

"And you as well," Jim said, returning the hug. "It's been too long."

"That it has," Tony said, as he reached for a glass and poured a small amount of wine. "That it has. Now, tell me, daughter Marie, what was your comment about continental drift slow?"

"I was just complaining that men are such slow learners," she answered as Aurora returned and took a glass and poured herself some of the wine. "I'm not sure how men make it through the day, as slow as you guys learn."

"Oh, honey," Aurora said, putting her arm around Tony's waist. "Men learn what they want to learn faster than a speeding bullet. It's just when it comes to the women they love, their brains are so overcome with emotion they can't think of anything except that."

Tony looked at Jim and said, "See, she thinks I'm Superman. That's why she always uses the phrase *faster than a speeding bullet*."

"You need to stop right there before I let them know what I'm referring to when I say that," Aurora replied, gently slapping Tony's hand from her arm.

"Mom!" Marie exclaimed. "Remember, there are people here!"

"Oh, hush," Aurora said, laughing and turning to kiss Tony. "Jim's the only *people* here and he's family. Now, you two sit down, and Superman and I will go take care of your meals."

"She can't wait to get me alone," Tony whispered, as he followed Aurora from the table. "We'll be back after you eat and bring a small bottle of something special."

"How long have they been married?" Jim asked, watching them leave.

"I think it's been forty-five years or so," Marie answered.

"And they still giggle like kids," Jim observed. "That's rare these days."

"Oh, I don't know," Marie replied. "Maybe they just feel free when they are around you. You never know how a couple of strangers really behave in private; most couples could be just as close … and giggly."

"You could be right," Jim said, refilling their glasses. "I guess I just see so many couples on the plane or at the hotel restaurants where I'm staying that don't seem to have any interest in each other."

"Could be because they are in public," Marie countered.

"No, it's easy to tell when they don't even look at each other or talk," Jim explained. "They just sit there staring at the walls until their food arrives and then eat silently. Makes me wonder why they even sit together."

"Comfort? Security? Habit?" Marie replied. "You know, sort of like the same old sweater you reach for when it's a little nippy.

"Maybe there's a hole worn in one of the elbows. Maybe the neck's a little frayed. But it's still your favorite and you pick it over the others that never get worn," Marie explained.

"I guess," Jim agreed. "People seem to have two sides. Two faces. One, they let the public see, and the other one, people may never know about. And the public face may not depict what's truly in a person's heart."

"And what's truly in your heart, Jim Lashley?" Marie asked as Aurora came in with a tray bearing their dishes.

"You, the twins, your mom and dad, and mattress wrestling," Jim said, as Aurora set the tray on the table.

"You're such an asshole, Jim Lashley," Marie said, shaking her head. "You say such sweet things and then go and ruin it with some comment like that. You need to learn when to just shut up."

"Oh, honey," Aurora said, putting her hand on Marie's shoulder. "If you're waiting for a man who only talks sweetness, you'll be waiting forever. And you'll probably find that's not the kind of man you really want.

"And don't try to change the man you want," she continued. "If he was what you wanted when you met him, accept him as he is. Now, you guys enjoy the shrimp scampi, and Superman and I will be back when you finish."

"I thought you said Tony was complaining about too many orders of shrimp scampi," Jim said. "I'm sort of surprised I didn't get lasagna."

Aurora looked at Marie, winked, and said, "Men. What would we do without them? They're never happy unless they have something to complain about. Just make sure it's not you they are complaining about. Let it be the shrimp scampi. Or the weather. Anything but you."

Chapter 7

"Okay, what can you tell me about this foreign nation?" Marie said, finishing her meal. "I thought you only worked in the States."

"I mentioned that to Gene," Jim told her. "And then he reminded me that I work for Black Water, and they alone decide which branch I work with. And he's right."

"Where are they looking at?" Marie asked. "France, Germany, Italy?"

"I believe it's South Africa," Jim answered. "At least the history and other information Gene gave me were concerning South Africa."

"What's so important down there?" Marie asked, as Aurora walked up to their table.

"Important down where?" Aurora asked, taking their empty plates.

"South Africa," Marie answered. "Jim thinks he's going down there for something."

"Don't they have tons of diamonds and gold?" Aurora asked, looking at Jim.

"I believe so," Jim told her. "But I don't believe that's why the company is interested in sending me there."

"Are you talking about American Airlines?" Aurora asked.

"No, mom," Marie answered. "Gene works for a company that does international security stuff, and he uses Jim sometimes as an advisor or sends him to look at whatever they are interested in."

"I thought he was just a retired military guy," Aurora said, taking the dishes and heading for the kitchen. "I'll tell Tony you guys are done and see if he has time for a quick drink. I know he's got a bottle of Courvoisier Cognac he's been saving, and having Jim here is as good a reason as I can think of."

A few minutes later, Tony came to the table with an unopened bottle and four crystal brandy snifters. "So, you're going to South Africa," he said, as he poured the brandy. Interesting place."

"I guess so," Jim said, accepting the glass as Aurora joined them and took a seat beside Marie.

"I don't know much about it," Tony continued, as he poured the remaining glasses. "I believe they've had some trouble of late. Something to do with farmers."

"I don't know, either," Jim acknowledged, as Tony sat and raised his glass. "I'm hoping Gene will fill me in when he gets here in a few days."

"To the future," Tony said, as everyone raised their glasses. "Be it South Africa, a trip home to Italy, or having my grandkids give me great grandkids."

"Let's not rush into that great grandkids issue," Marie replied, shaking her head. "Perhaps we should let them get married first."

"Speaking of marriage," Tony said, looking at Jim.

Jim shook his head and said, "I wasn't speaking of marriage. You and Marie were having that discussion, and I don't remember joining in."

"You just hush, Anthony," Aurora quietly said. "Jim and Marie are grown people and get to do what they think is best for them. And as for Seppa and Julie, let's let them enjoy being young for a few more years."

"You're right, of course," Tony said, topping his glass off. "I just know that I want my kids and grandkids to be happy. And I want great grandkids while I'm still young enough to enjoy them."

"Well, I don't think I'm ready for grandkids," Marie said, shaking her head. "And I'm not in a rush to get married again. And I know Jim isn't either. Both of us have lost spouses too recently and neither wants to experience that again."

"You don't have to be married to lose someone you love," Tony argued. "But I'll say right now, I'd welcome Jim into my family. Today. Tomorrow. Any time he's ready."

Jim raised his glass and said, "There's no other family I'd rather be with. From the twins up to the grandparents, there's no finer family I've ever known, but Marie and I will take that path when we get there.

"Regarding Julie and Seppa, I agree with Aurora. Let them get all of their mistakes out of the way before they decide to settle down," Jim said. "Looking back at my life, I'm blessed that I didn't turn a mistake of love into a disaster of a life. What's the old saying, you have to kiss a lot of toads before you meet a prince?"

"There's your problem," Marie said, laughing. "You've been kissing toads when you should have been kissing ladies. Not to mention, if I'd known you wanted a prince, I'd have suggested you get a townhouse in Oak Lawn. You'd be a big hit at JR's."

"Maybe I should rephrase," Jim replied, shaking his head. "I've had to kiss a lot of lady toads before I met my princess.

"Now to change the subject before I put my foot back in my mouth," Jim said, looking at Tony. "Gene has offered to bring some Wagyu steaks for the family and asks if you could be so kind as to grill them with lobster tails and asparagus."

"It would be my pleasure," Tony said, as he set his empty glass on the table. "Now, if you'll excuse my wife and me, we need to check on the rest of the guests."

Chapter 8

The following morning, after Marie had gone home, Jim was doing some very necessary housekeeping when he heard the doorbell ring. Opening the door, he saw Gene standing there with Butch North.

"Good morning, guys," Jim said, somewhat surprised. "Come on in. Could I offer you a cup of coffee or something?"

"Good morning, Jim," Gene said. "Why don't you come with us instead, and we'll go to breakfast?"

"Okay," Jim answered, tossing a dust rag on the table beside the door. "Do I get to pick the place, or have you two already made that decision?"

"It's been decided," Gene told him, as Jim came outside. "Butch says he wants to go to Denny's. Is that all right with you?"

Jim looked at Butch as Gene led them down the sidewalk to the black Suburban and asked, "Did you really pick Denny's?"

"Nope," Butch said laughing. "Gene said you were such a big fan of Denny's that you'd drop anything to go there. I picked Waffle House, but Gene just shook his head and reminded me that since he was buying, he got to make the decision.”

“Let me tell you about Gene’s buying,” Jim said, as they pulled away from the curb. “When that happens, you can rest assured Black Water is paying.”

“Company business,” Gene retorted, as they headed for the 635 Loop. You should know by now that almost everything I do is company business.”

“Of course,” Jim replied, as they joined 635 heading north. “Now, perhaps you’d care to explain why you and Butch are here on company business.”

“Of course,” Gene answered, as they crossed over US 80. “I flew in late yesterday after making sure Butch was going to be home. After driving out to meet him and explaining the situation in South Africa, he tentatively agreed to help us.

“Now, since he’s going to be involved with you, I wanted you to have a voice in the matter,” Gene continued. “So, I figured the best way to get everybody on the same page was to meet today before I have to fly back to Quantico.”

“When you say, ‘involved with me’, just what does that entail?” Jim asked. “If I’m not mistaken, you haven’t even explained exactly what I’ll be doing.”

“That’s part of what we’re here to discuss this morning,” Gene explained, as he took the exit for N Town East Blvd. “We, Black Water, have been gaming this problem for some time, and I want the two of you to listen to our basic operating plan.

“Since we’re still in the conception phase, I want to hear from you guys to see if you can see any major flaws,” Gene continued. "But mainly from you, Jim. Butch is mostly here to see if he thinks his portion of the plan is operationally sound and he has no issues with the scope."

"What is his part going to be?" Jim asked, as they headed east on N Town East Blvd.

"Since you and I both agree that his talent is more in the planning and management of an operation," Gene answered, turning north on E Emporium Circle. "I want him to see if he believes our concept will meet our objectives."

"And what is our objective?" Jim asked as Gene turned into the Denny's parking lot.

"Stop the genocide, ethnic cleansing, and expropriation of the Boers' farmland," Gene said, parking. "And a small matter of regime change."

"Regime change?" Jim asked, as they headed for the door to Denny's. "Is that synonymous with governmental interference?"

"There are levels of *governmental interference*," Gene explained, holding the door open for them. "It ranges anywhere from campaign contributions to blackmail to a more absolute solution."

"And where does our involvement fall in these levels of interference?" Jim asked, as the hostess led them to a table.

"Excuse me, ma'am," Gene said, as the hostess indicated a table for them. "Would it be possible to have that table in the rear by the wall? We may be longer than usual, and we don't want to interfere with the other guests."

"Of course, sir," she replied with a slight nod. "This late in the morning, there shouldn't be much of a problem.

"Would you care for some juice, coffee, or water?" she asked as they took their seats, and she handed them menus.

"Just coffee for me," Gene said, taking his menu.

"Coffee, also," Jim said, laying his menu on the table.

"Same," Butch said, opening his menu.

"Wonderful," she replied. "I'll be right back to take your orders."

Butch looked at Jim and asked, "Aren't you going to look at the menu?"

Gene laughed and said, "Jim has the menu memorized, at least the part he's interested in."

Chapter 9

As they were eating, Gene told them, "I'm trying to set up a meeting in Quantico in a few days, as soon as we can notify all of the other players, and I want to make sure you guys can make it."

"Depends on the exact day," Butch answered. "I have a three-day trip starting two days from now."

"Don't worry about that," Gene told him. "As Jim can verify, trips that interfere with Black Water business have a way of being needed by American for some training or Captain upgrades."

"But then that's just a coincidence," Jim said, laughing. "After all these years of working with Gene, it's surprising how many coincidences there are when he wants you."

Gene gave a quick look at Jim and continued, "Anyway, this operation is going to be massive, at least as far as the number of people involved."

"How many are you talking about?" Butch asked. "As many as we had going after Tren de Aragua?"

"More," Gene answered. "There are around three hundred thousand farms in South Africa. I realize it would be impossible to send a team to each farm to ensure their safety, so we've broken the country into three zones with about one hundred men for each zone."

"That's spreading it pretty thin, isn't it?" Butch asked.

"Not really," Gene told him. "We know the bad guys can't hit every farm at the same time. Also, many of the farms have already been hit, and many of the farmers are trying to get refugee visas so they can leave.

"One of the duties of the teams is to assist them with that," Gene explained. "And we're setting up a transportation system to get them out of the country."

"I'm sure you know how difficult that could be," Jim offered. "We don't have any military bases there, so you're pretty much stuck with the airport in Johannesburg."

"Yes, that does present a problem, both getting in and getting out," Gene acknowledged. "We've leased four Boeing 767s through a Swiss-based corporation. They will be flying in as part of a United Nations humanitarian team to investigate potential food supply issues. We have contracted for enough buses to take our teams to the locations selected for their portion of the operation.

"These same buses and planes will then fly out the refugees and our people at the conclusion of the operation," he finished.

"What's my part in the operation?" Butch asked.

"You'll be coordinating the movement of the teams," Gene answered. "You'll be at a secure location in Johannesburg with the necessary communication equipment to relay information from Black Water, back in Quantico, to whichever team you need to give directions or relocate as necessary."

"I'm guessing Debbie has already established means of locating the bad guys, manipulated their phones so she can listen and track them, learned all of their secrets, and put indecent photos of the President of South Africa's wife on the phones," Jim said.

"Pretty much everything you just said, except for the wife thing," Gene admitted. "And that lady has been busy. She's also managed to tap into the Starlink system to use the installed cameras."

"How the hell did she get permission to do that?" Jim asked.

"Did I say she had permission?" Gene replied.

"Forget I said anything so stupid," Jim replied. "Bracer knows no boundaries."

"How long do you expect this operation to take?" Butch asked.

"We're hoping for a week, possibly less," Gene answered. "If things go as planned, we hope we can convince the folks behind the genocide and ethnic cleansing to disappear before the week is over."

"How do you think you can do that within just a week?" Jim asked. "Even if you can cover three hundred farms a day, that's a thousand days. If you only have to cover half the farms, it's five hundred days."

"I can do the math," Gene replied. "What we're counting on is that once the bad guys see what's happening across the country, they will fade away."

"I understand," Jim countered. "But aren't you worried about them returning as soon as they discover we've gone?"

"That point is well taken," Gene answered. "Removing the folks who are killing the farmers and their families, raping, torturing, or whatever, is just part of the operation."

"What's behind door number two?" Jim asked, sitting back.

"We'll remove the head of the snake," Gene answered. "More accurately, the heads of the snakes."

"I guess that's where I come in," Jim replied, shaking his head.

"You didn't think you were going there for a summer vacation, did you?" Gene asked, signaling for the check. "Silly rabbit. Tricks are for kids."

"I have a thought about the UN involvement," Jim then said.

"What about it?" Gene asked.

"Don't you think they will be extremely noticeable?" Jim answered. "I mean, if you're going to use these UN vehicles to take our teams to the farms where we're going to take out the folks who are killing the farmers, that's sort of advertising we are there, isn't it?"

"What's your suggestion?" Gene asked.

"There are lots of tour groups, safaris, all over South Africa," Jim explained. "I'd think we could blend in much better if we were driving around in vehicles with Paul's Lion Country Safaris. Those blue UN vans stand out like a sore thumb.

"I can see using it to gain entrance to the President," he continued. "But I think it wouldn't help Butch's folks go unnoticed. I mean, how many blue UN vans are we talking about? I think you're just asking for some part of the South African security folks to follow you wherever you go."

"You've got a point," Gene finally agreed. "I'll have to see what we can manage. Maybe we can actually get the United Nations to man the refugee registration part. Give me a few days to work something out."

Chapter 10

"Can I get you gentlemen anything else?" the waitress asked as she approached their table.

"More coffee?" Gene replied. "And is it okay if we stick around a little while longer?"

"That's not a problem," she answered, waving her arm across the almost empty room. "I doubt if we get five more customers for the next hour or so. You guys just take all the time you need.

"I'll be right back with your coffee," she finished, turning to leave.

"Could you please bring our check when you come back?" Gene asked. "At least I'd like to take care of that in case you're not here when we finish our business."

"Certainly," the waitress answered. "I'll take care of it when I return."

"Back to business," Gene said, looking at Jim and Butch. "I've got a more comprehensive package for each of you to take home and review.

"There's a lot of information that you need to understand, and I don't have time right now to explain all of the details," he continued. "I'm just showing you the album cover right now. You'll have to listen to the music on your own."

"I haven't even had a glimpse of, as you call it, the album cover of the music I'm expected to sing," Jim replied. "And it sounds like I'll be singing a couple of solos a cappella."

"You're getting too far ahead of me," Gene said. "If you'll wait, I'm sure you'll have a better understanding of what your part in this 'concert' is going to be. And you aren't singing solo. You'll have a partner. So, it's a duet."

"Sorry, General," Jim said contritely. "I guess I was a little overwhelmed when I realized exactly what you had planned for me."

"And what do you think we have planned for you?" Gene asked as the waitress approached with a tray carrying two carafes of coffee.

"I hope these will take care of you," she said, setting the tray on the table.

"If you need anything else, just let me know."

Gene took the ticket for their meals, checked it, and handed her two one-hundred-dollar bills, saying, "Keep the change, miss. We appreciate you taking such good care of us. And if you need our table, please don't hesitate to tell us to go home."

She looked at Gene and said, "Sir, I'll let the manager know that you'd appreciate it if you could use the room as long as you need."

"Thanks," Gene told her as she turned away. "Now, back to my question, Jim. What do you think we have planned for you?"

Jim looked around the room quickly and answered quietly, "The assassination of the President of South Africa. And another person who is yet unknown to me. The head of the other snake."

"You assume correctly," Gene told him. "I'll get to that after I give you a little insight into both of the targets.

"Let's start with the first, and most important, of the snakes," Gene explained. "We'll call him 'Bull', just to ensure any conversation regarding him doesn't reveal his identity.

"And before you ask, he refers to himself as Bull," Gene added. "And we're calling the other one 'Steer'."

Gene paused, looked at Jim, and then asked, "Have you ever heard of a 'Phyllobates terribilis'?"

Jim glanced at Butch, and then back at Gene, saying, "Hell no. I doubt if more than a dozen people in the world would know what you're referring to. But I'm pretty sure anything with any form of the word *terrible* isn't something I'd want for breakfast."

"No, you definitely wouldn't want this for breakfast," Gene said, chuckling. "If you did, you'd never make it to lunch.

"Phyllobates terribilis is more commonly known as a *golden poison frog,*" he continued. "It's native to the rainforests down in Colombia and is possibly the most toxic animal in the world.

"The next most toxic animal is the puffer fish, which is more readily known for its toxic qualities," Gene explained. "I think it gained much notoriety in the movie, Kill Bill.

"One puffer fish has enough toxin to kill thirty people," he continued. "With the golden poison frog, an amount of the mucus, where the toxin is found, equal to three grains of salt, will kill a human within mere minutes.”

“The picture is coming into focus,” Jim said, refreshing his coffee. “My partner, a chef of some renown, and I will prepare a succulent dish of frog legs and asparagus tips with béarnaise sauce for the *Bull* and watch him die while no one lifts a finger.

“Of course not,” Gene retorted, shaking his head. “First off, frog legs are more often served with cheesy roasted green beans, a dry white Chardonnay, and Baileys Cinnamon Churros over a French Vanilla ice cream for dessert.”

Chapter 11

"Now, if you'll let me continue, I'll see if I can't add a little clarity to your unfocused picture," Gene said after a slight pause meant as a minor reprimand.

"The frog is important because the Bull has an affinity for reptiles," Gene explained. "He has various lizards, frogs, and snakes. The more exotic, the more he wants them.

"And the same goes for the ladies," he continued. "His taste for women has no bounds. Doesn't matter whether they're from India, Mozambique, Central America, or New Guinea.

"Before you jump in with another sarcastic remark, allow me to make the connection between the Bull, the women, and the frog," Gene quickly said, seeing Jim about to interrupt.

"The Bull is actually what psychologists refer to as an extrovert who is covering for severe feelings of inadequacy," he continued. "He uses numerous situations to demonstrate how his virility and physical dominance make him the most respected and sought-after by everyone, especially any female.

"Now, even though he believes every woman wants him, he thinks he must reserve himself for only the most beautiful, exotic, and unattainable women whom he comes across," Gene explained.

"And that leads us to the frog," he said, nodding his head. "As we've discussed, the mucus of the frog is extremely toxic.

"The natives used to rub the tip of a dart or an arrow across the frog's back to coat it with the toxin," he continued. "They could let it dry, and it would remain toxic for up to a year.

"There was an illegal market for these specific frogs, and since their habitat was fairly restricted, it became one of the endangered species, and people began breeding them in captivity," Gene explained.

Pausing, he continued, "The native wild golden frog's diet consisted of specific insects, which it is believed to be necessary for the production of the toxin.

"Those kept in captivity eventually lose their toxicity, and those bred in captivity are non-toxic," Gene told them. "Now, that's the key to how we'll eliminate the Bull.

"Specifically, he likes to demonstrate his virility by actually licking the back of the golden frog he keeps on display," Gene explained. "The frog, and I'm sure it's been replaced numerous times, is actually an orange black foot. It's not a true subspecies and exists only in captivity.

"So, when the Bull wants to impress some lady, he explains how toxic the golden poison frog is, and proceeds to slowly run the tip of his tongue up and down the back of his frog," he continued. "As he's licking the frog, he gives the lady his most suggestive look.

"Most of the information we have obtained leads us to believe what he thinks is seductive is viewed more as repulsive," Gene told them. "Regardless, this frog licking is how we're going to send the Bull to the butcher.

"If this *orange black foot* isn't toxic, how is that going to kill him?" Jim asked, shaking his head.

"We have gone to considerable effort to obtain actual toxin from a source in Central America," Gene answered. "You will administer a dosage large enough to kill twenty men while the Bull is distracted by your partner."

"I see where you're going with this," Jim replied. "But if it's known that the orange frog doesn't produce toxin, isn't that going to be discovered?"

"Possibly," Gene admitted. "But there will always be a reasonable speculation that this frog had somehow mutated or some genetic abnormalities caused it to become toxic.

"And, since you'll be gone by the time the cause of death is discovered, I don't see any major problem," Gene continued.

"How am I, or my partner, supposed to administer this toxin?" Jim asked.

"As I mentioned, he likes to demonstrate his invincibility by self-administering the most toxic material known to man," Gene explained. "While he's licking and looking, you'll have a chance to slip the toxin into whatever beverage he's drinking.

"We expect him to offer each of you a glass of Badenhorst Ramnasgras Cinsault Swartland," he said. "That seems to be what he believes will impress you as to his cultured lifestyle and actually is one of the finest wines from South Africa."

"How will I administer this shit?" Jim asked. "If it's as toxic as you say, just a drop on my skin could terminate any chance I have of finishing any remaining items on my bucket list."

"You'll be provided with a syringe holding about one milligram of the toxin," Gene answered. "It has been designed to keep the toxin from reaching the tip of the syringe unless six ounces of pressure are applied to the plunger.

"The plunger itself has a small tab that must be moved before you can depress it," he continued. "We have worked with this for some time, and you'll have a chance to practice while you're in Quantico."

"I guess that's when I'll get to meet my partner," Jim said, remembering a previous time they had used a similar method and some of the issues they had experienced.

"Yes," Gene told him. "And the two of you can develop whatever relationship you think will benefit the operation."

"By the way, what's the antidote?" Jim asked. "Just in case."

"There is no antidote," Gene answered somberly.

"Then I guess my partner and I had better develop a pretty close relationship," Jim replied. "I'd hate to go into a situation where my partner didn't trust me explicitly, especially since I'll be the one with the syringe.

"Sort of reminds me of the situation where a rattlesnake bit a fellow on the butt," Jim said. "He asked his partner to suck the poison out and his partner took one look at his exposed butt and said, "Sorry old buddy, but it looks like you're gonna die.

"And if this shit is as bad as you say, I don't think I'd offer much assistance myself if it came to sucking either," he finished. "No matter how exotic the lady was."

Chapter 12

"Now that you've decided how I'm to remove the Bull from the pasture, just how do you plan on getting me close enough?" Jim asked as he began wondering about his partner.

"Just having an attractive lady with me doesn't get me an audience, I wouldn't think," he continued.

"You remember I mentioned using United Nations humanitarian teams as cover for the folks going into the field," Gene answered. "Well, they will be your cover as well.

"You will be a special assistant to the Ambassador to South Africa, on loan from the United States Department of Agriculture," he continued. "You are there as part of a special envoy to encourage the Bull to resolve the destruction of the Boer farming community.

"Regarding that, he has refused to acknowledge any criminal activity," Gene said. "He says there have been no atrocities and everything seen on the news is politically motivated by our government to press him into accepting substantial increases in tariffs imposed on South Africa."

"Do we have proof of what's been reported?" Butch asked. "And if we have proof, who is behind it, if not the President?"

"First, we have absolute proof," Gene answered. "We have undeniable photographic evidence, some of the most heinous nature. We also have testimony from some of the Boers who escaped and made it to the US.

"As to who is behind it, it is both he and the man who is running against him in the upcoming election," Gene finished. "You've already heard his name for this operation."

"Steer," Jim said immediately.

"Very perceptive," Gene replied, nodding.

"I can't believe two political candidates for the office of President would conspire to destroy their country," Butch said, shaking his head. "Why would they do that? And who benefits?"

"First question first," Gene answered. "They don't believe they are destroying their country. Both of them believe they are righting the wrongs from years of apartheid and returning the land to the people where it rightly belongs.

"Second, they both benefit," he continued. "The Steer is running on a platform espousing the return of the land and expelling the white oppressors. The Bull is publicly condemning that policy.

"While the rest of the civilized world supports the Bull, even his strongest opposition from the South African population recognizes the long-term effect espoused by the Steer is unworkable," he explained. "So, the Bull is almost guaranteed to be reelected, as the Steer realizes, and when the dust settles, the Bull will ensure plenty of pastureland is provided for him and his herd."

"What if the Steer got elected?" Butch asked. "What then?"

"They have that covered," Gene explained. "If the polls show even a slight chance of him being elected, he will drop out before the election."

"How do you know all of this?" Jim asked.

"Bracer," Gene answered, smiling. "She's had bugs in every possible place they could meet. Bugs in their phones. And Black Water has had an inside assistant for the last year."

"How did they manage that?" Jim asked. "And are we sure the *assistant* isn't feeding us the droppings from the Bull?"

"Absolutely," Gene confirmed. "I'm sure you remember a certain lady who worked with you several times over the years. Red hair, slight build, intelligent, somewhat exotic looking, and can think on her feet."

"Jewell," Jim replied, nodding. "How'd she wind up there?"

"I've mentioned how the Bull likes exotic ladies," Gene explained. "Jewell, who likes to travel, managed to get on a tour of South Africa. An *unexpected* event involving the Bull occurred while the group was in Johannesburg.

"The Bull has extensive real estate holdings there, and she just happened to bump into him, so to speak," he continued. "We knew he was going to be in the area from telephone conversations he was having with his agent in Johannesburg. Someone a few levels above me had been looking for a way to get information from the country for quite a while and had been sending agents on these tours.

"It just happened that Miss Jewell was in the right place at the right time," he finished. "Just another coincidence. So, are we getting bull shit? Not a chance."

"What was, or is, her cover story?" Jim asked.

"She was publicly an advisor on US travel and leisure," Gene told him, almost laughing. "Privately, I don't know."

"Why aren't we using her instead of bringing in a new lady?" Jim asked. "She's already there. He's comfortable having her around. I'd think she'd be the perfect person to help me."

"She's on her way back here in a day or two," Gene explained. "The story is she's coming home to care for her ailing mother. The truth is that the Bull was looking for a new heifer."

"At least she didn't get run over or shot as she has been on so many of the operations where we worked together," Jim replied.

"Maybe because you two weren't working together this time?" Gene asked, smiling. "Maybe I should warn your new partner."

"Speaking of her, what's her name?" Jim asked.

"Megan," Gene answered.

Chapter 13

"Gentlemen, do you need anything else?" the waitress asked as she came to check on them.

"No ma'am," Gene answered, smiling. "But maybe some fresh coffee would be nice. These two seem to need the caffeine to stay awake while I conduct business."

"On its way," she said, turning away.

Moments later, after she had brought two new carafes, Jim asked, "What experience does Megan have with the company?"

"She's been with us for about three years," Gene answered, pouring himself some fresh coffee. "During that time, she's been the bait, so to speak, several times."

"Has she ever been on a wet mission?" Jim asked, filling his cup.

"Not one where she was actually a participant in the execution of the subject," Gene acknowledged. "But she's been on several high-risk jobs where things got out of control, and we had to eliminate a target in front of her.

"For example, we loaned her to the FBI for a sting operation where she was an exotic dancer at a club they were interested in, and a shooting ensued," he continued. "She was part of an operation where she played the part of a babysitter in a child pornography filming operation that was taking place in Thailand, and things got ugly.

"Most recently, she played the part of a lady engaged to one of our agents to trap a well-known congressman into making unwelcome advances," Gene said. "Once we had him on tape, we convinced him that unless he pulled his name from reelection, his wife would be getting an early Christmas present.

"So, she's had enough experience that I don't think you'll have any issues," Gene finished. "But you'll get to meet her when we get together in Quantico, and if you have any doubts, we'll revisit the issue."

"An exotic dancer, huh?" Jim asked. "Did you happen to mention to her that I was once a Chippendales dancer?"

"Oh, good Lord, Jim," Gene said, bursting out laughing. "Even I couldn't pull that one off. And I'm very skilled at shading the truth when necessary. But you? A Chippendales dancer? I doubt I could sell that one to a blind man. Just one touch and he'd know I'd fed him a line of crap."

"Now that hurts," Jim said, joining in on the laughter. "Marie thinks I look good without my shirt, wearing a black bowtie, French cuffs on my wrists, and tight leather pants."

"You're not a bad looking guy," Butch said, laughing. "But even I doubt if you could have pulled that off twenty years ago. No offense, but I've seen those guys, and the resemblance just isn't there. Not even slightly."

"Why, Butch," Jim replied, shaking his head. "I never thought you were the sort of guy who went in for the exotic male dancer stuff. Are you sure you weren't Navy?"

"Several years ago, I went with my girlfriend to a bachelorette party," Butch explained. "I was rather surprised to see so many men there besides me. And at least I didn't hold out dollar bills for the dancers. Some with their teeth."

"Can we get back on track here, gentlemen?" Gene asked them. "I know the lady said we could stay as long as we want, but I don't have time to indulge in the escapades of questionable behavior by you two."

"Okay," Jim finally said when he could quit laughing. "Back to Megan. Is she qualified with firearms?"

"Definitely," Gene answered. "But that's not relevant for this mission. First off, I doubt if you could sneak a gun past Bull's security. More importantly, this mission is supposed to resemble an accidental poisoning.

"I've given her the same information regarding the frog as I gave you," he continued. "Her biggest concern is getting the syringe past security."

"What's your answer for that?" Jim asked.

"It will be disguised as a Montblanc pen," Gene answered. "When you take the cap off, the tiny syringe will drop out. And you have to twist the cap to remove it. That was one of the safeguards to make sure it didn't accidentally expel the poison during travel or during an inspection."

"Am I carrying it in my pocket?" Jim asked.

"Yes," Gene answered. "We originally wanted it to be in your briefcase, but since your assistant will be carrying that, we decided this was the best way for you to have quick access to the pen. And it would seem normal for you to be removing your pen to take notes."

"My concern is accidentally getting some of that shit on me, or her," Jim told him. "Since there is no antidote, that's a death warrant for either of us. Not to mention finding two extra bodies in the President's office. Sort of blows the whole charade apart, doesn't it?"

"We've tested duplicate syringes repeatedly," Gene assured him. "We've dropped them from ten feet off the floor, both inside the cover pen and by themselves. We've stepped on it, hit it with a hammer, tried to break it with our hands. It's as solid as possible.

"The only time you could possibly be exposed is when you depress the plunger and some of the liquid splashes back on your hand if it hits anything except the wine in the glass," he finished. "We've done every sort of test imaginable, and that's the only flaw we can find in the operation."

Chapter 14

"What's the plan for the Steer?" Butch asked. "Are we trying to cover up that one as well?"

"No," Gene answered. "The plan is to shoot the bastard in the face the first chance we get."

"Won't that seem suspicious?" Butch asked. "I thought the whole operation was to keep our government's hands clean."

"Your side of the operation won't be clean," Gene informed him. "However, it's planned to put the blame on the Boers."

"How do you intend on doing that?" Butch asked. "And aren't we there to help them?"

"Of course we're there for their benefit," Gene answered, nodding. "But each incident will be viewed as a man protecting his land and family. There will be no inkling of our government's involvement.

"We'll get more into the specifics at Quantico," he continued. "Your part of the operation is monitoring what's happening in the field, which includes removing the Steer, who is your primary target.

"Most of the time, the guys running the actual field operation will be controlling everything within their area," Gene explained. "You'll be paying attention to the radios, but most of the time, the folks at Quantico will be working with them.

"That includes warning them of the approaching enemy, the number of them, and anything else they need to prepare for them before they reach the intended farm," he added. "You'll also be getting updates on the Steer's location and may need to pull one or more of the shooters from their location if he's in their area.

"We'd like to put a stop to this shit on day one," Gene continued. "However, I believe it's going to take three or four until they get the picture. Even when none of their operatives come back from what was formerly a walk in the park.

"I want every single person who is trying to disrupt the established farming operations to become an example," he informed them. "And by example, I mean a pile of bodies outside the boundaries of the farm they were targeting.

"If that doesn't get their attention, we'll escalate to putting their heads on spikes," Gene informed them. "As much as I despise such brutality, it's come down to what we faced before we dropped the bombs on Hiroshima and Nagasaki.

"The loss of life, both ours and the Japanese, would have been much worse if we had attempted a land invasion," he explained. "We tried to show how destructive an air attack would be by firebombing them. Even after the first bomb hit Hiroshima, the government refused to admit defeat.

"Unfortunately, it required a second example," he finished. "I'm hoping the first pile of bodies convinces these people that things have changed and the Boers are fighting back."

"How will they know it's the Boers?" Jim asked.

"First, they don't know anyone besides the Boers and their families who are at the farms," Gene explained. "We believe they will think the farmers are banding together to fight back. Our people will be out of sight and surrounding the farmhouse or where the farmer is at the time of the attack.

"The person at the farmhouse will actually be one of our people, dressed in the custom of the Boers," he continued. "We'll have removed the families as soon as we learn where the next attack will happen.

"Where are you keeping the families?" Jim asked. "I'd think it would be hard to hide that many people for very long."

"You're right, it would be difficult if there were more than one or two attacks planned in any single area on any given day," Gene answered. "We plan on moving those who are currently threatened to one of the other farms we believe to be a safe location."

"Do these people know about your plans?" Butch asked. "I mean, some farmer suddenly has an influx of people when he had no idea they were coming …"

"That's one part of the field teams' responsibilities," Gene answered. "When the folks at Quantico learn of the intended targets, which should give our guys in the field at least twelve hours to gather the families we're relocating and explain the situation to the receiving farm."

"Have you thought about designating the holding areas beforehand?" Butch asked.

"Of course," Gene told him. "The biggest problem with that is we could be broadcasting our intentions to the wrong people. Not to mention we don't know where these assholes will be striking next. We discussed this with the Boers who have been given asylum in the US, and they concur with not saying anything until we are ready to move the people.

"They are much akin to the farmer or rancher in this country," he continued. "They'll welcome any neighbor if they need help. And their grapevine will spread the word soon after the first day or so."

"Isn't that pretty much what you were concerned about by designating the holding areas beforehand?" Jim asked.

"Possibly," Gene acknowledged. "But once the operation starts, we don't have much of a choice. And the folks who've made it here believe their friends and neighbors who remain in South Africa will understand that they could be next if we don't succeed. No, I think this is the best option.

"There has never been a perfect means of keeping an enemy from learning your plans," Gene informed them. "But since it's in these folks' best interest to make sure no one knows, we're confident this plan will protect them.

"Now, if you have any other questions or recommendations, you'll have to voice them when we meet in Quantico," Gene said, standing. "I have to get back to Quantico and see how the planning is progressing."

"I have one quick question," Butch said.

"What's that?" Gene asked as Butch and Jim stood.

"Do I get an exotic assistant as Jim does?" he asked.

"Of course," Gene said, leading them toward the door. "The lady who'll be working with you is a somewhat chubby forty-seven-year-old lady from Puerto Rico. But she has a great personality. She has a small dental problem, but our dentists are working on that. Oh, she has a slight, I mean a very slight speech impediment, but I think you'll get the gist of whatever she's saying."

Butch stopped and looked at the smiles on Gene's and Jim's faces and said, "I'm not sure I want to go to South Africa with either of you. You damn Marines stick together, don't you? Semper fi, and all that stuff. You think you've had a tough time in the field?

"Well, I'm here to tell you that being an Air Force pilot meant being sent around the world to some pretty dismal locations," he continued without a trace of a smile. "Hell, at some of the more remote locations, the Officers Club didn't even have a decent eighteen-year-old single malt Scotch.

"We had to suffer with a twelve-year-old single malt," he finished completely deadpan. "And most of the time, our steaks were overcooked, and the lobster was stringy."

Jim and Gene looked at each other and then burst out laughing as they passed their waitress, and Gene shook his head, saying, "Sorry, Miss. One of the guys thinks he's a comedian. And thank you for your outstanding hospitality."

Chapter 15

That afternoon, Jim had just finished mowing his yard and gone inside for a glass of tea when the phone rang.

Seeing it was Marie, he answered, "Hi, Marie. How are you?"

"Good, I just got off the phone with the girls, and they are coming down tomorrow," she answered. "I don't know if that's too soon to make arrangements for Gene to get his steaks and have dinner with us or not. What do you think?"

"I don't think he'll be able to make it," Jim answered. "He was here this morning and said he had to get back to Virginia."

"Oh, he was here?" she asked.

"Yes, he came by with Butch North and took me to a late breakfast at Denny's," he answered.

"Well, at least you got to go to Denny's," she responded. "That should have made your day."

"Always," he replied. "I don't know why so many folks avoid Denny's. I like their chicken-fried steak, the place is clean, with clean restrooms, and the price is reasonable. What more can you ask of a restaurant?"

"Not much, I guess," she answered. "What did Gene want to talk about? I know he didn't fly all the way down here just to take you to breakfast."

"No," Jim admitted. "He told me a little bit more about Johannesburg and what he was asking me to do."

"And that was?" she asked.

"Something to do with trying to get the President of South Africa to do something to stop taking the farms from the rightful owners and all the killings," he answered.

"And just why does he think you can convince him of anything?" she asked. "Isn't that something our government should be involved in? Isn't that why we have ambassadors all over the world?

"There's got to be more to this than just having you fly halfway around the world to discuss farming with the President of a foreign country," she finished. "Just what did Gene tell you?"

"He said the government, our government, had asked Black Water to help negotiate some dispute about who owned some land and how their government was wrong to be taking it from the people whose families had been farming it for generations," he explained.

"Again, I ask, why does Gene, or anyone, think you can waltz over there and solve what appears to be none of our business anyway?" she repeated.

"Look, I only know what Gene's asking me to do," Jim replied. "He said they were having a meeting in Quantico sometime soon and he would have more details."

The phone was silent for a moment, and she asked, "When are you going and how long will you be gone?"

"To Virginia or South Africa?" Jim asked, already knowing what she meant.

"Let's assume both," she answered.

"I don't know," Jim told her. "All Gene said was that we would be meeting in Quantico soon, and I don't know what soon meant. I'm guessing in a day or two, but he didn't give me a date.

"As to how long, I'd guess one day, maybe two," he continued. "Now, as to South Africa, I don't know. He didn't give me any dates for that either.

"The only thing he said was that he hoped it could be done in one day," Jim explained. "Now, I'm not a diplomat or know much about how those people negotiate, but I'd be surprised if it didn't last at least a week.

"Hell, it's at least an eighteen- or nineteen-hour flight from here to there," Jim explained. "And South Africa is about seven hours ahead of us time wise. We'd have to take off from Texas or Virginia, roughly a day before the meeting, given eighteen hours to fly and the time difference.

"I think that pretty much shoots down the one-day thing," he continued. "And then I'm betting our government isn't going to let me sign any formal agreement, so toss in another day or two for me to tell some shoe clerk in Washington what the agreement was, another day for him to tell his boss, another day for a meeting at some junior congressman's office to discuss the details, and then another day to tell me to sign it.

"Hell, I'd bet it would be more like two weeks," Jim admitted. "I mean, look at Korea. We signed a ceasefire with them thirty years ago, allowing us to negotiate an end to the war, but we still haven't formally ended the war.

"What I'm trying to explain is that I don't have a clue when Gene wants to meet in Virginia, how long that will be, when he wants me in South Africa, and I know he doesn't have a clue how long that will take," Jim finished. "But I promise I'll tell you when I find out.

"I think it's impossible for anyone to know how long the meetings, and I'm sure it won't be just one, in South Africa will take," he added. "And you're getting pissed at me for something I can't possibly know?

"Hell, Marie, I don't think even Gene knows," he continued. "I'll even bet his boss at Black Water doesn't have a clue either. Nor do those muttonheads in Washington, DC. I'd be willing to bet that even Jesus H. Christ himself doesn't know. So how the hell do you expect me to know?"

Chapter 16

"Then how can you agree to something so open-ended?" Marie asked. "That's like him asking you to take an assignment to a place he doesn't know and do something he hasn't been told about.

"Would you say yes?" Marie asked.

"Probably," Jim answered. "As long as I've known Gene, something like that has never happened. Usually, he has all the information I need to make my decision.

"And if I find out later that it's something I don't want to be involved in, I'm sure he'd be okay with that," he continued.

After a short pause, he said, "All I can guess, and it's just a guess, is that it has something to do with what's been in the news lately."

"What's been in the news?" Marie asked.

"It sounds like the South African government is stealing the land from the white farmers," Jim answered. "And there have been rumors of farmers and their families being tortured and killed.

"I've heard denials from their President, but then why would he want to acknowledge something like that happening in his country?" Jim continued. "Now, why Black Water is involved, I don't have a clue. But I can't think of anything else."

"That leads us back to why our government isn't taking care of the problem, if it even exists?" Marie countered.

"My guess, and I'm still guessing here, is that our government can't be viewed as meddling in another country's internal business," Jim posed. "We can't just walk over there and demand the return of the land to the rightful owners.

"Even if we had proof, all the South African President would have to say is for us to look at what we did to the Native Americans when we, the Europeans, came to America," Jim explained.

"And not just the Indians," he continued. "We took the land from the Mexicans as well. When you look back on our history, the white man has been about as evil a race as you can imagine.

"With Apartheid being the rule in South Africa for so long, it seems almost normal for the black population to seek retribution," he explained. "We have our 'reparations' issue, which is similar.

"So, I don't see this as a winning issue for our government to step in and condemn a situation which bears amazing similarities to our own," he finished. "So maybe the solution is to send a nongovernmental organization in to negotiate.

"I'm not a political science guy, but I think this is called backdoor negotiations," Jim said. "Our government can deny it if it fails but can also send in an *official* delegation if it proves to be to our advantage."

"Let's assume you are correct," Marie replied. "Why you? When did you become such a successful negotiator?"

"I never said I would be the negotiator," Jim argued. "I am just guessing that's what this is all about. I may only be a bag carrier for some experienced former diplomat who will actually be talking to the South African President.

"Or it may be some low-level schmo who will pass it on to the next level schmo, etc., until it reaches someone in an office who has the President's ear," he continued. "I may be the schmo who talks to their schmo. Or I could just be carrying the bag for the schmo and acting as his personal assistant.

"Of course, I could tell you that I would be the one who was meeting with the President of South Africa because of my charismatic personality and unbelievable ability to convince anyone of the subject I'm obviously a master of," he said. "But I know it's more likely I'll be carrying the bags for the lowest level of schmo there."

"I guess you're trying to tell me you're hoping to find out how low a level schmo you are when you get to Virginia," Marie replied.

"I never said I was any level of schmo," Jim countered. "I said I was even lower; I'm just carrying his bags. But yes, I'm hoping for a better explanation when we meet.

"I'm expecting to be more of a personal bodyguard assignment for one of our Ambassadors or some dignitary from the United Nations. That's a little more likely given my field of expertise," he continued. "Or my absolute lack of negotiation skills.

"Now, if you'd like to come with me and get the story firsthand," he said. "I'll ask Gene if it's okay for you to come with me."

"You think he'd let me sit in on stuff he hasn't even discussed with you?" she asked. "There's not a chance."

"No, you're right," Jim agreed. "He'd never let you do that. But you'd have a chance to talk to him after everything is taken care of regarding the operation, and maybe he'll have more to tell both of us exactly what I'm doing over there.

"As much as I wish I could tell you, I just don't know myself," he finished. "So, if you want to go, I'll ask."

"What would I do while you're having your meetings or whatever?" she asked, already planning to go.

"I don't know," Jim answered. "I'm sure there are lots of museums or art galleries around there. Or you could just sit around the hotel until we finish and meet for dinner.

"Why don't you do a little research on the area and see if you'd be interested before I ask Gene," Jim suggested.

"I'll think about it," Marie answered, nodding her head. But if I do decide to go, I'm going to need to go shopping for something appropriate for dinner and stuff. Probably a couple of new outfits. And shoes. I'll need at least two or three pairs. I'm going to need at least three days' notice before we go."

Chapter 17

No sooner than Jim had hung up than his phone rang again. Thinking it was Marie with another comment, he answered, "What is it now, Marie?"

"I'm not sure what it is now with Marie, but I wanted to let you know we have set the date for the meeting in Quantico for three days from now," Gene replied.

"Sorry about that, General," Jim said contritely. "Marie and I had just finished a marathon discussion regarding this operation, and I naturally assumed it was her with another *last word.*"

"Maybe assuming is natural in some parts of the world, but I tend to refrain from *naturally assuming*," Gene replied. "Not a good trait in our business."

"Again, my apologies," Jim said. "Have you made travel arrangements, or do I need to get a ticket?"

"I'm sending a plane down to pick up you and Butch," Gene answered. "It will be at Love Field at ten o'clock. I've talked to Butch, and he said he'd swing by and pick you up if you wanted."

"Not necessary," Jim replied. "However, that does bring up a question."

"Ask," Gene said. "I'll always have an answer, even if it's a tentative answer."

"I sort of alluded to Marie that she may be able to come with me," Jim told him.

"That's not a question," Gene corrected him. "That's what we in the business, or those who have studied basic sentence structure, call a statement.

"Overlooking that, what brought this up between you and Marie?" Gene asked.

"She's been questioning what I'm supposed to be doing in South Africa and wondering just why you chose me to be a negotiator for the problems," Jim answered.

"Where did she get the idea you were going over there to be part of a negotiation team?" Gene asked.

"From me," Jim admitted. "I couldn't very well tell her about the frogs and the rest of the operation, could I? So, I used the farmland reappropriation issue as to why I was going over there."

"I understand," Gene told him. "And I understand her concern about your involvement. Especially since she discovered some of the falsehoods, we've led her to believe about what Black Water actually does.

"So, I recognize the situation and realize you really had no other choice," he continued. "We're pretty much at the point of trying to put the toothpaste back in the tube regarding any future operations you become involved with.

"Either we include her a little more, or you'll risk creating a divide between the two of you, which will ultimately lead to each going their separate ways," Gene said. "Since you don't want that, the only option is to let her know a little more about this operation. At least the part that's already in the public domain.

"I sort of anticipated this and have a tentative solution, if you believe we can pull it off," Gene offered after a slight pause.

"At this point, I'm willing to listen to any solution, tentative or not," Jim replied. "Just what is your idea? We both know she can't learn the actual truth, and any lie better be believable and have some facts to support it."

"I know," Gene said. "Since you brought up the negotiation issue, which I'm sure she knew was completely unreasonable, given your lack of any training or experience, we have to somehow make your job dovetail with what she already thinks about what Black Water, and you, do."

"I told her that I didn't know exactly what I would be doing on the negotiating team and suggested I would possibly be providing personal security for one of the Ambassadors or something," Jim told him. "I was searching for something believable, and that is all I could come up with."

"Then that's exactly what you'll be doing," Gene said, nodding. "I'll make sure everyone she's likely to run into understands the ruse. Now let's return to your question.

"I believe it would be advantageous to all involved that she comes up with you," Gene said. "We can lead her down the path to the water, so to speak. I'll let her know more about the history behind the current situation and possibly draw some parallels with our own history.

"I'll let Butch know since he'll be on the plane with you guys, and I'll get everyone else on board with the story," he said. "And, I'll make sure Butch has a story that would be reasonable under the circumstances, with a little embellishment.

"Are there any other land mines in our paths you've planted in your discussions with Marie?" Gene asked, shaking his head.

"None that I can think of offhand," Jim answered. "But you know I occasionally suffer from hoof and mouth disease."

"That I know all too well," Gene said, chuckling. "I only wish I knew of a cure, but medical science can do only so much."

"I only know of one way to prevent this issue from arising over and over as long as I'm involved in Black Water," Jim replied.

"And that is?" Gene asked.

"Let her know the full story," Jim answered. "Otherwise, I'll be fabricating some different story over and over again. Sooner or later, my story from three missions ago will conflict with another, and Marie will start questioning how honest a man I truly am."

"Let me think about that," Gene said. "I'm sure we can never let her know everything about some of our operations, such as this one, but maybe we can convince her that when we're involved with bad actors, we have to respond in kind.

"You just keep her believing you're coming as personal protection for some Ambassador or Embassy toad until I can figure out just how far I'm willing to go to satisfy her curiosity," Gene finished. "I love Marie as if she were my own daughter, and I'm glad you've found a lady who makes you happy after the tragic death of Jennifer.

"But my obligation is to protect Black Water and our relationship with our government," Gene finished. "Perhaps I'll have a better solution when we meet in three days."

Chapter 18

As soon as he had ended the call with Gene, Jim called Marie to let her know when they would be leaving for Virginia.

As she answered, he told her, "Gene says you're welcome to come along, and he's sending one of the company planes to get us."

"When?" Marie asked.

"In three days," Jim replied. "We need to be at Love Field in the morning before ten o'clock."

"That's not much notice," Marie complained. "Today is almost over, and if I have to be at the airport three days from now means I only have tomorrow to get everything for the trip."

"I don't think you really need to go to much extreme for this," Jim explained. "You'll be on the airplane with Butch and I, and possibly another person or two, and nobody really cares how you're dressed.

"I'm wearing jeans and a t-shirt," he added. "That would be fine for you as well."

"I'm not going dressed like some country bumpkin," she said. "And who knows who else will be on the plane. I'm guessing that Butch is the same guy I met last time we went to Quantico.

"And I'm sure he'll be talking to Amanda, and I don't want her to think I don't have appropriate attire for occasions such as this," she continued.

"First off, yes, Butch is the same guy you've already met," Jim told her. "And I can guarantee you that he doesn't care what you're wearing. And I sincerely doubt he'll even think of mentioning it to Amanda.

"Guys don't think that way," he added. "Women are the only ones who care what they are wearing. And both Butch and Amanda have seen you dressed, as you call it, appropriately."

"I'm not sure I even want to go, now," Marie said. "I'm sure there will be other ladies there, just as there were before, and I'm not going to embarrass myself in front of them.

"That was a unique occasion," Jim reminded her. "It was a formal affair due to having the Border Czar there. This will just be a dinner or two with some of the normal guys like me. What you'd wear if we were going to dinner at Denny's would be entirely appropriate.

"But, if you don't believe you have whatever you want to wear, by all means, take tomorrow and get what you want," he finished.

"I plan on it," she replied. "Now, how many days will we be there? I can't wear the same thing to dinner every night."

"Gene didn't say," Jim told her. "I'd guess we'll meet for dinner twice, maybe three times. I'd bet that's about as long as this will take. The first night will probably be just us and Gene. Probably Butch as well."

"Is Amanda coming with Butch?" she asked.

"I don't know," Jim answered. "I don't think she's involved with this operation, and I haven't talked to him about it."

"How do you know he's coming then?" she asked.

"Gene told me Butch offered to pick me up and go to the airport with him," Jim explained. "I haven't actually talked to him, so all I know is he's going to be on the same plane."

"Why don't you call him and see if Amanda is coming?" Marie asked. "It would be nice to have someone there I already know."

"No," Jim said. "Butch didn't say anything about her. Neither did Gene. I believe it's safe to assume she isn't coming with us."

"But you don't know if she'll be there," Marie argued.

"No, I don't," Jim replied, becoming exasperated with the direction of the conversation. "And I don't care. If you still want to come, do whatever you want. I'm just trying to tell you this is going to be as informal as me coming to your dad's restaurant.

"But, if you want to spend all day tomorrow buying four new outfits, with matching shoes and purses, I don't care," Jim finished. "As far as I'm concerned, and I'm sure Butch will agree, none of this warrants anything more than what we'd wear if we were meeting for a beer at a local bar."

"I don't care what you and Butch think," Marie answered. "But I don't plan on having any of the other people who will be there thinking I dress like some floozy at the local bar."

"I've told you what I think," Jim replied. "You can certainly wear whatever you want. The only reason I called was to tell you Gene said you were welcome to come, and to let you know when."

Jim paused and then said, "I've got to go take care of some stuff here since we only have one day available. If you don't mind, it would help if you spent the night here tomorrow night.

"That would make it easier to get to the airport before ten," he finished. "But you need to let me know so I'll know if I need to leave the house an hour earlier to come by your house."

"I'll let you know tomorrow," Marie replied, before hanging up. "Now I've got to figure out what I want to wear and plan my shopping since I only have one day."

Chapter 19

Three days later, as Jim was loading his pickup truck for the drive to Love Field, he asked, "Marie, is there anything else before we leave?"

"No," she answered. "Did you get your suitcase?"

"Of course," he answered, smiling. "It's buried somewhere beneath the pile of your suitcases."

"We're not going to go there again, are we?" she asked, getting into the passenger seat.

"Of course not," Jim replied, getting in. "I've tried beating a dead horse before, and it never helps. Neither does milking a dead cow."

"And all of that means?" Marie asked, as Jim started the pickup.

"It means I'll just shut up and drive," he replied.

Thirty minutes later, Jim parked beside the General Aviation terminal and said, "Why don't you go on in and I'll bring the bags."

As he was removing Marie's bags from the rear seat, Butch walked up and asked, "Can I give you a hand?"

Jim turned and stuck out his hand, saying, "That would be great. How was the drive in?"

"Not too bad," Butch answered, picking up two suitcases. "Just a little over an hour. Most of the commuter traffic had gotten off the road, and there weren't any accidents to slow me down.

"It would have been closer for me to use the Dallas Fort Worth airport," he continued, carrying the bags to the terminal. "But since it's the company's plane, I guess they can land wherever they want."

"I think they like Love Field because it doesn't have the traffic DFW has," Jim said, as they entered the terminal. "Just sit the bags over there beside the door since I don't see the plane on the ramp."

"I know better than to say anything, but since I know you'd only bring one suitcase and it probably only has a shave kit and two changes of underwear, does Marie think we're staying a month?" Butch asked as they saw Marie coming from the lady's restroom.

"Yeah, you'd be well advised to avoid that subject completely," Jim whispered as Marie approached.

"Marie, I'm sure you remember Butch," Jim said, as Butch reached out to shake her hand.

"Of course," she answered, shaking his hand. "And I remember the lady you were with, Amanda. Such a nice lady."

"Will she be meeting us there?" Marie asked, as they saw a Gulfstream V taxiing to the front of the terminal.

"Not that I know of," Butch answered. "I don't think she's involved with this operation."

"Let's grab the suitcases and head out to the plane," Jim quickly suggested, to forestall any conversation involving Butch's private life as he was picking up two suitcases.

"Right behind you," Butch said, grabbing the remaining two. "This is going to be my first time flying a private jet. What's it like?"

"Pretty nice," Jim said, as Marie followed him to where the plane had parked and the boarding stairs were being lowered. "Beats the last row on the Super Eighty across the aisle from the toilet."

"I've been there before myself," Butch replied, nodding as a man with three stripes on his epaulets came down to greet them.

"Just sit those down and I'll take them up," he said, as he reached where they were standing. "I'm Trey Taylor, and I'll be assisting Captain Rob Sproc on the flight to Quantico."

"Nice to meet you," Jim said, shaking his hand. "If it's alright with you, Butch and I can take the suitcases up the stairs and put them wherever you want them."

"That'll be fine," Trey answered. "Just sit them inside the door and I'll store them in the luggage area. You guys go ahead and find a seat while I do a quick inspection of the plane, and Rob takes care of the paperwork.

"Oh, yes," Trey added. "There are a couple of folders in the passenger area for you two. And there are some snacks in the galley area. Just make yourselves at home."

Jim took the seat where the folder bearing his name was and waited for Marie to take the window seat beside him. Sitting down, he wondered if he should open the folder with her sitting beside him.

Knowing Gene had anticipated that, he decided to take a look. Pulling the elastic band from the button holding the folder closed, he pulled out a file holding numerous papers and took a quick look.

"What's that?" Marie asked, looking at the paper Jim had set on the small table in front of him.

"Looks like a document from the US Department of Agriculture transferring me to the United Nations Humanitarian Rights Council," he replied, amazed that Gene had been able to mount such a fabrication in such a short time.

"This one seems to assign me to the Assistant to the Under Secretary of the UN Refugee Agency," he continued. "And here's another one assigning me to someone named Megan Foxworthy as her personal security officer."

"What do you have?" Jim asked Butch as he saw him shuffling through his file.

"A bunch of papers describing me as some administrative assistant to some assistant to the Director of US Customs and Immigration," he answered.

"Hell, look here," Butch said, pulling a laminated badge from the file. "I've even got an official badge."

"And a no-shit badge," he continued, holding up a gold badge with ICE embossed on a blue background.

"You've got me beat," Jim said, searching through his file. "All I have is a bunch of papers signed by some schmo with an official seal stamped into the papers."

"Maybe you're undercover," Butch suggested. "Maybe they don't want anyone to know who you are or what you're doing."

"You're just a shoe clerk stamping paperwork for people wanting to claim asylum in the United States, and you get a shiny badge?" Jim asked incredulously.

"Oh, grasshopper," Butch replied pinning the ICE badge to his knit shirt. "You're speaking to an official of ICE and using defamatory language. I could toss you out of the country for that."

As Butch was simulating polishing his badge with his bare forearm, Captain Sproc stepped in and walked back to where they were sitting. "Good morning, folks, I'm Captain Sproc, but please just call me Rob," he said. "It's gonna be a quick flight, no clouds, smooth air, and a hundred knot tailwind.

"But if you have any questions, please don't hesitate to let either Trey or I know," he continued. "I'm aware that both of you guys are pilots for American Airlines, so naturally, I assume you are quite comfortable back here.

"But if the lady has any apprehension, please let us know," Rob said. "Now, if there are no questions, I'll get back to work and we'll head east at almost six hundred miles an hour, counting the tailwind.

"Again, don't hesitate to call on us if you need anything," Rob finished, seeing Trey enter the plane and give him a thumbs up.

Chapter 20

After landing and taxiing to the ramp at the Quantico Marine Corps Air Facility, Jim noticed a black Suburban waiting just yards from where they parked. As the engines wound down, the Suburban moved to a position just feet from where the stairs on the left side of the Gulfstream would be lowered.

"You guys go on down," Trey said, stepping from the cockpit. "I'll bring your bags to the bottom of the stairs."

"Thanks, Trey," Jim said, letting Marie out from her window seat. "You guys did a great job."

Following Marie down the stairs, Jim was surprised to see Fabio standing there helping Marie take the final step. "Fabio," he said. "I never expected you see you here."

"I asked for the job when I heard you were coming in," he replied, as Jim stepped off the stairs and shook his hand. "I can't think of anyone who is as glad to see you again as I am."

"Marie, this is Fabio," Jim said, introducing them. "He was my driver back in Indianapolis. Not only did he do a terrific job, but he also watched my back every second."

"Nice to meet you, Fabio," Marie said, shaking his hand. "Someone has to watch out for this guy. He can't seem to stay out of trouble."

"He wasn't any trouble, ma'am," Fabio replied. "I've got to say working with Jim was the most interesting job I've ever had being a driver."

"Just normal, take me here, take me there," Jim countered. "Where are you taking us now?"

"General Barker has made reservations at the Embassy Suites in Springfield," Fabio told him. "It's about a thirty-minute drive, and the General thought there would be more for Marie to do while you guys are meeting on base."

"That sounds great," Jim said. "There's a lot more up there, Arlington National Cemetery, tours at the White House, probably more art galleries and museums than a person could see in a year."

"For sure," Fabio agreed, as he took two of the bags Trey had set at the base of the stairs.

Jim and Butch picked up the remaining bags and carried them to the Suburban where Fabio tossed them in the rear.

"Any idea what Gene has planned for this evening?" Jim asked, as they got into the Suburban.

"I'm to drop you and Butch off at Black Water and take Marie to the hotel," Fabio answered. "I'm not sure what he wants at the headquarters building, but I know he's made dinner reservations for you guys at five this evening."

"Do you know who's coming to dinner?" Marie asked, as they headed for the entrance to the Black Water headquarters.

"No ma'am," Fabio answered. "All I know is I'm supposed to drop you off and return to get Jim and Butch at four o'clock. I'll be back tomorrow morning at seven to take them back to Black Water for the day.

"Then, I'll pretty much be at your disposal if you want to go see the sights," he finished.

"You mean I'll have you to take me anywhere I want?" Marie asked excitedly.

"Yes, ma'am," Fabio answered, as he headed for the Black Water headquarters. "As long as I can be back to get Jim and Butch at four o'clock."

"Private jet and my own chauffeur," Marie said, sitting back. "I'm going to enjoy this."

"Sounds like you better have a map of all the popular tourist spots," Jim said, as they approached the outer fence surrounding the massive concrete building that housed Black Water.

As they approached the first gate, a Marine Sergeant stepped from the guard shack and said, "Could I see your identification, please?"

"Just me or everyone?" Fabio asked, taking his ID from the visor over his seat.

"Everyone," the Sergeant said, looking at Fabio's ID and checking it against a list on the clipboard he held.

Handing it back, he looked at Jim and asked, "How about you, sir?"

Jim handed his ID over and waited for his name to be checked. Handing his ID back, the Sergeant snapped to attention and saluted, saying, "Thank you, Colonel."

Next, he took Butch's ID he had already pulled from his wallet. Checking his name on the list, he announced, "If you'll wait here, I'll notify the folks who are coming to get you. Sorry, but only Colonel Lashley and Mr. North are cleared past this point."

"That's not unexpected," Jim told Marie. "Access is pretty restricted here."

As he finished speaking, the inner gate slid open, and they saw Gene on a four-seat golf cart heading their way. As he approached the gate where they were waiting, the Sergeant waited for the inner gate to completely close and then opened the gate to let Gene through.

"I'll see you at the hotel in a couple of hours," Jim said, getting out of the Suburban.

"Jim, nice you see you," Gene said, stepping from the cart and walking over. "And you too, Butch."

Leaning down, he said, "Welcome to Quantico, Marie. Has Fabio told you the plan?"

"Yes," Marie answered. "I get to roam around the city all day while you boys discuss secret missions or whatever you guys do here."

"That's pretty much it," Gene agreed. "Toss in a pool game and a couple of beers, you've summed it up."

Turning to Fabio, he said, "I'll be bringing Jim and Butch this evening, and tomorrow evening as well. Just please be ready to pick them up at seven in the morning and the following morning for their return to Texas."

"We're only here for one day?" Jim asked after kissing Marie goodbye.

"That's the plan as of now," Gene said. "If everything goes as planned and we don't have any surprises, we should be done by four o'clock tomorrow.

"Oh, we'll also have dinner at the hotel tomorrow evening," Gene told Marie. "So, if you'll finish your tour by four o'clock or so, I've made reservations for five of us at five."

"Who is the fifth?" Marie asked.

"If she's able to make it, it's the lady Jim will be working with in South Africa. Johannesburg, to be more precise," Gene answered. "I want them to have a little extra time to make sure there are no slip-ups when they are dealing with whoever is representing the President.

Chapter 21

Once they had entered the windowless building, Gene turned to a dark glass set into the wall and said, "General Barker with Jim Lashley and Butch North."

A moment passed as unseen cameras scanned their faces, and then a slight click was heard, and the door slid open. Nodding to the unseen operator behind the glass, Gene said, "We'll first head to the cafeteria for a quick snack. I'm sure you didn't have time for breakfast this morning, and it's going to be a while before we have dinner, so there's just enough time to grab something before we meet with Debbie in the main auditorium."

"How many of our people are here today?" Jim asked, taking a tuna fish sandwich and a bag of chips.

"I'm not exactly sure, but I know there are over two hundred," Gene answered, selecting a chicken salad sandwich.

"I have a question," Butch said, as he grabbed a ham and cheese hoagie.

"Go ahead and ask," Gene said, getting a glass of tea.

"Why is it a tuna fish sandwich and a chicken salad sandwich?" Butch asked, getting a glass of tea. "I mean, if it's a tuna *fish* sandwich, shouldn't it also be a chicken *bird* sandwich?"

Gene stopped and looked at Butch for a moment and then replied, "You've been spending way too much time around Jim. I'd expect some smartass thing like that from him.

"But if you're really interested in that, there is an excellent library here, or you can pose the question to Debbie tomorrow during her briefing, and see what response you get," he finished, taking a seat at a long table.

"Oh, no," Butch said, sitting across from Gene. "I've heard about that lady. No way I'll let her have a chance to humiliate me in front of an audience of two or three hundred people."

"Bracer doesn't need an audience to humiliate someone," Jim replied, almost laughing. "I think she prefers it, but it's certainly not necessary. I've seen her send a grown man to his knees, blubbering uncontrollably, just because he questioned her ability to know where anyone is at a specific time. The lady doesn't suffer fools gladly."

"Why do you call her Bracer?" Butch asked.

"That goes way back," Gene explained. "There was an unknown computer hacker who was wreaking havoc with governmental computers and getting into systems we thought unbreakable.

"We launched a nationwide search for this person known only as Bracer due to the signature left just to tantalize us," Gene continued. "We tried to follow every lead that used those letters in any combination or had some hidden meaning.

"We used every known language, dialect, or anything to decipher some hidden clue," he explained. "It's unbelievable the effort spent trying to learn the identity of this person who seemed to be able to waltz in and out of the most secure programs involving our Defense Department, programs involving defense contractors, banking systems, you name it. Bracer was everywhere, but invisible.

"Then, while we were doing random checks through the Department of Motor Vehicles, the DMV, down in Texas, we stumbled across a fellow who looked at the word Bracer, and smiled in recognition," he continued. "We had gone through every motor vehicle registration licensing across the country.

"Every combination of letters and numbers assigned to a license plate was scoured to locate this menace," Gene said, shaking his head. "No hits. Then we happen upon this small DMV office in Texas, where someone recognizes the word.

"Turns out that the man we were talking to had gone to school with a lady and had a major crush on her," Gene continued. "The lady was a barrel racer and had put custom plates on her horse trailer. B racer. Barrel Racer?

"Since the plate was not being used, it wasn't entered into the computer system," Gene explained. "But this poor heart-struck fellow remembered the day she came to pick up her vanity plates. Most importantly, he knew her name.

"Once we had her identified, the rest was easy," Gene finished. "We, Black Water, offered her two choices. One, we could turn her over to the Feds and let them decide her fate, which probably meant crocheting doilies in some federal prison.

"Or she could come to work for us," Gene finished. "The choice she made, you already know."

"Whatever happened to the guy who recognized the license plate thing?" Butch asked.

"He married a fat woman from a neighboring town, and they have twelve children with learning disabilities because unbeknownst to either of them, they were actually half sister and brother to each other," Jim answered. "Their mutual father was a Postal worker who made too many special deliveries. What the hell difference does it make?"

Butch looked at Gene for confirmation and then said, "Bullshit. I was just wondering if she, Debbie, knows who outed her."

"She figured it out," Gene replied. "Since she was aware of her own trailer tags, it didn't take long to add two and two. The only flaw in her plan was that someone from her distant past would recognize the plate that led to her. And the odds of that were astronomical. But to answer the unasked question, she didn't even attempt to contact him."

"Hey, just another love gone wrong song," Jim said, finishing his sandwich. "I'll see you guys in the auditorium."

Chapter 22

"Hey, Debbie," Jim said, walking up to the podium at the front of the room. "About to get a grip on the situation?"

"Have you ever tried to get a grip on a puff of smoke?" she responded. "Or hold a handful of fog?"

"Can't say I have," Jim replied, looking around at the number of people milling around the auditorium. "What's your biggest issue regarding this operation?"

"Are you referring to resolving the genocide issue or the Presidential issue?" she asked.

"Aren't they related?" Jim asked, spotting Gene heading toward him with a woman walking by his side.

"On the macro side, yes," Debbie replied. "But on the micro side, two entirely different issues."

"Let's take the farm issue," Jim said. "What's the major stumbling block?"

"Computers," Debbie answered. "I thought tracking all the players in previous operations was difficult. That was a piece of cake compared to this."

"How so?" Jim asked.

"Sheer numbers," she explained. "Here, there are three hundred thousand farms. If you estimate four people at each farm—the typical family—to estimate the number of targets we have to monitor…that's over a million targets.

"And that doesn't include our people, another three hundred or so, and an unknown number of opposition players. I don't have enough computing power to monitor each of them," she finished.

"I'm sure you'll come up with something," Jim said, shaking his head. "I would already guess you've developed some priority system which updates the most likely areas of concern every millisecond."

"No," she corrected him, smiling. "But I've got it down to a tenth of a second."

"More to my part of this effort," Jim responded. "How's that portion going?"

"That one's fairly simple," Debbie told him, as Gene walked up. "I've been monitoring that situation for months and can almost predict every move the Pig makes, given any situation."

"I believe you mean the Bull, don't you?" Jim asked.

"No, I mean pig. The man is a pig," Debbie repeated. "Hog. Swine. Sus domesticus. I don't think I've ever been disgusted with a male of any species as I have been with this pig.

"I've had to watch hours and hours of his activities and listen to hours and hours of conversations," she continued. "A bull is a magnificent animal. Thick neck and chest, proud stance, pure animal, masculinity on display.

"Our man is more physically aligned with a pig," Debbie explained. "A pot-bellied pig. Narrow shoulders, protruding stomach, flabby arms. Nothing attractive or masculine about that poor specimen.

"And he's got what I call a dickie-do-belly," she said, shaking her head.

"What's a dickie-do-belly?" the lady with Gene asked.

"That's a belly that sticks out further than his dickie do," Debbie informed her. "Toss in a frog butt and you can get the picture. A most repulsive, repugnant, disgusting person. And then there's the grunting."

"I guess I'm the lucky lady who gets to deal with this gentleman," she said, shaking her head. "Lucky, lucky, lucky."

Gene took a second and then said, "Jim, this lucky lady is Megan. And as you can tell, she's anxious to meet our Presidential Pig down in Johannesburg as soon as possible."

"Hi, Megan," Jim said, with a slight nod. "I'm pleased to meet you. I'm sure Debbie has done some embellishment of the object of our mission."

"I'd say she's understated it," Megan said, looking from Jim to Debbie. "I haven't watched as much of this man as Debbie, I'm sure. However, what I've seen confirms her description is on target.

"Now, this assignment wasn't my first choice," she continued. "Especially when I read the man's biography and studied every facet of his life, but I couldn't let someone else deal with this. That would be too easy.

"No, I knew there would be some unpleasant assignments when I joined Black Water," she continued. "But I agree with Debbie. This is probably the top of the list of unpleasant assignments.

"The only shining light is that the man will cease to exist when we complete our assignment," she finished. "And knowing how it will end, even with the expected licking of the toad, brings a certain joy to my heart."

Chapter 23

"I have a package for you to take back to the hotel and review this evening," Gene said. "I'll give it to you when we leave."

"Is there some shift in the mission?" Jim asked.

"Not really, but since you've led Marie to believe you are just a bodyguard for the actual negotiator, we've decided it would also be best for the mission to switch your and Megan's roles," Gene answered. "So now you're her assistant.

"Another factor we looked at is we don't think President Pig, and we've got to stop using that term, would allow a presumably armed person to be as close as you'll need to be," he continued. "Everything else is pretty much the same.

"Oh, I almost forgot," Gene added. "We're putting the Montblanc pen in the briefcase. We ran several tests with metal detectors, and it rang the bell every time. That would require you to remove it, and they would probably handle it. Unnecessary exposure.

"However, having a pen in a briefcase full of documents needing signatures seems more realistic," he explained. "Not to mention, not too many men carry a pen in their shirt pocket anymore.

"When Megan asks for documents which are in the briefcase, you'll be reaching into it several times," he continued. "Once that becomes routine, you won't be noticed when you reach in for the pen.

"One other factor in reversing positions is taking advantage of the Bull's propensity to attempt to impress any woman he sees as desirable," Gene added. "Given all of these reasons, you've been demoted from negotiator to bodyguard to assistant to the assistant of an assistant.

"Now, back to the package. You need to be very familiar with it before the operation begins. It's a dossier on Megan's past experience in negotiations, time with the State Department, various embassies, and as an assistant to several ambassadors," he explained. "You'll be very surprised at the accomplishments she has achieved in such a short time."

"What you'll be surprised with is the amount of bullshit that can be fabricated in such a short time," Megan said, shaking her head. "I've never even heard of some of the people or places where I'm supposed to have been instrumental in the negotiation crap when I have no idea what crap is being negotiated."

"The company is rather proficient in slight embellishment when it comes to the resumes of their people," Jim said, nodding. "Half the time, I have no idea of what mine says, but I've been assured I'm invaluable in whatever area where I'm the most qualified person. At least that's what the company tells whoever I'm being sent to deal with.

"If you were to believe everything they put in my various biographies, you'd believe I can run faster, dive deeper, and come up dryer than any human possibly could," Jim said, laughing. "I guess that since I'm so invaluable, I can expect a hefty raise following every mission where I've proven once again my invaluableness."

"Maybe if you were a bodyguard," Gene said, smiling. "But you're just an assistant to an assistant for an assistant. Your compensation follows your position during any operation."

"Has the company, on behalf of our government, requested an audience with the Bull?" Jim asked.

"Of course," Gene answered. "That's one of the reasons we don't have an actual date for the operation yet.

"We're sending the same package I'm giving you to their Chief of Staff, requesting a date at their earliest convenience," he continued. "The package will also contain a photo of Megan, which should elicit some response when it's shown to the Bull. We believe that will get us a quicker response."

"And my resume?" Jim asked.

"Of course it was attached," Gene assured him. "It will be one page depicting your position, assistant, with a small black and white photo at the top of the sheet."

"That might get a quick glance," Jim replied. "And that's probably all I'll get from the Bull."

"That's exactly the point," Gene told him. "We want his attention on Megan. He has a rather dismissive attitude to anyone he sees as inferior and tends to forget they are around.

"Put a beautiful lady in front of him, I doubt you'll warrant even a glance," Gene explained. "Given all of the circumstances and things we've learned about him, this change in your positions should enhance the chance of success."

"Let's talk about that," Jim said. "Have there been any preparations made for our extraction should things go off course? It would be nice to have some way of getting us the hell out of there if I get caught squirting something in the man's drink."

"I guess the best answer I can give you is no, there are no workable plans to get both of you out of there," Gene answered. "Even the car you'll be taking from the hotel we've booked for you to his place in Johannesburg will be driven by one of his people."

"Why?" Jim asked. "Why don't we provide our own driver? At least then, I'd have an asset who could possibly help us get out of there safely."

"That's not how he usually does things," Gene answered. "He has control issues and wants only his people handling every aspect. That includes bringing guests to his house in Johannesburg."

"I think you should look into how I can use the car to get us out of there," Jim suggested. "Is there some way to get one of our people on the property who can disable the driver and get us somewhere for an extraction? At least put a weapon of some sort in the car where I can get to it."

"I'll have Debbie look into how we can put someone there," Gene said, nodding.

"How about as a FedEx driver?" Jim suggested. "I'm sure there are frequent deliveries when the Bull is in residence there. And I'd bet there are few, if any, searches of either the vehicle or the delivery guy."

"That's a good idea," Gene agreed. "We'll take a look at it. The biggest issue will be the timing. We can't have him get there too soon, or worse yet, too late. That's going to take some planning."

"We'll be wearing some sort of communication system, won't we?" Jim asked. "Something like we used in Indianapolis."

"No," Gene answered. "We thought that would probably draw attention."

"Put it in the briefcase," Jim suggested. "The stuff Debbie uses has a range of several feet, doesn't it? Or use our phones. Even if they take them from us to prevent us from using them to record the meeting, they should be close enough to pick up our conversations. And I doubt they would do much of an inspection of my briefcase.

"Or, if Debbie has some bug planted in his phone, use it," Jim continued.

"I'd rather rely on our own assets," Gene told him. "He may leave his phone in the toilet or somewhere we can't guarantee monitoring the situation. Let's use the briefcase."

"Back to the timing issue," Jim said. "Let's come up with a phrase that would be normal during the negotiations but would tell the FedEx guy to get his ass to the house.

"Do some research on how far away from the residence he can park without drawing attention," Jim continued. "We know he can stall for a couple of minutes pretending to look for the package he's delivering, so work out a time frame for me to let him know we need assistance, and he can be at the front door waiting.

"And make damn sure he's armed. I'd like it even more if he were entering the house with a twelve-gauge in a cardboard box," Jim finished. "I'd suggest a Kel-Tec KSG Bullpup. It's compact and carries twelve shells plus one in the chamber."

"I'll make it happen," Gene said, as Debbie walked up.

"Shall we get this started, General?" she asked.

"The stage is yours," Gene answered, as he led Jim and Megan away.

Chapter 24

"Okay, folks," Debbie said, taking the podium. "Please take a seat, preferably in the section divided to replicate the areas where you will be operating when you get to South Africa.

"For clarity's sake, area one is to my left, area two is directly in front of me, and area three is naturally to my right," she said, watching the people milling about.

"It's not that important that you are in that section, but it will make it easier when we get a little farther into this afternoon's program," she continued. "And speaking of this afternoon's program, we don't have all afternoon. So please move as quickly as you can without knocking someone down."

As soon as the majority of the people had found a seat, she said, "We still don't have an exact starting date, but I've been assured it won't be long from now.

"That does not mean that we are sitting on our asses," she told them. "We've sent agents to South Africa to scout various farms that have been abandoned. It will likely be one or more of these that we will use if there's any resistance from families still on their land.

"We did a quick survey and found that many of the families who are still trying to maintain their lives are worried that having a family who is trying to leave the country could place them in greater jeopardy," she explained.

"These same agents will be incorporated into the teams in the areas where they have been scouting," she told them. "That should expedite learning your areas, save time searching for an individual farm, and provide current intelligence regarding your specific area.

"Now, I'm going to introduce you to the gentlemen who will be directing the operation," Debbie said, turning to Butch. "First, Mr. Butch North will be responsible for ensuring our assets, which basically means you people, are where they need to be, when they need to be there.

"Then I'll let him introduce the three gentlemen who will be in charge of the individual areas," she finished and stepped aside, motioning for Butch to take the microphone.

"Good afternoon, everybody," Butch said, stepping to the podium. "As Debbie said, I'm Butch. Disregard the Mr. North. I'm probably the most un-mister you will ever meet in your lives.

"As far as directing the operation, that's actually happening here in this building," he told them. "And the person behind that is the lady who just told you I was in charge. I am in charge of making sure the instructions from here are provided to you, the operators.

"The best way of doing that is to have short lines of communication and a limited number of contacts," he explained. "Under normal conditions, I'll be relaying information directly from Debbie and her folks watching over us to the fellow in charge of your individual area.

"I'll be monitoring each area's operation as well as I can, but I only have two ears," he continued. "Debbie has hundreds. But she also has hundreds of frequencies to monitor. Some are not connected with our operation at the farms, or possibly not connected with our mission of eradicating the bad actors and possibly assisting those seeking refugee status.

"There is one major role we will be playing in addition to what I've mentioned," he said, looking at Gene to see if he could broach the subject. "There is a single target that we are especially interested in."

Seeing Gene nod his approval, Butch continued, "This target is the highest priority of our entire operation. He is, in fact, the man behind the rapes, murders, and theft of the farmland from the rightful owners.

"Each of the areas has been assigned three sniper-qualified shooters. I will have direct contact with these guys. If I need to assign one to this target, it requires immediate action," he said, looking at each face as he scanned the crowd. "Every one of you will be given a photo of the man, and you are to contact me directly if you spot him. Or think you've spotted him.

"Time is critical on this issue," Butch explained. "We can't take a chance of missing the only shot we may ever get if I can't get the shooter in position as quickly as possible.

"The man will be highly mobile, possibly using a helicopter, and has no restrictions as to where he can travel," Butch warned them. "He's also going to be well guarded.

"Now, if there are no questions, and I hope there aren't because I'm as clueless as you are at this point, I'll turn it over to the gentlemen who are your primary contacts for operations in your areas. I hope by now, you've at least met them. If not, please get with them when Debbie dismisses us for the evening."

Chapter 25

After the meeting had concluded and Gene was driving Jim and Butch to the hotel, he asked, "How do you think it went?"

"Reasonably well," Jim answered. "But what more could you expect from such a short meeting where there wasn't shit for information and nobody knew anyone."

"That's rather harsh, don't you think?" Gene countered. "What did you expect anyway?"

"Pretty much what I got," Jim answered. "Look, this could have been just a travel day for everyone. This meeting was purely a chance to count noses and let the people see who was running the show, so to speak.

"You could have sent them photos with bios and asked them to notify Black Water when they had checked into their hotels," Jim finished.

"So, you think it was all a waste of time," Gene replied.

"No, that's not what I said," Jim explained. "I think getting the people together, especially where they can see who they will be working with, is somewhat worthwhile.

"I think having the operators from the field meet the man they'll be working under was important," he continued. "But all of that could have been done at the motel with an open bar or buffet table."

"In other words, it was a complete waste of time," Gene restated.

"No," Jim replied. "I think Butch's revealing the main objective was extremely important. We couldn't have put that in any brochure, but I believe it brought focus to the people and reminded them of the real reason we're here.

"I think his emphasis on the critical time issue was the exact thing to tell them," he continued. "Yeah, we're there to help the farmers who want to leave. But that's not a critically time-sensitive operation.

"And we're going to be there to eliminate the bad actors who are following the orders to enact this genocide," Jim added. "But narrowing the focus to a single face was the pivotal point, I believe.

"I'm not sure if you looked around as Butch was talking about the Steer, but I was," he explained. "You could see the look on the faces change when he told them about the priority of the Steer. It's as if each eye squinted slightly and mentally focused on that single issue.

"Before that, they were casually looking around, probably wondering why it took so many men to hand out refugee visas," he added. "You asked if I thought it was a waste of time. Definitely not."

Jim paused for a moment, and then said, "If I could pick one moment out of the entire hour or so we were there listening to how we didn't have enough information to add to their knowledge on the operation, that moment was when Butch looked at you and you nodded your approval.

"Everything prior to that could have been handled with a photo and a three-paragraph description of where the operation stands right now," Jim continued. "Then those few words Butch spoke brought this operation into something more personal and with greater focus. As I previously said, that was a pivotal moment."

Gene was silent as he continued to drive for several minutes, and then finally glanced at Jim and said, "You're right. This could have been handled with informational packets left in their rooms. No, we didn't tell these people anything new. They knew why they were going to South Africa.

"Or they at least thought they did," he corrected himself.

He continued to head for the hotel and then suddenly looked at Jim and said, "Damn it, I hate it when you're right. I know it happens so infrequently, but it's still irritating."

Glancing in the rearview mirror, Gene asked, "Butch, does it irritate you as much as it does me to listen to him when he knows he's right?"

"I've never experienced that before," Butch said, grinning. "I was dumbfounded. Granted, I haven't known him as long as you have, but you'd think I would have heard some inkling of intelligence and awareness during that time."

Jim turned and looked at Butch for a moment, then said, "After I make up nice shit to say about you, and making up nice shit about you is a monumental effort, you collude with the General to impugn my ability to discern the veracity of events I behold."

"Oh, shit," Gene said, laughing. "Now we've got him using every big word he knows. I should have kept my mouth shut. Let this be a lesson to you, Butch. Never provide a man with a platform to demonstrate his acumen of the English language. Especially when it's his second language."

"I thought he grew up speaking English," Butch replied, as he tried not to laugh. "English isn't his first language?"

"Somewhere down the list a ways," Gene answered, as the hotel came into view. "Jim is extremely fluent in Texican, profanity, and gibberish. English? He can get by with a little help from his friends. But that's about it."

Chapter 26

"Okay, guys," Gene said, letting Jim and Butch out at the entrance to the hotel. "I'll go park and head to the restaurant. I'll see y'all and Marie in a few minutes."

"Sounds good," Jim said, before shutting his door. "Maybe she's ready. I know it's only four thirty and you told her the reservations are for five, so my bet is I'll come down and wait for her to join us.

"I have never understood why some people think that a five o'clock reservation means after five o'clock," Jim continued. "Granted, it's not for three, or even four o'clock.

"But you don't need to come down at five thirty and not expect there to be a reservation after yours," he added, shutting the door. "Hell, I'd rather come down at four and enjoy a drink at the bar instead of feeling rushed to finish my meal because I was thirty minutes late for my reservation."

"Don't poke the bear unnecessarily," Gene advised. "You know her habits better than I, but women seem to get their back up when they get rushed when they're dressing for a night out. Doesn't matter if it's already past the reservation time; they've got to check the lipstick one more time. Or change shoes because the ones she's wearing clash with the purse.

"All I'm trying to tell you is that perhaps waiting for her to be ready might be the best option," Gene advised. "Butch and I can be found at the bar if the table isn't ready, which I'm betting it will be this close to five o'clock. Just do as you think best, and we'll see you and Marie when you get there."

Jim headed for the door with Butch following, and asked him, "Do you need to go to your room before dinner?"

"Nope," Butch answered. "I'll just go check if our table is ready and wait there with Gene until you guys come join us."

"Okay," Jim said, heading for the elevators. "Hopefully, you won't have to wait too long."

"Understand," Butch said, pausing beside Jim. "Just remember what that ancient philosopher Tao Nail once said."

"What's that?" Jim asked.

"A wise man never puts his private parts in the hornets' nest," Butch answered, laughing as he turned and headed for the restaurant.

"Asshole," Jim said under his breath as he pushed the up button on the elevator. "I really doubt there was an ancient philosopher named Tao Nail anyway."

Getting off on his floor, he saw several people he thought he recognized from the meeting at Black Water. Nodding to them, he walked down the hall until arriving at his door.

Knocking to let Marie know he was about to open the door; he was mildly surprised when she opened it.

"I was starting to worry," she said. "I thought you were going to be here about four."

"I believe Gene said he hoped the meeting would be over at four, and it was," Jim said. "And then we came straight here.

"Looks like you're ready," Jim said, heading for the bathroom. "I'll just wash my face, and we can head on down. Butch and Gene are already down there."

"Does this look alright?" Marie asked, following Jim to the bathroom. "It's pretty casual. I'm saving the nice one for tomorrow when we have dinner with the other lady."

"It looks just fine," Jim said, drying his face. "I told you; a pair of jeans and a t-shirt would be acceptable. And I have to tell you; I find you particularly attractive in jeans and a tight t-shirt."

"I know that," she said, turning to look at herself in the mirror. "But you are just like all men. The fewer clothes and the tighter they are, the more you are attracted to them."

"I'm sorry, but you are so wrong about that," Jim said, heading for the door. "There aren't too many men who are attracted to a six-hundred-pound lady who wears a halter top that exposes and highlights the eight rolls of fat leading down her sides to the too tight shorts which fail to cover the top of her t-back pink undies, and more hail damage on her thighs than a fifty-seven Buick left outside during a thunderstorm in the Panhandle of Texas.

"Your statement would be correct if you were wearing those same clothes," Jim said, holding the door open for her. "But due to my jealous nature, let's stick to just wearing them around the house where they'll be easy to pick up an hour later after I rip them off with my teeth."

Chapter 27

"Nice to see you again, Marie," Gene said, rising as they approached the table where he and Butch were sitting. "I hope you weren't too bored this afternoon while Jim and I were drinking beer and shooting pool."

"I got by," Marie said, giving Gene a hug. "We'll have to wait and see how tomorrow goes."

"Wouldn't Gene and Jim let you play pool with them?" Marie asked Butch, giving him a hug.

"I was supposed to play the winner, but they never finished their game," Butch replied, as Marie took the chair Jim was holding for her. "Maybe tomorrow I'll demonstrate my prowess on the field of green."

"If you two would take a look at the menu, I'll see if I can get the waiter's attention and he can take your drink order," Gene said, looking for the man who had waited on their table.

Jim set his menu on the table as the waiter arrived and said, "I'd like a Jack and Coke, please."

"Manhattan, please," Marie told him, as she also placed her menu on the table.

"Excellent," the waiter said, scribbling on his pad. "And if you're all ready to order, I'll turn in your requests to the chef before returning with your drinks."

As everyone told him their order, Jim glanced around the small restaurant and saw a couple from the meeting at Quantico. He also noticed that their table was as private as they could get in the small restaurant.

"I apologize for the limits of the menu here," Gene said, looking at Marie as the waiter left. "But I figured you'd rather be close to the interesting areas around Washington than have a more extensive menu."

"This is fine, Gene," she said, placing her hand on his. "Any place I can be with my favorite men needs nothing more than a place to sit and enjoy time with them."

"You're too gracious," Gene replied, with a slight nod. "I enjoy every minute I get to spend with you and ole what's his name … oh, yes, Jim."

"You were going to tell me a little about this South Africa thing, I believe," Marie said, leaning back in her chair.

"Oh, yes," Gene replied. "I'll try to keep this as short and on point as possible, but you've got to bear with me as I go back in the history of the country, some of which I've already discussed with Jim.

"First, both our country and South Africa were discovered by Europeans who were searching for a route to China," he began. "Columbus never found that route; however, the Portuguese sailor who sailed around the southern end of Africa did.

"Knowing this route from Europe to China and back would require replenishing the food and other necessities for the ships traveling the route, the Dutch East India Company decided to establish a colony on the southern tip of Africa for that purpose," he continued. "Much like the British established colonies in America.

"As business grew, more and more Dutch came and established the farms that provided the produce required by the ships and the increasing demand from the other people coming into the country," he explained. "The majority of the land was uninhabited, no records of ownership, so the farmers, known as Boers, just did what might be called homesteading.

"Things chugged right along for years, but major issues developed between the black population and the whites," Gene told her. "This is similar to the interaction between the American settlers and the Native Americans.

"In the late 1800s, there was legislation in South Africa called the Native Location Act," he continued. "It was followed about thirty years later by the Native Land Act. These were meant to restrict the black ownership of the land.

"I'm going to jump back to a similar system of dealing with the indigenous people, Native Americans, also known as Indians, here in our country," Gene said. "What started as a fairly loose association as the colonies were being settled, it soon became apparent that the Native Americans had some land that the government thought should belong to the white settlers.

"In 1830, President Andrew Jackson signed the infamous Indian Removal Act which demanded all the tribes east of the Mississippi abandon their ancestral land and move to the Indian Territory, now known as Oklahoma.

"The tribes most affected were what was known as the five civilized tribes," he explained. "Those tribes were the Cherokee, Choctaw, Chickasaw, Creek, and Seminole, who inhabited the land from the southeast portion of our country, roughly from North Carolina down through Florida. This was roughly during the same period as the Native Land Act in South Africa.

"So perhaps you're beginning to see the parallels between our countries," Gene said, looking at Marie.

"Yes, I do," Marie said, nodding as their drinks were delivered. "I'd like to ask why the five tribes you're talking about were called civilized? I thought the Indians were pretty much seen as savages."

"These five tribes were recognized as civilized by the US government because they adapted many of our customs. They became Christians, attained some level of literacy, and had agricultural practices," he explained. "They also maintained political relations with the white population."

"So, they were forced to give up their land, but were given land in…what did you call it? Oh yeah, Indian territories," Marie replied, taking a sip of her drink. "What did the South African do to provide land for the blacks?"

"Pretty much nothing," Gene answered, as they saw their dinner orders coming."

"Maybe it wasn't fair, but at least we made sure the Indians had somewhere to go," Marie replied, as her meal was set on the table.

"You haven't heard the entire story yet," Gene told her, as his meal arrived.

Chapter 28

After eating and engaging in casual small talk during their meal, Gene looked at Marie as the table was being cleared and asked, "Are you ready to finish this little discussion about South Africa, its history, especially that part that mirrors our own?"

"Sure," Marie answered. "Would it be possible to get an after-dinner drink before you start?"

"Certainly," Gene said, looking for their waiter. "What would you like?"

"I'd love a small glass of Cuarenta y Tres," she replied.

"What the hell is that?" Butch asked, wiping his lips. "I don't think I've ever heard of it."

"It's a Spanish liqueur," Jim answered. "I found it on a trip to Mexico City a couple of years ago. It's damn good."

"Then I'll give it a try," he said, nodding.

"Do you folks have Cuarenta Tres?" Gene asked as the waiter arrived.

"Yes, sir. We have Cuarenta y Tres," he answered, subtly correcting Gene's pronunciation.

"Then I think we'll all enjoy a glass," Gene replied.

"On the rocks or neat?" the waiter asked.

"Neat, please," Jim answered. "As my great-great-grandfather always said, 'Never water down delicious'."

After their drinks arrived, Jim raised his glass and said, "Here's to the most important things a man can have…friends."

"For sure," Butch agreed, raising his glass. "To friends."

"To friends," Gene and Marie repeated, raising theirs.

Butch took a sip and exclaimed, "This shit is delicious! I've got to get a bottle. This will be perfect after a mesquite-grilled steak. Damn, it's good."

"I think you've impressed the boy, Marie," Gene said, laughing. "I hope he doesn't spill any. I believe he'd be licking the table so as not to lose a drop."

"Can't say I'd blame him," Marie said. "After Jim brought a bottle back, I fell in love with it myself."

"Okay," Gene said, after taking a sip. "Back to the Indian Removal Act. There were over one hundred thousand members of the five tribes who were forced to march to their new homes in Oklahoma. Fifteen thousand died on what became known as the Trail of Tears.

"Once they arrived, they were restricted to establishing their settlements on the eastern half of the state," Gene continued. "The west half was to be reserved for communal hunting grounds.

"Then, following the end of the Civil War, that land designated for hunting was revoked and opened for white settlement," Gene explained. "The Homestead Act of 1862 allowed settlers to claim one hundred and sixty acres of public land if they lived on it for five years and improved the land.

"We also need to include the Louisiana Purchase in 1803," he added. "We bought the entire territory of Louisiana from the French, approximately eight hundred and twenty-eight thousand square miles, for fifteen million dollars. That's about eighteen dollars per square mile.

"How much were the indigenous people who lived in the Louisiana territory paid for their land?" Gene asked. "None. You also need to remember that during this century, the 1800s, there was a policy known as Manifest Destiny.

"Basically, that meant that our government felt it had a supreme right to all land from the Atlantic to the Pacific. From sea to shining sea," Gene explained. "It's not surprising how horribly we treated the Indians. We thought we had a right to their land, regardless of how long those people had lived there.

"And I haven't even touched the Mexican American war, where we took land in California, Arizona, New Mexico, Colorado, Utah, and Nevada," Gene continued. "Land that had belonged to generations of Mexicans. And let's not forget the annexation of Texas, which was most likely the cause of the war.

"So once again, the white government of our country takes whatever it desires with total disregard for the indigenous people," Gene said. "You can draw a parallel with the white government of South Africa.

"You may have heard the term Apartheid. Basically, it was a government controlled by the minority of the population, the white population, and was felt unfair by the majority black population," Gene explained. "This became a major issue when gold and diamonds were discovered in South Africa.

"Since the mines were owned and controlled by the government, you can guess who benefited from the proceeds of the mines, which were on public lands," he continued. "Needless to say, this didn't seem fair to the majority of the population, the black population.

"After finally gaining its freedom from British rule, another parallel, in 1934, South Africa became a Nation State, and later a Republic with democratic elections," Gene explained. "Then in 1994, the African National Congress gained a majority in the government.

"This was most likely the impetus for the black majority to believe they were owed what we call reparations," he continued. "And that leads us to today, and the expropriation of the land the Dutch had settled and lived on for generations. This expropriation led to some of the most brutal acts of rape, torture, murder, and destruction of those people on the farms. Entire families. And the farms were burned to the ground in several instances.

"As a sovereign nation, we, our government, have no business interfering with their internal affairs," Gene explained. "That's why Black Water was asked to go through the back door to their government and see if we could find a solution."

"Couldn't we just use sanctions or tariffs, or something else to put pressure on them to stop the genocide and ethnic cleansing?" Marie asked. "I guess I understand why we're there, but it really comes down to do we have the right to meddle in their affairs?

"What if South Africa decided we needed to have reparations as our black community wants? Would we accept their interference?" she continued.

"This expropriation isn't the only reason we need to be involved," Gene said. "This involves some very critical issues that have nothing to do with who gets the farms, or the gold and diamonds. As far as our government is concerned, that is their business.

"After all, gold and diamonds are merely jewelry," Gene said. "Status symbols to show others the level of some success you have attained. None of that is the true reason we're there. And that's why this negotiation is so vital.

"Then what is the real reason?" Marie asked.

"Rare earth elements," Gene answered. "South Africa has some of the largest deposits of many minerals and metals than anywhere else in the world. And their purity is among the best."

"Why is that so important?" she asked, as their waiter came to ask if they would like anything else. "If we don't have them here, can't we buy them from someone else? Some other country?"

Chapter 29

"The major supplier, outside of South Africa, is China," Gene explained, after they had ordered another drink. "We can't depend on them to supply us with such critical materials should our relationship with them deteriorate. Our defense, our computer industry, and other vital industries need these minerals.

"And it's essential that other nations do not know the extent of our requirements," he added. "That's one of the major reasons we need a source outside of China."

"What's so important about some other country knowing how much of this stuff we're using?" Marie asked, taking a sip of her fresh drink.

"Guess now's as good a time as any to delve into a little history regarding our need for secrecy of defense projects," Gene answered. "Back in the 1950s, we were looking for a replacement for the aging F106 interceptor.

"That was our frontline defense against the threat of Russian bombers carrying nuclear weapons from finding their way into the interior of our country," Gene explained.

"We needed something with superior speed and a reduced radar signature.

"Lockheed's Skunk Works division in the Los Angeles area, run by a gentleman named Kelly Johnson, designed a replacement known as the A12, a single-seat fighter," Gene continued. "You also should know that the U2 program, our previous only true reconnaissance aircraft, a spy plane that was used to photograph areas in Russia, was discovered to be vulnerable to surface-to-air missiles.

"After Frances Gary Powers was shot down over Russia in 1960, we needed an immediate replacement for the surveillance program," he explained. "The A12 seemed the logical choice. A Mach-3 aircraft with stealth capabilities.

"The A12 had one major flaw," he continued. "It's skin, the outer shell, was made of aluminum. And aluminum couldn't withstand the extreme heat generated when traveling at Mach-3.

"Mach one is seven hundred and sixty-seven miles an hour," Gene explained. "That makes Mach-3 about two thousand and three hundred miles an hour. That means it would take only about an hour and twelve minutes to fly from Los Angeles to New York.

"Now to produce enough of these surveillance aircraft, now known as the SR-71, a two-seat version of the A-12, we needed a special metal that could withstand the heat," he continued. "That metal was Titanium. It was lightweight, strong, and could survive the extreme temperatures. The only problem was that we didn't have any.

"The only source was Russia," he said. "And we needed great quantities. There was no way we wanted Mother Russia, who was our number one enemy at the time, to know we needed the Titanium or why we needed it.

"So, we set up dummy companies around the world to order small quantities that would go unnoticed," Gene added. "This allowed the development and production of a fleet of SR-71s to go basically unnoticed."

Gene paused for a moment to let the information sink in and then said, "Here we are today in a similar situation. We need certain rare earth elements in large quantities, and the only source is currently our number one enemy, China.

"That is a major reason for the negotiations," he explained. "Now, we don't intend to divulge why we need these elements, but we can use South Africa's need for revenue as a carrot.

"There are several factors which we believe will result in a fairly quick agreement," Gene said. "First, we'll provide them with the data showing many of the expropriated farms are failing to produce anywhere near what was previously produced. The new farmers don't have the knowledge or experience to manage the farms.

"The farms where the owners are seeking refugee status are not producing a single tomato or ear of corn," he continued. "This decline in production is quickly leading to a humanitarian crisis, potentially a nationwide famine.

"If this happens and there is no quick solution, the population will riot when there's no food on the table for their families, and the current President will possibly be removed from office," Gene told them. "That by itself is reason enough for him to take some action to stop the violence against the Boers, regardless of any expropriation actions.

"The stick is we'll put tariffs on their gold and diamond exports that will cut their revenue stream to a mere trickle since we are one of the major purchasers of jewelry material," he added. "Then we'll sanction the sale of the rare earth elements.

"The whole package accomplishes several things we want," Gene finished. "We get the President to put a stop to the violence occurring across his country using whatever means necessary. We'll agree to stop soliciting the refugee visa participants in an attempt to forestall any famine caused by the farms being unproductive, and we'll negotiate a lucrative contract for the rare earth elements we desperately need.

"And since there is a Presidential election on the near horizon, we secretly designate a portion of the rare earth elements contract to his campaign fund for his service as an agent," Gene said. "Much like a realtor's fee. Or a musician's agent."

"Isn't donation to another country's election sort of discouraged?" Marie asked.

"Discouraged is far short of a more correct term for meddling," Gene answered. "But you have to remember, the government, our government, has nothing to do with that little behind-the-scenes agreement. And the issue of the fees for bringing two parties together for the purchase of the material will never be put on paper, at least not the names of the true players, therefore unprovable."

Gene looked at his watch and finally announced, "Guys, this has been a most pleasant evening, but I've got to get back to Quantico and ensure everything is ready for tomorrow's briefing."

Getting up, he signaled for the waiter and told them, "You guys head on up to your rooms. I'll take care of the bill, and I'll see you tomorrow morning when Fabio picks you up at seven o'clock and brings you to Quantico.

"Marie, I'll see you tomorrow evening for dinner," he continued, as he handed the waiter his credit card. "And enjoy your tour of Washington or wherever you have Fabio take you while we finish our pool game and drink beer back at Quantico."

Marie kissed Gene on the cheek and said, "Thanks for a great evening. And now I think I understand why you and Jim are involved with this operation. I had my issues before with him being gone and me not knowing why or for how long, but now I see why both of you and Butch want to be part of it, regardless of how long it takes. And I look forward to meeting the lady who'll be working with Jim tomorrow night."

Chapter 30

The next morning, Jim and Butch were waiting in the lobby for Fabio to pick them up and take them to Quantico.

"Have you noticed that nothing has been said about your part of this?" Butch asked.

"Of course, I've noticed," Jim answered. "I'd have been surprised if it had been."

"Why?" Butch asked. "Don't you think the other people need to know what you're doing to support the overall mission?"

"Definitely not," Jim replied. "There's no reason for them to know because it has zero bearing on their part. Regardless of the outcome of my side of the operation, they are still going to try and protect the Boers and expedite the refugee visas. That still goes on.

"You need to remember, there's an exponential increase in risk of disclosure for every person who knows what my mission actually is," Jim told him. "Let's look at the potential result of that information reaching the President's office.

"Best case, at least for me and Megan, they deny our access to the President," Jim explained. "Next possibility, they let us in and immediately place us in custody and then parade us in front of the world stage, showing how the US government is meddling in the internal affairs of a sovereign nation.

"That's probably the worst case for our government," he continued. "If you think saving face is purely an Asian custom, you are sadly mistaken. Our government is extremely sensitive to the notion of being humiliated on the world stage.

"That's one of the factors why Black Water was hired to try to resolve the ethnic cleansing and genocide without them being involved," Jim said. "Now, let's put Megan and me on stage with the evidence, the frog juice, and you have a major political disaster.

"Next, let's look at what, to me at least, is the worst outcome," Jim continued, as they saw Fabio pull up to the front doors. "Megan and I walk into the President's office, and his people put a bullet in our heads. Then the news hits the world stage."

"Why did Gene allow me to mention the removal of the Steer to everyone if we're concerned about the information leaking out?" Butch asked as they headed for the exit.

"The Steer isn't the President of the country," Jim answered. "His name was never mentioned, but that is sure to come out sooner or later, and he is not a major public figure on the world stage, yet.

"Yes, he's in the public," Jim continued as they got to the black Suburban. "But when he's shot from a distance, it could have been anyone.

"Hell, the blame could even be placed on the current President since the Steer is running against him in the next election," he explained, opening the front passenger door.

"That's a far cry from the President knowing his assassin has asked for a meeting.

"Let's assume the information on assassinating the President leaks out," Jim continued, as Butch got into the rear seat. "He has our names and the times. He can take every precaution and intercept us at any point he desires.

"Regarding the Steer," Jim explained. "There are no dates, times, or locations mentioned. There are especially no names associated with any assassination attempt. Hell, there are probably rumors of assassination plots floating around on a daily basis.

"No, there's not even a sliver of similarity," Jim said before turning to Fabio and saying, "Good morning, Fabio. How's your day going?"

"Excellent," Fabio answered, pulling away from the hotel. "Looks like it's going to be an easy day. Take you guys to the base, come back and pick Marie up for a quick tour of some tourist attractions, and then bring her back to the hotel by four o'clock. Piece of chocolate cake with chocolate fudge icing."

"Oh, grasshopper, you underestimate the situation," Jim said, laughing. "If I were to give you any advice, it would be to make a list of the most popular sites and take her to each.

"Have a time schedule that allows the maximum number of sites but ensures the return to the hotel by four," Jim advised. "Make this as close to one of those scheduled tour buses as possible.

"Don't give her any options," he continued. "If she suggests something that's not on your list, make sure she understands she must skip one of the things you're recommending. But if that's what she truly wants to see, then accommodate her.

"If you've ever taken a lady to the mall to buy a pair of shoes, just a pair of shoes, you'll have a glimpse into the amount of time and number of detours you'll be taking before you even enter the shoe store," Jim said. "But also remember, a lady is always right. But also know it'll be entirely your fault if she's not back at the hotel by four.

"And lord help you if she doesn't have time to fix her hair, apply her makeup, and change her mind as to what to wear several times after she gets back to the hotel," Jim finished. "It's a no-win game for you, my friend.

Chapter 31

"Good morning, guys," Gene said, as Jim and Butch came into the auditorium after clearing security. "Have y'all had breakfast?"

"No, sir," Jim answered. "There wasn't a Denny's at the hotel, and I didn't see one on the way here."

"You know there are restaurants besides Denny's," Gene told him, shaking his head. "Let's just go to the cafeteria. They aren't Denny's, but they have a pretty good breakfast buffet set up.

"I guess Marie is excited to go touristing this morning," he continued, as they entered the cafeteria. "I'm glad she's gotten on board with this mission. Makes it a little easier for your home life."

"That it does," Jim replied, taking a tray from the stack at the starting end of the buffet. "I don't like lying to her, and even though what we told her was nowhere near the truth, I don't see any other way."

"I don't either," Gene said, following Jim down the buffet line. "Unfortunately, in this line of work, there are very few people you can discuss things with. And even some of the people you're working with can't know either."

"I knew that when I signed on," Jim replied, taking a glass of orange juice. "I guess being married to Jennifer for so long without any real issues makes this rather uncomfortable."

"You're forgetting what you were doing back then," Gene explained. "First, you were a Marine pilot flying in Vietnam. Then the missions you went on for Dark Water were done in conjunction with a 'Marine' deployment.

"Following that, after you retired and started flying for American Airlines, the missions pretty much fell in line with your flying schedule," he continued. "The few times she knew about an operation, it was pretty easy to explain.

"Now, with Marie, you pretty much left the door open to her imagination when she found out Black Water was responsible for finding her husband's killer and you were involved," Gene finished. "Toss in the little incident in Honolulu, then her seeing you on TV in Indianapolis, she's developed some trust issues."

"It would be so much easier if I could just tell her about some of the more … unpleasant missions," Jim said, taking scrambled eggs and ham from the line.

"You and I both know that's not possible," Gene replied, getting a breakfast burrito and some hashbrowns. "And I really don't think she'd want to know. What do you think she'd do if you told her you shoved fentanyl up someone's nose and watched them die?

"Or you poisoned a city councilman and watched him die?" Gene continued. "Just what do you think she'd think of her airline pilot boyfriend then?"

"Life would be much simpler if all I had to worry about were a couple of horses and a few cows, like Butch," Jim said, as he looked for a place at one of the long tables that would hold the three of them.

"You can have that life, if you really think you'd want it," Butch said, taking a seat across from Jim. "But I don't think you'd be happy with it. You'd probably turn into someone like Mike.

"I think he's seen too much of the bad side, and not much of the good side," Butch continued. "Watching so many of his friends die in Vietnam and having repeat disasters with married life has made him rather bitter.

"I love the guy, but he's got serious anger issues," Butch said, slicing off a piece of his omelet. "No, that life is definitely not what fits your personality. You like people too much. It doesn't bother you to kill them. But you still like people … I should say you like a few people … some of the time."

"You do have the option of leaving Black Water," Gene told him, taking a fork full of hashbrowns.

"I know," Jim answered, picking up his coffee cup. "My problem is that I agree with every mission I've been handed and see what a positive difference it makes in every instance.

"And I guess I do enjoy the adrenaline rush," Jim confessed. "There doesn't seem to be a way to do the things we do, and I know I can't tell the woman I want to spend my life with. Not to mention what her twins would probably think of me. Or her parents."

"That's the problem with a double life," Gene said. "Sooner or later, one of the lives has to go. And I know which life you'd get rid of. Why don't you take a break after this operation and give it some thought?

"I'll stand behind you regardless of your decision," he finished, looking at his watch. "I'd hate to lose you. But I'd hate to see you lose something I think is more important to you. Now, we need to finish breakfast and get to the auditorium, or Bracer will be on our case."

Chapter 32

As they entered the auditorium, they saw Debbie at the front looking at the huge screen on the wall behind the podium. Seeing most of the seats filled, they took three together at the rear.

"Have you met the three guys who will be running the three areas?" Gene asked, as Debbie turned to the podium and scanned the crowd.

"Briefly," Butch answered. "I plan on getting together with them after this meeting. I'm hoping we learn more about what the company expects regarding the disposition of those groups who are attacking the farms.

"I'd like to know if we need to move some of our people from one of the areas to another based on current data," he continued. "It looks like the initial assignments were just based on area size versus actual farms or valid threats."

"You are probably right," Gene replied. "I know the Northern Cape, Western Cape, and the Eastern Cape cover about half of the total area of the entire country.

"I believe the North-West, Free State, and KwaZulu-Natal area cover about one third of the country, he continued.

"That leaves the Northern and Eastern Transvaal for one-third of the teams we've assigned.

"However, there are definitely more farm locations in the lower provinces, or Capes, and damn sure more square miles to cover," he explained. "The northern areas, the Transvaal's, shouldn't have too many targets.

"But since it is home to one of the three capitals, Pretoria, the seat of the administration, we initially planned on that area being potentially important, especially since it's so close to Johannesburg," Gene continued.

"Johannesburg, the largest city in South Africa, has a population of about eight million people," he added. "And the Bull has extensive real estate holdings in the city. He also uses one of them as his 'home away from home'.

"The entire country has a population of a little over sixty million," Gene said. "The two other capitals, Cape Town, where the parliament is located, and Bloemfontein, the judicial seat of the country, are each located in one of the other areas.

"Looking at the country from a population standpoint, the division into three areas seems logical," he explained. "But neither population nor pure land mass gives us a true picture of where we expect the problems.

"Another issue we've had to include is the fact that there are twelve official languages, and that complicates any interaction or cooperation between various groups," Gene added. "And after considering the terrain, we just started with the most logical division, roughly equal areas with recognizable boundaries."

"What about the Steer?" Butch asked. "Where do you expect to find him?"

"He spends more time in the more populated areas, as you would expect," Gene answered. "That was another factor we considered. Since there are three capitals and he could be at either one on any given day, we wanted to make sure we had a sniper team in each area.

"One issue we've had is a lack of information about the exact number of targets we expect to attack the farms," Gene told him. "We have good information on the leaders, but most of the others don't have phones, so that makes it almost impossible to know how many people are headed for any single location.

"We can only guess at that from conversations we pick up from the various leaders when they are discussing an operation against one of the farms," he explained. "There is at least a loose command structure to help prevent sending too many people to the same farm at the same time, or one that was taken over the day before.

"We know that the Steer has been trying to establish a more formal command and control system, but there are so many conflicting factions, it's proven to be almost impossible," Gene added. "It would be much easier for us if we knew of their overall strategy. But even they don't seem to know what that is.

"We're left grasping the few tidbits of information from the several leaders who are the focal points scattered across the country," he explained. "But sometimes these guys don't know what another group is planning, even when they are hitting neighboring farms.

"This has been described as herding a group of cats," Gene finished, as Debbie asked for everyone to take a seat. "And that's about as accurate as I can think of. However, I've never tried to herd cats. Hell, herding cats could be a relatively easy endeavor."

"I'd use tuna," Jim said, as the noise level began to subside.

"Just how would that work?" Gene asked.

"Stop thinking of the problem as herding, which implies pushing them toward the goal, to leading," Jim answered. "The old ranchers used to have a lead steer, and he was accustomed to following a horse. The rest of the herd, being herd animals, would fall in line behind him and go where you wanted them.

"In this case, the tuna is just the lead Steer," Jim finished, just as Debbie started speaking. "At least if we're still talking about herding cats."

"Let's please get in our seats, folks," she announced. "There is a ton of information we need to cover, and I understand that General Barker has assured several people that they would be headed home this afternoon following the briefing, or no later than early tomorrow morning."

Chapter 33

"Good morning, General," Debbie said, walking back to where he was sitting with Jim and Butch. "And you guys as well."

"Any major developments since last night?" Gene asked, standing.

"Quite a few, actually," Debbie answered, as Jim and Butch joined Gene in standing. "I'll hit the high points, and we can get together at lunch and see if you have anything to add or recommend.

"First, we've heard from those close to the Bull that he's open to meeting with Megan regarding whatever negotiations she's authorized to present," she continued. "However, he demands that she come alone. No assistants. No secretaries. Alone."

"Not negotiable," Gene said, shaking his head. "That's an unreasonable demand, and I won't have that fat son-of-a-bitch dictating terms or who is on our negotiating team. We're not telling him who his negotiators may be, and I'll be damned if I'll let him decide who we send.

"And I know damned well the reason is because he wants to be alone with Megan," Gene continued, with his temperature rising almost as fast as his voice. "Send word back immediately. And by immediately, I mean right now.

"We don't need to proceed any further with this briefing if a key part can't be accomplished," he continued. "And make sure it's delivered from the Department of State with the appropriate seals or whatever and stamped IMMEDIATE RESPONSE REQUIRED.

"I know the issue with the time zones, but I want that fat piece of shit to be hand-delivered the response, even if he has to be woken up if he's gone to bed, or regardless of where he is," Gene emphasized. "And I want an answer within two hours of transmission. I don't care whose signature is at the bottom of our reply, but make sure it's someone who will get his attention."

"Yes, sir," Debbie replied. "I'll have your response on his desk within an hour. We know he keeps a member of his staff in his office at the Pretoria capital to handle any emergencies that arise when he's not in the Capital. He's currently in one of his houses in Johannesburg, where he stays when he's not in the Capital.

"I'll be able to monitor any activity within his office and on his personal phone," she continued, "and I'll stay with my folks, who are taking care of this until I have a firm answer.

"I have left some maps with the current data on locations of the hit teams and numbers of men, at least as close as we've been able to verify," she said. "I'll tell the folks to get maps of their areas and take a look while I'm getting this message sent.

"I shouldn't be more than ten minutes making sure the Bull has the message, so I'll just start the formal part of the briefing when I return," Debbie said, before turning to leave.

"He normally only has one guard at his residence, while there's an entire contingent of security personnel at the capital," she finished. "So, we're hoping he will set the meeting for his Johannesburg home."

"I'm going to pick up one of the maps Debbie was referring to," Butch said, glancing at the rear of the auditorium where several people were milling around. "I've found it beneficial to know at least as much as the people you're supposed to be controlling. Personally, if I find anyone who knows more than I, I make him my assistant."

"And when you discover that everyone knows more than you, what do you do then?" Jim asked, following him to the rear.

"I just tell them if they find a problem, ask the man working next to them what he'd do, come tell me what he said, and I'll tell you what to do," Butch answered. "Usually, it only takes two or three times before they figure out it saves them time and avoids me having to give them my world-class, you've got to be shitting me look.

"A good stare with a disapproving frown is sometimes as effective as knowing what the hell they are doing anyway," Butch finished, as he reached the table with the various maps.

"Guess I'll need one of each," he said, picking up several of the different maps.

"Why don't you just stare at a couple of the people here getting their own maps?" Jim said, picking up the map depicting the northern area where he would be working. "Why should you be bothered knowing where your people are or what problems they'll encounter? Just toss in your infamous disapproving frown, and you can probably catch the next flight back home with a job well done text from Gene."

"Who am I supposed to text?" Gene asked, as they returned to where he was waiting for Debbie's return.

"Nobody, General," Butch answered. "Jim's being his normal wiseass self. I swear, I couldn't stand the man if I didn't like him."

Both Gene and Jim just looked at him quizzically and then looked at each other, shaking their heads.

Chapter 34

"He was just handed the message," Debbie reported when she rejoined Gene. "He's none too happy, but he told his assistant to prepare an answer agreeing to the entire negotiating team, which includes Jim.

"He also directed his assistant to hold the reply until one hour and fifty-nine minutes from the receipt," she added. "As I heard him say, 'Those arrogant white assholes from America cannot dictate what I do in my own country. I'll respond when I'm damn good and ready.

"And then he added, 'Tell them there will be no negotiations at my office in the capital'," Debbie continued. "He also said, 'They will not be accorded the honor. They will come to my home where there will be no welcoming ceremony or honors normally shown to officials, such as their Ambassador, that whiny little pudgy twirp'."

"Good," Gene told her. "Let's get this rolling since we can't expect the President of a sovereign nation to be kept waiting for our formal acceptance of his kind invitation. Prepare a response and send it the second you receive their notification, requesting a date and time with a deadline of four days from today."

"Shouldn't I just suggest a deadline of four days?" Debbie asked.

"Absolutely not," Gene told her. "He's already shown we have the upper hand by agreeing to let Jim attend and responding within two hours. And I don't intend to let him think he's running this show now. Not a single aspect of it."

"I'll take care of it," Debbie replied. "Oh, by the way, Jim. This fits our original plan since his collection of exotic reptiles is kept in his home. We would have had to do some major revisions if he had insisted on meeting in his office."

"I guess we are just covered with good luck," Jim said. "Now, I have a couple of thoughts to augment the FedEx addition that we can discuss following this meeting."

"Good," Debbie answered. "Just remember, we only have four days to implement any new plan. If you'll just jot down what you're thinking, I'll review it this evening after the briefing and let you know something before you head back to Texas tomorrow."

As she walked back to the podium, Jim turned to Gene and asked, "Is she running the operation?"

"Pretty much," Gene answered. "I've got all the confidence in her, and it's her assets that will be supporting it. But if you have any questions about anything she decides, you can always come to me with your concerns.

"But for now, she's got the ball," he finished. "Having said that, what are you looking at regarding you and Megan?"

"I've been thinking of what we could do to ensure we send the Bull to the slaughterhouse should we be unable to administer the frog juice," Jim answered. "Since I probably can't get a weapon into his house, I want Debbie's people to see if they can locate any pistol or other weapon, he may have in wherever room they believe the meeting will take place.

"Then I'll get his weapon, and we can stage a little gunfight at the OK Corral," he continued. "To do that, I'll need to draw the security guard into the room before I call for the FedEx delivery.

"If we can manage to catch one of the Steer's men between now and the meeting, we can have him in the FedEx truck on the day of the meeting," Jim explained. "If things go to shit, the FedEx driver can bring him in, and I can take the gun the captive has with him. Now, that gun must be traceable to someone in the Steer's group of supporters.

"I'll have the Bull calling for his guard," Jim continued. "I will be holding Bull's gun on him and demand that the guard hand his weapon to Megan.

"Then, when the FedEx man delivers his package, Megan will shoot the captive with the guard's gun," he explained. "The driver will shoot the Bull with the weapon he took from the captive and then shoot the guard.

"I'll then replace the Bull's gun, after a thorough wipe down, and the three of us will calmly walk out to the FedEx truck and depart the scene," Jim finished.

Pausing while Gene thought through the scenario, he added, "This will look like a passionate Steer supporter managed to get into the Bull's house and assassinated him before the brave guard managed to prevent the shooting. However, he did manage to shoot the assassin before succumbing to the fatal shot he received."

"Have you discussed this with Megan?" Gene asked.

"No, I wanted to see if you thought it would be a workable backup plan," Jim answered.

"What if she's hesitant about shooting someone?" Gene asked.

"Then I'll hand her Bull's gun, have her hold it on him," Jim answered. "I'll take the guard's gun and shoot the captive. All Megan has to do is make everyone think she'll shoot the Bull unless the guard hands me his gun."

"Hell, I can't think of anything better if you can't doctor his wine," Gene replied, nodding. "However, I think you should plan on just having Megan holding the gun, as in your second scenario. As we discussed, she's never pulled the trigger, and this definitely needs to be a split-second operation. There can be absolutely no hesitation. Nor can we miss the target. There won't be a chance for a second shot at any of them. Not if you expect to leave there alive.

"We'll talk about it with her on the way to dinner this evening," Gene decided. "If she's the least bit hesitant, you've got four days to come up with another plan.

"Just bear in mind, no matter what you decide, it can have no chance of casting any blame on our government," Gene reminded him.

Chapter 35

"Has everyone picked up the map of your area?" Debbie asked, as the huge screen behind her lit up, showing the entire South African country.

Waiting until she saw a predominance of nods, she continued, "As you've probably already seen, the first sheet is South Africa, showing the three separate areas.

Using a mouse on the podium, she highlighted each area and said, "I'm going to overlay each area with the names and numbers of the people assigned to that area.

As the names began to appear, she continued, "As you can tell, there are too many names for us to have floating around on the map. They cover some important features and would detract from the data your leaders need. Specifically, where the enemy is, how many, direction of movement, and most importantly, where their targets are."

Changing the screen to the southern tip of South Africa, she said, "This shows area one, Northern Cape, Western Cape, and Eastern Cape. You can see all of the major cities, but more importantly, we can remove them if we wish.

"As you can see, I can remove a single city or every city from the map," she explained as various cities disappeared and reappeared on the screen. What you're more interested in is where the farms are located."

Again, the screen became a blank slate, and she started adding the farms located in that area to the screen. As the screen became covered, she said, "It's still too much data to be efficient.

She continued as she began removing farms from the screen, "The only farms that need to appear on the iPad you will be given once you are in the country are those that have been targeted.

"It's easy to understand that if every farm, all hundred thousand of them in your area, were constantly cluttering the screen, there would be no room for the important information," she said as she removed three-fourths of the farms. "Even twenty-five thousand farms are too many.

"We've now reduced the screen to five farms," she continued as the screen cleared. "This is an accurate depiction of where we've been able to determine the next strikes against the Boers will occur.

"There's not much we can do today except warn the families," she explained. "Those few people we have over there are letting the farms targeted know they have only twenty-four to forty-eight hours to get to safety.

"We've set up emergency locations, primarily in farms which have been raided in the past, where we can offer some protection," she continued as the screen began showing red dots moving toward the five farms.

"Here you can see where the killer teams currently are and how close to their targets they are," she explained. "We get this information from the phones the killer teams' leaders are using.

"We're using a combination of the phone's GPS locator and triangulation of the transmission towers scattered throughout the country," she continued. "We can also hear when orders are given regarding any future plans, such as how they plan on surrounding the farm, which farm, actual time of attack, and any worthwhile intelligence.

"It should be intuitively obvious how beneficial this system can be when you're trying to plan for the dispersal and movement of your teams," she said as the screen changed to depict the next area.

"Here's area two," she told them. "I've only included the data showing the target farms and the killer teams that are headed for them.

"Here's area three," she said, changing the screen again. "The one thing we do not have on the screen is the deployment of your teams.

"Once you are deployed to your areas, we will be able to monitor the exact location of each member using a new piece of equipment," she explained. "You'll be provided with a unique pair of glasses before you leave tomorrow," she continued. "These are similar to the ones we've previously used, except they have a transmitter and receiver built into the earpieces.

"This was necessary to prevent a reoccurrence involving one of our operational leaders just a short time ago," she said, looking directly at Jim. "The predecessor of these glasses required a connection to the phones the company provided.

"Unfortunately, one of our people left the phone in his vehicle, and when he entered a store, the connection between the glasses and the phone was broken, thus rendering the entire system useless," she explained. "Here, the glasses will attempt to use the phone to transmit or receive data, but should it fail to connect after two attempts, the transmitter and receiver in the glasses will try to establish communication with us here in Quantico.

"Please understand that while the phone isn't necessary for communication, it has a much greater range than the glasses by themselves," she continued. "For those of you who have never worked with the glasses, the lenses are the screens for any photos we need for you to see.

"The camera is in the hinge point of the right temple, that's the part that goes over your ear, and the picture will appear in the upper right quadrant of the right lens," she explained. "There is an almost invisible tube that runs from where the plastic part of the temple begins into the right ear.

"We no longer need the old-style ear pod, or bug," she added. "And the transmitter is located in the right nose pad. It's capable of picking up voices from approximately two feet. Plenty good for us to hear the wearer's voice.

"Here's where the phone has a definite advantage," she said. "They can pick up voices from distances up to twenty feet.

"The other reason to carry your phone is that it has the GPS locator system and the glasses don't," she explained. "Yes, we may be able to hear you and communicate, even with the ability to display photos on your glasses, but we can only locate you via the phone.

"If it's back in your hotel room and you're out in the field, we can't tell you if there are any threats around you, give you directions to your target, or tell you where your teammates are," she finished. "So, we've done everything possible with current technology to try to keep you safe and provide intelligence for you to use when you need it to perform your missions, it's only as good as the man who's using it."

Taking a final look around the crowd, she finished, "Now, I hope I've expressed how valuable these glasses and the other technologically advanced equipment you'll be given are to ensuring mission accomplishment and getting you back home safely.

"But all the smart devices in the world can't overcome the stupidity of some people," she finished, with a slight bow in Jim's direction.

Chapter 36

"Now I'd like to do a quick explanation of how we'll locate and track every one of you," Debbie announced. "You've seen how crowded the screen can become if we try to upload too much data.

"Well, your name is data," she explained. "So, we've devised a system using less 'data', but which allows us, and your team leader, to quickly locate you and pass any important information efficiently."

Returning to the screen depicting area one, she showed them the effect of having over one hundred names on the screen and said, "Now, you can see how much of the screen is useless. Even removing the first names doesn't clear enough of the screen to allow us to provide accurate data on the location of our people and the killer teams."

Clearing the screen of the names, she replaced them with three or four-digit numbers saying, "Here's the same information but using numbers to locate each member of our teams. More precisely, the members of the area commanders' teams. Here, the number one, one, two, four represents area one, team one, and member twenty-four of team one.

"That's even too much data," she said as she removed the first digit. "Now, since you know you're in area one, and the commander is only assigned to an area, that's unnecessary clutter. So, the commander of area one is simply a one. Area two commander, two."

"The team leaders are numbered however the commander decides, so the leader of team two is one-two," she explained. "The fifth member of area one, team two, will be one-two-five. The only exceptions are the snipers.

"This is because we may need to move a sniper from area one to area two if he's the closest to the target," she explained. "So, for the snipers, the designator for them will be the letter 'S', obviously standing for sniper, number one, two, or three, for the area assigned, and number one, two, or three, for the number assigned to that person.

"For example," she said, manipulating the screen. "Here's S-2-1, who I happen to know is Connor Stewart. Easy to understand once you know the snipers on your team.

"Here, the sniper is assigned to area two and is the first one on the list of names," she explained. "It should be easy to keep track of three names, especially since they are part of the most important aspect of this entire operation.

"One additional feature is that the commander of any area can expand his coverage to include a maximum of two hundred miles outside of the borders of his area," she told them. "This allows him to track his sniper as he enters the adjoining area, and to potentially see if any of the killer teams have changed direction from the adjoining area and headed for him before they enter his area.

"The single issue we haven't resolved is who is in charge of the sniper once he is activated," she admitted. "If we knew the sniper would only be working within the area where he is assigned, we'd let the area commander be in charge of the hit. However, we can't be sure of that.

"The target may be headed for Johannesburg, which is in area three, and suddenly head south to Bloemfontein, one of the nation's capitals," she explained. "Who's in charge of him while he's activated in area three due to intelligence from the morning?

"Then the helicopter taking the Steer where we thought he was going suddenly turns south just as we learn he's going to be speaking at a rally in Bloemfontein," Debbie continued. "Who's in charge as he heads north? Who's in charge when he turns south but is still in area three?

"We've already told you how important this target is," she continued. "And how critical time is for recognizing, tracking, intercepting, and having a reasonable shot.

"You have probably hours to move men around the farms if updates vary from where you have assigned teams based on last night's intelligence," she said emphatically. "But in the case of the snipers, they may only have minutes, or luckily an hour, to move, get into position, and take the shot.

"Now we've decided that the snipers will be under the central control of Mr. Butch North," she told them. "I'm sure you've seen him here since yesterday, and up until now, he was only here to coordinate with the area commanders."

She paused for a moment and looked at Butch before continuing, "The snipers will be directly connected to Butch for activation and deployment, but the area commanders will be responsible for his field support.

"In other words, he's your responsibility for safety, housing, food, and transportation, just as the other members of your teams," she concluded. "But once activated by Butch, you'll only provide transportation to whatever location is given and wait for the sniper to rejoin your teams after successful completion of his mission. Or if there's no shot.

"Now, I hope there are no questions at this point," Debbie announced, as she finished and switched off the screen. "But I'm sure the area leaders would like to have a little discussion with Mr. North while we break for a quick lunch. Please be back in your seats in forty-five minutes."

Chapter 37

"Well, what do you think?" Debbie asked, as she walked up to where Gene, Jim, and Butch were standing.

"I think you blindsided me," Butch answered. "Why the hell wasn't I told about this before it was made public?"

"You can blame me for that," Gene told him. "We had the spooks who reside in the bowels of Black Water Headquarters perform statistical, hypothetical, and mystical wizardly simulations all last night regarding the control of the snipers.

"They presented their findings this morning while you were having breakfast," he continued. "I've had an operational study team analyzing those findings, and they presented them to Debbie right before the briefing.

"I had already seen the findings and told Debbie to announce it during the briefing," Gene explained. "I could have told you, but I think it was important to tell everyone while she was discussing how the information regarding our people and the killer teams, and I credit one of the spooks from the basement for that moniker … killer teams, would be tracked.

"Now, if you think you'll have any problems with it, I can get another one of our operational folks who aren't currently active to do it," Gene said. "I just thought you'd have plenty of time to take care of it, and it made sense to me since you are aware of all of the teams and are tasked with moving them as needed based on the intelligence and your birds-eye view of the playing field."

Butch hesitated for a moment and finally said, "No, you're right about me being the most logical. I know Jim's going to be using every available brain cell he has trying to sneak some toxic agent into the President's wine.

"And I doubt if he'd have a clue about what's going on in the field," he continued. "I'll take care of it."

"Excellent," Gene said, putting his hand on Butch's shoulder. "There is a slim chance Jim can come help if his little negotiation wraps up early on the first day, but I don't believe that any more than I believe in the tooth fairy.

"Speaking of the negotiations," Debbie broke in. "I have a possible solution for your weapon request."

"What's that?" Jim asked.

"I believe Gene told you about an asset we have within the Bull pen," Debbie said.

"Yeah, he did," Jim acknowledged. "I also think he said she's on her way back here. Something to do with her mother."

"That's correct," Debbie confirmed. "However, she still has access to the Bull pen."

"You really think she can sneak a gun into the room where Megan and I will be meeting him?" Jim asked.

"She's positive she can," Debbie answered. "I gave her a quick call right after we discussed how you planned on sending the Bull to the butcher if the frog juice option was off the table.

"Over the last few days, I've had several discussions regarding how things operated in the Bull pen," Debbie explained. "We discussed security, manpower at his offices in the various capitals, and in his home in Johannesburg, where he does most of his ... entertaining.

"Since she's been almost a constant fixture at all of those places, she's rarely given a thorough security inspection," she continued. "She's already snuck in cameras, recorders, and listening devices.

"Granted, a weapon, even a pistol, could be a little more difficult," Debbie said, smiling. "But she explained to me that even though the guards enjoy the pat down a little more than she does, they tend to smile, wink, and tell her to come back soon.

"When it's something important, she puts it in her purse," she continued. "She says they seldom do more than ask her if there's anything in it, or possible open it for a perfunctory glance. When they ask her what's in it, if it's something she doesn't want them to know about, she just smiles and says, 'Oh, you know. Perfume, lipstick, some hand lotion, and I almost forgot…some feminine products I may require. You know, it's that time of the month'.

"They can't seem to look away fast enough," Debbie said, laughing. "She's planning on taking a small thirty-eight caliber when she goes there in the morning to say goodbye to the Bull.

"He's headed back to Pretoria and won't be back until his meeting with you and Megan," Debbie continued. "She'll tell me where the gun will be located after she leaves for the airport, which should be around six o'clock our time tomorrow morning, if she's successful.

"That will give us some time to refine our plans, or come up with a new one," Debbie finished.

"That sounds great, but I'd still like to know if he has a weapon in the room and where it is," Jim said, nodding. "I sort of like to have a multitude of options when my life is on the line. Especially if my host can get to a weapon before I can."

"I'm still working on that," Debbie told him, as she followed them to the cafeteria. "And Jewell is probably our best source for that, also. We're monitoring everything in the Johannesburg house, which may bear fruit. Especially if some mention of it occurs, such as the guard asking about it, or he takes it out when he goes to Pretoria.

"We're using every asset we have," Debbie assured him. "We know the risks you and Megan are taking, and we're well aware of the repercussions if we fail. Not just your lives, but the damage to the country.

Chapter 38

"By the way, where is Megan?" Jim asked as they entered the cafeteria.

"She's been with some State Department twit all morning," Gene answered. "She's taking this negotiation thing seriously."

"But she knows how the story ends, doesn't she?" Jim asked, reaching for a tray at the start of the buffet.

"Oh, yeah," Gene assured him. "But I admire her effort. And I believe, as she does, if she's fluent in the issues, the genocide, the ethnic cleansing, the rare earth elements, the failing food supply due to inept people taking over the food production, she'll be more capable of keeping his attention while you hold up your end of the operation."

"I see your point, sir," Jim replied, taking a tortilla from the steam tray. "But I'm just as sure that if she read nursery rhymes while wearing a revealing blouse and a short skirt, she would be able to hold his attention.

"And if this lecherous old man is as bad as I've been led to believe, and Megan being as attractive as she is, the Bull would be rolling his upper lip and sniffing as if she were a heifer in heat the minute we enter the room," Jim continued, heaping fajita meat and Pico de Gallo on his tortillas.

"Excuse me, gentlemen," came a female voice from behind them on the buffet line. "Would you folks mind if I joined you for lunch?"

Gene turned and looked past Debbie, Jim, and Butch, saying, "Why, Megan. Of course, you're welcome to join us. And we were just talking about you."

"I know," Megan replied. "I believe I heard most of it. At least the part beginning with me reading nursery rhymes."

"Mea culpa," Jim said, with a slight bow. "I definitely didn't mean anything derogatory. I just …"

"I understand," Megan said, interrupting Jim. "Just as I understand exactly why I was selected for this operation."

Pausing while she picked a Chef Salad from the buffet, she said, "Now, having laid our cards on the table, I want to be able to converse intelligently with him in the event he thinks I'm just there to seduce him and to get him to agree to whatever terms we present.

"I've read all the reports," she continued. "And I fully expect him to behave exactly as you so graphically described as a Bull in a pen with a small herd of heifers.

"I can assure you, I understand the mating habits of Bulls since I grew up on a ranch just north of Fort Worth," she said, smiling as she took a glass of tea. "And I'm also familiar with the various techniques to, as we used to say, change his interest from ass to grass."

"I think this is going to be fun," Jim said, smiling and shaking his head, as he headed for an open space on the long table that would accommodate the five of them. "It's been a while since I've heard barnyard talk."

"I understand you grew up somewhere up in the Texas Panhandle," Megan said, setting her tray across the table from Jim. "That 'barnyard talk' you referred to sticks to you no matter how long it's been since you've seen beef on the hoof that wasn't wrapped in plastic."

"What's that old saying? You can take the boy out of the country, but not the country out of the boy?" Jim asked. "I guess that includes the country girls as well."

"Not to interrupt you two's reminiscing and barnyard talk, but we only have a few more minutes before we need to get back to the briefing," Debbie reminded them. "Jim, I think this would be a great time to discuss your backup plan with Megan."

"Of course," Jim replied, taking a sip of tea. "Megan, I know you've had some experience with firearms. My question is, do you think you can convince our Bull that you would blow a hole through his face should he not do as told?

"I'm not asking this because you're a female," Jim hurried to explain. "But it's something I always ask someone who has your back but never faced a situation where that was the only option.

"I say the same thing when someone asks me what sort of weapon they need for self-defense," he continued, looking at Megan. "I always ask the same thing; can you pull the trigger when your gun is pointing at another human face?

"It has nothing to do with male or female," Jim said. "It has to do with the aversion to seeing a human's head explode before your very eyes.

"Then I advise them to forget the gun if they can't use it to defend themselves," he finished. "Because if you can't carry through without hesitation, the man you're trying to defend yourself from with have no qualms about taking your gun and blowing your face off."

Chapter 39

"Hey, guys, I've got to get back to work and make sure everything is ready for the last part of this briefing," Debbie said, rising with her tray. "I'll see you inside."

"Okay," Megan said, picking at her salad. "Exactly what are you asking me to do on your backup plan that requires me to shoot someone?"

"First, I'm hoping we don't need to enact the backup plan," Jim said, seriously. "I'm hoping you can keep him distracted, and I have no issues pouring the toxin in his wine.

"That's my goal, no guns required," Jim continued. "This was the plan the Black Water folks came up with, and it will keep suspicion off our government.

"It's conceivable he accidentally poisoned himself and we had nothing to do with it," Jim explained. "Especially if we can be gone for some period of time before he's discovered.

"Once we introduce weapons, the story of any accidental death becomes unbelievable," Jim continued. "Especially since there will be three dead bodies. I'm just hoping you and I aren't among the three.

"If things go as I plan, I don't plan on you shooting anyone," Jim told her. "But that doesn't mean it's not a possibility.

"In a fluid situation, especially when there's a highly trained bodyguard, almost anything can happen," he explained. "If you're just holding a gun on the President when the guard comes in, and he believes you'll shoot his protectee, he may react to remove the threat, you, before you can shoot.

"I'm hoping the guard will see his best option, as far as he knows at that point, is to hand me his gun and try to negotiate the President's freedom," Jim continued. "But if he sees a lack of determination in your face, your eyes, he'll probably go for his weapon."

"I see what you're saying," Megan said, nodding. "Let me see if I can give you a little reassurance that I'm capable of convincing the guard and the President that I'm serious.

"If I can convince a fat-assed, puss-gutted, repugnant piece of shit that I would possibly enjoy any physical contact whatsoever, I think I can convince him that I'm serious," she explained.

"First, I've got to do some real first-class Hollywood acting to convince him he has the slightest chance of even touching me," Megan continued. "For me to act as if I'd blow his face off, that would be about as natural a reaction as any woman would have.

"Would I?" she asked. "I really don't know. As you said, I don't know if I can look anyone in the eyes and pull the trigger. But the disgust of imagining that ball of blubber just touching me will be written on my face as soon as I get the chance to drop the charade.

"I've even wondered if I can keep the disgust off my face when he begins his act of seduction," she continued. "That's part of the reason I'm filling my head with the data and logic behind the negotiations. I can always look down at a sheet of paper, or a photo, if I start to gag."

Jim sat looking at her for a moment and finally said, "I think you'll do fine. But if you have any self-doubts once I call for the guard, don't hesitate to hand me the pistol and step behind me.

"I can take care of the situation using the gun that's being planted for us, but that screws the pooch with our cover story that a third party killed the President and the guard before getting shot himself," Jim continued. "But I'd rather be standing in front of some commission explaining how things went wrong than to be lying in a pine box while some scarlet robe wearing preacher extolls my life, about which he knows Jack Shit.

"Bottom line, if you want out of the weapons issue at any point, let me know the second you make that decision, and I'll try to make sure both of us walk out of there," Jim finished.

"I guess we'd better get back to the auditorium and take our seats before Debbie starts her spiel," Gene said, standing. "I'd rather face the President's guard who has an Uzi than face Bracer's wrath."

"Who's Bracer?" Megan whispered, as they left the cafeteria behind Gene and Butch.

"Debbie," Jim whispered back, following her from the room. "I'll tell you the story behind the name later."

Chapter 40

They had barely taken their seats when a man wearing a knit shirt with 'Black Water' embroidered above the left breast pocket stepped up and said, "General Barker, I believe you need to see this."

As Gene read the note, he nodded to the man and rose, saying, "Thanks. Yeah, I needed to see this."

Leaving his seat, he headed up the aisle toward the front of the auditorium, shaking his head. As he neared the podium where Debbie was just about to resume the briefing, he motioned for her to join him at the side.

"We've just been told that we must meet with the President in three days," he told her. "I don't believe the audacity of this pompous, arrogant asshole. We give him four days to prepare, so he gives us a date that's one day short.

"I guess he has to appear to be in charge and dictate the terms," Gene continued, handing Debbie the note. "I guess you'd better get this meeting over and start preparing to figure out how to get all our people and equipment to South America a little sooner than planned."

"Yes, sir," Debbie said, shaking her head. "Why couldn't he just accommodate us as most reasonable diplomats would. At least make it a request instead of a demand?"

"Because he's a minor player on the world stage and he wants his country to think he's a major player and rules the rest of the world with a single finger," Gene answered.

"Well, I've got just the finger for him," Debbie replied, as she turned to the podium.

As Gene headed back to his seat, Debbie announced, "Folks, I've just been informed we only have three days to get this operation started."

Pausing for a moment, she continued, "I'm going to give you the most abbreviated version of the rest of the briefing I can, and I'm leaving it up to each of you, mainly the commanders of each area, to begin initial deployment plans.

"I want you to give my people, whose names and numbers are on the brochure on the table at the rear, everything you think you'll need initially to be ready in your area in three days," she told them, as she put the map of South Africa with the three areas depicted back on the screen.

"Coordinate with Mr. North as you determine where you want your teams initially located, where you plan on stationing the snipers, and what logistical support you'll need," she directed. "Use the data I showed you this morning as to where the killer teams are and which farms they plan on attacking.

"We'll be sending updates to your iPads as we get further intelligence," she continued. "I know this is akin to hunting black cats in the dark, but we've got to start somewhere, and I'll see if I can't provide a little illumination over the next couple of days.

"I'm asking Mr. North to meet with each of you this evening and make sure he's in the loop regarding the initial deployments. Especially the snipers," she continued. "Now, I've got fifty pounds of shit to stuff into a twenty-five-pound bag in the next two days to arrange transportation for three hundred people to go half way around the world, weapons, vehicles for you once you get to your staging areas, communications for everyone, and all of this under the radar of our friends who we hope aren't aware of our impending arrival.

"Please let my folks know your exact requirements as soon as you determine them," she finished, before stepping off the platform. "We've estimated everything we figured you'd need, but it's your asses on the line over there, and we may have overlooked something crucial. Good luck, folks."

Butch shook his head and said, "I guess I'd better cancel dinner with you guys tonight. It looks like I may be here for several hours by the time I've spoken to all the area commanders and tried to connect all the dots.

"Would it be okay if I asked Fabio to bring me back to the hotel when I'm done?" he asked, as the crowd began to leave their seats.

"I've got something better in mind," Gene said, looking for the man who had brought the note.

Spotting him standing by the exit waiting for a response to the note, Gene told Butch, "Come with me. Jim, Megan, I'll be right back."

"I've got a request," Gene said as he and Butch reached the guy. "No, make that a demand. I want a room tonight for Mr. North here, and I want Fabio standing by to take Mr. North to the airport in the morning, if he's ready to head back to Texas.

"Butch, you let me know when you're ready to fly home, and I'll have a jet standing by," Gene told him.

"Yes, sir," the man acknowledged when Gene turned back to him. "I'll take care of that right now."

Extending his hand to Butch, he said, "I'm Jerry Clower, and I'll leave my number in your room. Call if there's anything I can do for you."

"Nice to meet you," Butch replied. "Your name sounds familiar. Have we met before?"

"No, sir," Jerry answered. "You're probably thinking of the Mississippi comedian who made jokes about his southern upbringing.

"So, don't look to me for anything too humorous, but I can handle almost anything else," he said, before turning. "General, let me know if there's anything else."

Chapter 41

As Gene left with Jim and Megan, Butch looked for the three area commanders. Finding them, he walked over and asked them to keep their folks in the auditorium.

When it appeared everyone was still around, Butch walked to the podium and asked, "Would all of you please have a seat. I've got a couple of things I'd like to say, and then we can all go back to our rooms.

"And please, can I ask for everyone attached to area one to take the left side, the right side from your point of view, area two in the center, and area three in the remaining seats."

As the people retook their seats, he started, "In case you don't recognize me, I'm Butch North. Just Butch will suffice.

"Let's start out with establishing a couple of procedures," he said. "I'd like for each of you, starting with area one, to stand and state your name.

"Area commanders first, then team leaders, then their members, if you've managed to get that far," he continued.

As the commanders, the team leaders, and their people did as he had asked, he said, "Now, my memory is about as short as my … you know what. So, pardon me if I don't remember every one of you three hundred people in ten minutes.

"First, I'd like for us to start by using the system of identification Debbie asked for," Butch continued. "It becomes easier if you start now, or as soon as the area commanders decide who is on which team."

Butch paused while they thought about it, and continued, "Now, let's set some ground rules. First, keep communication to a minimum while we're in the field.

"I don't know how technically advanced these folks are, by that I mean the killer teams," he explained. "But let's not underestimate them. There was a system we used in the Air Force called 'Zipper'. It was when you received an instruction, understood it, and would comply, you just keyed your mic twice.

"This let the sender know his instructions had been received and would be complied with," he continued. "This reduced the chance of triangulation of your position based on your transmission to a minimum amount of time.

"I'm going to ask Debbie to make sure our radios are using random frequencies, changing every second or so, to preclude any chance of someone hearing the entire communication," he said. "We had a radio system called 'Have Quick' that did that automatically, but it was rather cumbersome.

"With the technology we have today, I'm positive it would be a simple program in each phone tied through a central computer via some satellite floating over our heads.

"Now, let's get down to tactics," he continued. "One, how do you intend to handle the killer team headed for a farm in your area?"

The area one commander stood and said, "I'd like to catch them on the road to the farm and stop them before they can get there."

"Two, what's your plan?" Butch asked.

"Pretty much the same," the area two commander replied. "But I'd ambush them as they turned into the farm."

"Three?" Butch asked.

"I'd wait at the farm where I could be hidden out of sight and start shooting when they get there," he said.

"And how would you deploy the team?" Butch asked.

"Just have them on the sides of the farmhouse and wait for them to get out of their cars," he answered.

Butch paused for a moment and said, "Here's my thinking about catching them on the road. You've got to hide your vehicles. You've got to position your men, possibly with little cover, and there's a chance that tail-end Charlie, the last car in their convoy, may turn and run.

"Waiting at the entrance to the farm presents some of the same issues," Butch told them. "To me, waiting at the farmhouse is the most logical and tactically sound option.

"However, the folks in the house may be injured," he continued. "So, let's start with moving the family. If time is critical, have them in the barn. Or at least in a room at the rear of the house.

"And I'd send three teams," he explained. "Have one inside the house, where they are out of sight. Position the other two on either side of the house.

"Then, when the killer teams exit their cars, the teams on the sides can fan out at about a forty-five-degree angle from the house as the team in the house begins firing from any window or door that's available," he continued. "The reason for the forty-five-degree angle is to prevent what we used to call a circular firing squad.

"Do any of you need a further explanation of the concept?" Butch asked.

Not seeing anyone raise their hands, he continued. "I'd like for each team, or teams, to practice this technique prior to any actual contact. Now, are there any questions as to what to do after the shooting stops?"

"What about survivors?" someone asked.

"Are you familiar with Santa Anna's attack on the Alamo?" Butch asked. "As Santa Anna commenced his attack on the defenders within the walls, he carried a black flag signifying no quarter would be given.

"Meaning there would be no one left alive," he explained. "Once they had control, they systematically went through the place and bayonetted anyone left alive. That's where the battle cry Remember the Alamo originated.

"That's what we're doing here. This is a Black Flag operation," he continued. "When you've defeated the killer teams, you're to inspect each body and shoot anyone who is still alive in the left eye. Or right eye. As long as there are no survivors.

"Then you're going to search the bodies for any electronic devices, phones, pagers, note pads, anything that may lead us to other members of the other teams, or their leaders," Butch said. "If that leads us to ten people, maybe those ten will lead us to ten more each. That's over a hundred. Cast a wide net, catch more fish.

"Once you're sure you have anything useful for Debbie's wizards here at Black Water, pile the bodies back in the cars they came in, drive the cars back to the road that led to the entrance to the farm, and torch the cars," Butch said.

"Isn't that a little overkill?" someone asked.

"No," Butch answered, looking directly at the man who had asked. "What we are trying to do is send a message to whoever sent them that the burning, raping, torture, and murder of the farmers will not be tolerated. This genocide and ethnic cleansing of the Boers will stop right now.

"Not next week. Not tomorrow. Now," he told them. "Now, if you don't think you can follow this directive, tell your team leader. He can tell his commander. His commander can tell me, and I'll find a replacement for you.

"While we're on the subject, I expect all of you to strictly adhere to the chain of command, just as you learned when you were in the military," he told them. "If you were never in the military, ask someone who was."

After letting his directive sink in, Butch continued, "None of this is my idea. This comes from someone well above me. Someone above Black Water. I would hazard a guess that the person making this decision is very near the pinnacle of our government. But I've sworn to follow those orders.

"If you know your history of World War II, you should remember how we finally convinced the Japanese to surrender," Butch explained. "We knew from fighting our way up the island chain to reach mainland Japan that the Japanese would fight to the death.

"Look at the Kamikaze pilots," he continued. "They considered dying for the emperor an honor, and to fail would dishonor himself and his family.

"The number crunchers in Washington figured if we did a land invasion, the death toll of Japanese soldiers and civilians would be astronomical," he told them. "Not to mention how many of our men would die.

"We initially fire-bombed Tokyo, hoping that would convince Emperor Hirohito to surrender," he continued. "The next step in the escalation was a nuke on Hiroshima. Still no surrender. Next came Nagasaki.

"Finally, the emperor figured out, or so he thought, that we'd eradicate every major city on the island," Butch explained. "Of course, he didn't know we only had two nukes.

"Now, I don't know if the number of Japanese dead was more or less than predicted, but I do know it saved tens of thousands, if not hundreds of thousands, of American lives," he said.

"We're hoping this fire-bombing will send the message," Butch added. "If the message isn't received and the lesson learned, we can expect an escalation. I don't know what that would be, but I do know that we won't stop until the genocide, ethnic cleansing, and expropriation of the farms ceases.

"I'll be available all night if there are any issues," Butch then told them after a slight pause. "Your commanders can reach me by calling any Black Water number and have them patch you to my room.

"If it's after I leave for home back in Texas in the morning, they can patch you to my cell phone," he finally told them. "But just remember it's an unsecure line and if security was ever important to a mission, this is probably the most important one you'll ever be involved in.

"So, with that, I'll leave you to your commanders if he has any final words," he said, looking around the room. "So, I'll bid you good night, and I'll see you on the plane in a couple of days when we head for South Africa."

Chapter 42

As Butch was winding up his instructions to the men who were going to be in the field and Gene was driving Jim and Megan to the hotel in Springfield, Jim asked, "Gene, do you think you can give Debbie a call and see if the gun Jewell leaves for me can be traced to some crime or has some tie to any incident or person living in Johannesburg?"

"I can give that a try," he answered, reaching for his phone. "But this may be a little late in the game for her to manage that."

As Gene was talking to Debbie, Jim turned to Megan and asked, "What are you going to do with your couple of days off when you get home?"

"I was going to do some grocery shopping on the way back to Decatur, but I forgot my grocery list," she answered. "I guess that's never happened to you before, has it?"

"Constantly," Jim answered. "Hell, most of the time I make the decision to go shopping is when I'm passing a store and remember I need something.

"Then, I just grab a cart and make a pass by the veggies, dairy products, chips, and soda aisle," he continued, shaking his head. "I prefer to go buying, not shopping, because I hate wandering up and down the aisles and having to wait behind someone who has to read the label on every can on the shelf.

"A week or so ago, I was headed home from the airport after a three-day trip, and remembered I needed some pickles," he continued. "You know, those oval dill pickles that go so good on a hamburger?

"Anyway, I grabbed a cart and headed for the aisle where the condiments were displayed," he explained. "As I turned into the aisle, there was this very, very large lady pushing her cart toward me.

"I just stopped, trying to decide if I could squeeze my cart past her since the pickles were behind her, or just back out of the aisle," Jim said, slowly shaking his head. "Well, I guess I had one of those deer-in-the-headlights looks, and the lady gave me a stare that would cower a rabid dog. Then she asked, 'What? Do you think I'm too fat, or something?'

"That's when I should have just kept my mouth shut and backed out of the aisle," Jim said. "But noooo, I didn't. Matter of fact, I blurted out, 'Lady, I've only seen five fat people in my life, and you happen to be four of them'.

"Needless to say, I left without my pickles," Jim finished. "And I'm sure Walmart has a couple of carts that need some major repair after she charged into my cart. But I guess I'm lucky I escaped with just a lump on the back of my head from a ten-pound bag of sugar!"

Jim had just finished his story when Gene hung up his phone and said, "Jewell already has the gun. She got it from a man she met who works with the Johannesburg police.

"She doesn't know if it has some history, but at least if they track it, it will show up as being sold in South Africa," he explained. "I think that's about as good as it's going to get, seeing as how she's leaving in a day or two."

"That'll work," Jim said, nodding. "I just didn't want a weapon sold in Burbank, California, to wind up killing the President of South Africa.

"Speaking of that, who will become President afterwards?" Jim asked. "Do they have a Vice President?"

"They have a Deputy President," Gene explained. "And before you ask what difference a change in administration will accomplish, that's been taken care of.

"Some crafty folks from some black operation hidden deep within the CIA's underground sources of disreputable people have been wooing the deputy for some time," Gene explained. "Which actually makes our 'negotiation' irrelevant since the deputy has already agreed to everything we want.

"That includes, most importantly, the sole rights to the rare earth elements," he continued. "And somehow, the deputy managed to designate ten percent of the proceeds to The Big Guy. I have no idea how he's going to shelter that much money, but since he'll only be President for a year or so before the next election, that could be his retirement package."

"Isn't he going to be running for President?" Jim asked, as they neared the exit of the hotel.

"Is a frog's ass water-tight? Of course he is. And we'll voice our support for such a democratically inclined individual," Gene answered, with a look of disbelief at the question. "Once we acquire the minerals we need, it's actually to our benefit to have him in office.

"With all of the dirt we have on the man, he'll be in our pocket forever," he explained, as they arrived at the Embassy

Suites. "Looks like we've got a couple of minutes to spare before our five o'clock reservations.

"Guess I'll just run a washcloth across my face and head down to get our table," he said, parking. "I'll see you guys in a couple of minutes."

"I'm going to do the same," Megan said, opening her door. "I'll wait until after dinner to shower because I don't want to put my sweaty body in a clean set of clothes since I only brought enough for one day."

Chapter 43

When Jim got to his room, he saw Marie standing in front of the bathroom mirror, fussing with her hair. "You're a little later than I expected. You're almost late."

"Almost late, isn't that a synonym for on time?" he asked, as he looked at her dress. "You look nice, but I think I need to tell you that the only other female will be wearing jeans and a t-shirt."

"So? Why should I care what she's wearing?" Marie asked, as Jim took a washcloth from the rack and soaked it in the sink.

"I don't know," Jim said, washing his face. "We had this discussion back home before we came. And I just assumed you were dressing as you are because you thought Megan would dress the same.

"But it's definitely your decision," he added, toweling his face dry.

"I'm dressed and we don't have time for me to change," she replied, applying a quick brush of mascara to her eyebrows. "Why are you so late, anyway?"

"There was a major change we didn't receive until after lunch, and we needed to make several adjustments before we left," Jim answered, lifting his arms to see if there were any sweat stains.

"Why were there changes?" Marie asked, rechecking her makeup once again.

"Timeline got moved up a day," Jim said, turning to look at her. "Anyway, I'm here, almost late, and we *will* be late if we don't get down to the restaurant. Gene's probably already down there waiting."

"Is Butch going to make it?" Marie asked as they walked to the elevator.

"I don't think so," Jim answered, pushing the down button. "The accelerated timeline affected his operation more than it did mine, so he had to stay behind and make whatever adjustments necessary to do whatever he's doing over there."

"Isn't he going to be with you and Megan?" she asked, as the doors to the elevator opened.

"No, I think he's going to be out in the country working with the farmers," Jim answered, getting on the elevator.

"I was hoping I'd see him this evening. He seems like such a nice guy," Marie said, as she watched the numbers over the doors counting down. "Will he be with us going back to Dallas?"

"I don't know," Jim answered, as they stepped out on the ground floor. "I'm not even sure if I'll see him again regarding this operation. He may be there longer than I'll be, and I doubt he'll be anywhere near where Megan and I will be meeting the President."

"Maybe you can invite him over some weekend," she suggested, as they walked into the restaurant. "Do you know if he's seeing anyone?"

"No, I don't know much about his private life," Jim answered, looking for Gene. "And weekends don't always mean days off for airline pilots, as you already know."

Spotting Gene sitting toward the rear of the restaurant with Megan, Jim nodded to where they were sitting and said, "There they are. Looks like they didn't wait for us to order drinks."

As they walked up to the table, Gene rose and said, "You certainly look nice this evening, Marie. Did you enjoy your tour of our nation's capital?"

"It was nice," Marie said, as Jim pulled out a chair for her. "Fabio was a superb guide. But there's just only so much I could see in just one day."

"Maybe next time," Gene said, as she sat down. "Marie, I'd like to introduce Megan, the lady Jim will be working with in South Africa. Megan, meet Marie."

Megam looked across the table and said, "Nice to meet you, Marie. It's nice to have another female to talk to after a day in the testosterone atmosphere of an all-male assembly. And I do love your dress."

"Nice to meet you, too," Marie said, taking her seat. "I believe Jim said you're some sort of diplomat?"

"No, I'm just the assistant to an assistant of the special assistant to someone in the State Department," Megan answered, smiling. "I get to fly somewhere, usually not an island paradise, and spend days trying to convince some self-important dweeb underling to some vice-someone, to recommend whatever I'm recommending to someone a step above him, to someone at a higher level, where one of our esteemed Congressmen, or Senators, can get a photo, or hopefully a televised segment shaking someone's hand, while they exalt the importance of this earth-shattering agreement."

"Sounds like you get to travel a lot," Marie replied, as the waiter arrived at their table.

"Life out of a suitcase is not my idea of fun traveling," Megan said, as Marie and Jim placed their drink orders. "And I'm sure Jim will agree, since he spends half of his life going from place to place, with just enough time to grab a few hours of sleep before getting on the road again.

"No, I'm about ready to get a job holding up one of those slow/stop signs you see around road construction on two-lane roads," Megan said. "At least I could sleep in my own bed every night. And I'm sure I'd get to meet some very interesting people while they're waiting for me to spin my sign from stop to slow. Perhaps Mr. Right will pull up, notice how hot and thirsty I look, and offer me a frosty beverage in the rear seat of his Mercedes limo while I'm waiting to spin my sign."

"A girl can always dream," Marie replied, as her drink was set on the table.

Chapter 44

Following dinner, Gene reminded them of the flight back to Love Field and asked them to be downstairs by seven o'clock so Fabio could get them to Quantico on time, and he was heading for the exit as Jim, Marie, and Megan went to the elevators.

"What floor, Megan?" Jim asked, as the doors slid open.

"Five, please," she answered, getting in behind Marie. "Where are you?"

"Seven," he answered, after punching in the floors.

"So, I guess I'll see you in the morning," Marie said, as the elevator began to rise.

"I suppose so," Megan replied, watching the numbers count upward. "Maybe we'll have a chance to chat a little on the flight back to Texas."

"Of course," Marie said. "And maybe Butch will be on the plane with us. You know Butch North, don't you?"

"I met him today at lunch," she answered, as the doors slid open on the fifth floor. "So, I can't really say I know him. Anyway, you guys have a good night, and I'll be downstairs around six-thirty for something to eat.

"I guess you know they have a made-to-order breakfast, don't you?" she continued, holding the doors open. "I'm just going to get a breakfast burrito or something to eat on the drive back to Quantico. And coffee, of course."

"We'll probably meet you there then," Jim said, as she released the doors. "Good night."

Nothing was said as the elevator carried them up two floors, and when Jim opened the door to their room, Marie said, "Wow! Megan is a beautiful lady."

"Yes, she is," Jim said, heading for the bathroom.

"You really think she's beautiful?" Marie asked, kicking off her shoes.

"Do I really think she's beautiful? Is that what you asked?" he asked, as he pulled off the t-shirt he had been wearing.

"Yes, do you?" Marie repeated, slipping off her dress.

"Yes, I do," he replied, taking off his jeans. "And you said you think she's beautiful. Hell, if you asked fifty guys, or ladies, you'd probably get fifty-five hell yeses.

"What's this all about?" Jim asked, turning on the shower. "Hell, you've met several of the flight attendants I've flown with who were just as good-looking as she. What's the problem?"

"There, you just said it," Marie replied, crossing her arms. "You said the flight attendants were just 'good looking', but she's beautiful."

"Marie, I really don't want to get into this," Jim said, testing the warmth of the water. "I've had a long day, and I've got to leave one day after we get home.

"Can you at least wait until I get out of the shower?" he asked, slipping off his shorts and stepping into the tub.

"Do you want me to leave it running when I'm done?" he asked, pulling the shower curtain closed.

"No, I had my shower after I got back from my guided tour," she answered.

A few minutes later, as Jim shut off the shower, he heard Marie say, "You know, I'll bet she got the job because of the way she looks."

Not getting a reply, she continued, "I guess I can see why the company hired her. What do you think?"

Jim finished drying and replied, "I think you're somewhat correct. Maybe her looks got her noticed. But her brains got her hired.

"And yes, she's definitely an asset when we're dealing with our mainly male clients," he continued, pulling on clean shorts. "But the bottom line is, she produces results."

"Just how do you know that?" Marie asked, walking into the bathroom to remove her makeup.

"I read her resume," Jim answered. "Just as I read the resume of anyone I'm asked to protect. I want to know if there are any habits, traits, or anything I think has a bearing on my ability to protect them.

"And it's my life, too," he finished. "I'd like to spend just a few more years with a beautiful lady I know."

"And who would that be?" Marie asked, as she turned off the bathroom light.

"If you'll remove that red t-shirt you're wearing and get in bed, I'll show you," Jim answered, reaching for the light on the nightstand.

Chapter 45

The following morning, as Jim and Marie were having a quick breakfast with Megan, Butch came walking in saying, "Good morning, folks. Ready to head back to Texas?"

"Good morning, Butch," Jim said, standing to shake hands. "Did you stay here in the hotel last night?"

"Oh, no," he answered, giving a nod to everybody. "I spent the night at Black Water Headquarters dealing with a multitude of problems.

"I finally got to go to bed about four hours ago, couldn't get to sleep, got up and made a pot of coffee, of course, after drinking that, I really couldn't sleep," he continued. "Then I went to the cafeteria and had breakfast. I ran into Fabio there and decided to ride with him up here to get you guys."

"Is Fabio waiting outside?" Marie asked. "Why don't you ask him to come in and have coffee or something while we finish breakfast?"

"I asked him before I came in," Butch answered. "Anyway, I thought I'd carry your bags to the car while you finish eating, so if you'll point them out, I'll take care of that."

"I'll go with you," Jim said, wiping his mouth. "I'm done, except for a to-go coffee, and I'll get that when the waitress stops by."

"Good," Butch said, as Jim tossed his napkin on the table. "I don't mean to hurry everybody, but I'd sort of like to get the hell out of here and go home so I can get some rest before this shit show starts all over again."

As Jim and Butch carried their suitcases to the car, Butch said, "I'd like your advice on something when we get in the plane headed for Texas."

"What's it about?" Jim asked, as Fabio got out of the car and opened the rear door.

"I'd rather not have anyone around when we talk," Butch responded, handing one of the bags he was carrying to Fabio.

"Good morning, Jim," Fabio said, putting the suitcase in the rear beside Butch's. "Are you guys about ready to head down to Quantico? I checked before Butch and I came up, and the plane's ready any time you get there."

"I've just got to go take care of the bill and grab some coffee to go," Jim answered, setting two suitcases beside the car. "Can I get either of you anything?"

"Not for me," Fabio said, setting another suitcase in the car. "I'd need four or five stops between here and Quantico if I drank any more coffee."

"I'm good," Butch said, picking up one of the suitcases Jim had set down and handing it to Fabio.

"I should be back in just a couple of minutes," Jim said, turning back to the hotel entrance. "I'll try to hurry the ladies along, but they may need to visit the little ladies' room before we make the drive."

Walking up to where Marie and Megan sat talking as they sipped their coffee, Jim said, "Ladies, if you're ready, we need to get going. I'm going to go pay our bill and get a to-go cup. Do either of you want anything?"

"No, we're ready," Marie answered, setting down her cup and standing. "I just need to make a quick pit stop."

Megan set her cup down and said, "I'll just go with Marie, and we'll be ready as soon as we get back."

Jim looked for their waitress and signaled for her to bring their check. As she walked toward him, he placed three five-dollar bills on the table.

"Thank you very much, sir," she said, as she stopped beside the table. "Is there anything else I can do for you?"

"Just a large coffee to go," Jim answered.

"I'll be right back with it," she said, putting her tip in a pocket on her white dress.

Marie and Megan walked up just as the waitress was handing Jim his coffee, and Marie looked at it and asked, "Do you think that gallon of coffee will get you to the airport, or will we need to make a stop on the way?"

"It's only about a quart, and no, I don't think I'll need any more coffee before we get there," Jim replied. "However, I may need to use the empty cup for an emergency relief container."

"You wouldn't dare," Marie said, playfully slapping his arm. "I've heard about those 'piddle packs' you guys used to fly with, but I believe we can find a restroom down here on the ground."

As Jim followed them to the exit, he said, "And now that I've become more gentlemanly, I certainly wouldn't want to embarrass anyone with such crude behavior as public urination."

Chapter 46

An hour later as the Gulfstream V headed southwest toward Dallas, Butch quietly asked Jim if they could take two seats at the rear away from where Marie and Megan were talking.

Nodding, Jim got out of his seat and walked to where there were two club seats on the right side of the aircraft. Taking the seat which faced forward, Jim motioned for Butch to take the seat across from him and asked, "What's happened that you'd need my advice on?"

"You know how much effort Debbie and the folks put into setting up the teams and dividing the country," Butch replied. "I've spent a lot of time looking at it, discussing it with the three area commanders, and I'd like to propose a change."

"Okay," Jim said. "I'm not sure why you need my advice just to make a proposal, but if you want me to look at the change you're proposing, I'd be glad to do it."

"That would help," Butch said, pulling a sheet of paper from his shirt pocket. "I've sort of scribbled some notes and diagrams about the areas when I finished talking to the area commanders.

"Basically, I'd like to further break each area down into sectors," Butch explained, spreading the sheet on the small table separating their seats. "I've done some rough sketching, but I'll need more time to refine my idea."

Jim looked at the sketches and notes before saying, "You are in charge of managing these areas and the people Black Water assigned to them. I can see the benefits of smaller areas, and it looks like you've decided to break them down into areas based on the number of farms per area.

"I'd look at it with some adjustments for distance between farms, and from the staging areas the commanders select," Jim explained. "But, if this is what you and your commanders think is the way to go, you don't need my advice, and you certainly don't need my approval."

Jim sat waiting for Butch to come to the real reason he sought his advice, until he finally said, "I'm just worried that she won't appreciate me telling her she's wrong.

"I've seen how she can demean a guy for some slight comment, or question her," Butch explained. "I know I don't have all the answers on the best division of the areas and the teams, but I'll spend whatever time necessary to optimize them. There are almost one hundred thousand farms for each area commander.

"He has a hundred men, that's a thousand farms for each man," Butch explained. "We couldn't cover that if we had ten thousand men. The country is too vast, and the sheer distance between farms makes this nearly impossible."

"I see your point," Jim replied. "But, if you think your idea will be even marginally better, you should go to Debbie. If nothing else, she can plug the parameters you believe to be constraints into her computers, and they can spit out options faster than a cat laps milk."

"I'm sure she can," Butch agreed. "The lady has done some amazing stuff technologically, but her proposed area ideas aren't operationally effective."

"She's not an operational person," Jim explained. "She's never been on an operation, as far as I know. And as you know, the things in the field don't always mirror just pure numbers.

"I think she'll understand the situation and be more than happy to help you design a better allocation of the assets as you've shown me," Jim said. "So, what's the real issue?"

Butch paused for a moment, then finally admitted, "The lady scares the crap out of me. I'd rather deal with an angry badger with hemorrhoids than tell her she's wrong. I mean, she's been with the company for years, and I'm the new guy. Who am I to question her?"

"She's been with the company for years as a technician," Jim told him. "This is her first time trying to plan an operation of this scope. Usually, she's asked to design some gizmo to support a specific request.

"Now, she's been directed to do the initial planning for the operation and provide the technical side for implementing it," Jim continued. "Sometimes even the most operationally experienced General needs to be shown the ingredients of the sausage before it's put in the oven.

"Especially if it's pork and all he's ever dealt with is beef," Jim said. "You were brought on as an operational commander. You're expected to look at the operation differently and make recommendations.

"Regarding Debbie's reaction, I think she'll surprise you," Jim added. "Yeah, she can be a little brusque when she's dealing with someone who hasn't come prepared.

"But I've never seen her react that way when someone genuinely tries to get some clarification or expresses some possibly opposite point of view regarding a specific situation," Jim told him.

"I'll be glad to approach her, if that's the way you want to handle it," Jim said. "But here's the risk you're running. First, you know what you and your commanders decided were the changes you need. I know I couldn't explain that as well as you.

"And possibly more important, she's going to wonder why you didn't approach her yourself," Jim explained. "If she thinks you don't have the huevos to tell her when you believe she's wrong, you'll have a hard time ever getting her respect again.

"Everybody makes a bad decision sooner or later if you make enough decisions," Jim finished. "The only thing you can do is admit when you've made a bad decision and learn from it."

"Would you a least come with me when I explain what I'm trying to accomplish?" Butch asked.

"Hell, no," Jim answered, standing up. "The lady scares the shit out of me."

Chapter 47

As Jim and Butch discussed how to approach Debbie with the changes Butch thought necessary, Marie and Megan were having an entirely different conversation.

"How did you get interested in negotiations?" Marie asked, as Megan sat looking out the window at the passing clouds.

Turning to her, Megan said, "My father was a diplomat for most of his life. He was sent all over the world to help resolve differences between countries that were bordering on war.

"I remember my first introduction to the process when I accidentally walked in on a rather testy dialogue between my dad and some guy wearing a white robe and a scarf around his head. I later found out that the scarf was called a Ghutra, and was typical for men from his country," she explained. "I had no sooner walked in when the man looked at me and said, 'What a precious child. Is she yours?'

"Dad nodded and replied, 'Yes, but she knows better than to interrupt two men who are having a discussion'," she said. "Then Dad told me to go back to my room.

"The man shook his head and said, 'She reminds me of my daughter, she's about that age, please let her stay'," Megan continued. "So, I walked to my Dad, he sat me in his lap, and they resumed talking. But the tone of the conversation was much more subdued.

"After they had finally come to an agreement, the man walked over to me and said, 'You should bring this child to every negotiation. She reminds us that it's for her sake we try to work out our differences'," Megan continued. "Then he made a slight bow and left the room.

"After that, Dad welcomed me, especially when things had gotten to a stalemate," she said. "Occasionally, he would use a signal we worked out to come in, uninvited, of course.

"After all the negotiations where I was present, I learned just how important it was to put a human face, especially a child's, into the equation," she finished. "That's when I decided I wanted to be a negotiator. To put a human face on any negotiation."

"Jim said you've been a very successful negotiator," Marie said. "How much of that do you contribute to being an attractive female when negotiating with mainly men?"

"Some," Megan admitted. "But an analysis of my success shows that I'm actually only two percent above my male counterparts when dealing with men. I'm over ten percent above when dealing with women.

"So, I don't think it's that important," she explained. "But then again, I'm pretty picky when I accept an assignment. I don't accept those where I don't think I have a good chance to resolve the issue. That probably has more to do with my success rate instead of just being a female."

"What do you do when you sense some, let's call it flirtation, during a negotiation?" Marie asked.

"I just ask the man, or woman, and that also happens, if they would rather try to resolve the issue under discussion, or would they rather go somewhere they can pursue something they seem to be more concerned about," Megan said, as Jim came up the aisle.

"What do you think your chances are with South Africa?" Marie asked.

"I don't know," she answered. "I'm just going to try and paint a picture of what's going to happen if he continues the expropriation he's doing. That and the ethnic cleansing and genocide are going to cause a famine. The picture I want him to see is of the thousands of children all over Johannesburg, and the rest of South Africa, who don't know why there's no food on the table, and their bellies are hurting.

"But there are people out there who care more about some perceived injustices from the past than the harm their actions are going to cause in the future," she finished. "There's a reason why the windshield is five feet wide, and the rearview mirror is only five inches wide. The future is more important than the past."

"How's the flight, ladies?" he asked, stopping beside them.

"Enlightening," Marie answered. "I'm learning how to be a good negotiator."

"That never hurts," Jim replied. "Much better to negotiate than sulk when you're not getting your way. I'm heading to the cockpit. Is there anything you guys need?"

"Not that I know of," Megan answered. "Do they have a better idea of when we're landing at Love Field?"

"I'll ask," Jim said, as he headed for the cockpit.

Sticking his head in the open cockpit door, he asked, "Excuse me, Captain, do you mind if I step in for a second?"

"Come on in," the Captain answered. "And please, just call me Buzz, everyone else does. How are things in the back?"

"No complaints," he replied. "I do have a question, though."

"What's that?" Buzz asked.

"Do you have a secure radio or phone I can use to contact Black Water?" Jim asked.

"Yeah, we have a secure satphone," he answered. "Is there anything wrong?"

"No, I just need to contact General Barker about something," Jim replied. "I'd I need to make the call privately, if possible."

"No problem," Buzz told him. "I'll just make the call, and when they answer, you can take the phone back to the cabin."

"That would be perfect," Jim said, as Buzz reached behind the console and removed a bulky cell phone that had been connected to the aircraft's power.

Waiting for the call to be transferred to General Barker, Jim asked the copilot, "What's the latest ETA?"

"Looks like we'll be there just a little before noon, Texas time," he answered. "Weather's clear and there have been no reports of delays."

"Thanks," Jim told him.

"They are paging General Barker," Buzz said, handing Jim the phone. "Just remember, there's always a slight pause after any transmission. So, I'd recommend giving a second or two after they talk before saying anything."

"Got it," Jim said, taking the phone. "I shouldn't be too long."

"Not to worry," Buzz replied. "I'm not expecting any calls, and we have a printer here if they need to notify us of any changes."

"Thanks, again," Jim said, turning to leave. "I appreciate your help."

Chapter 48

Jim took a seat at the front of the passenger area and waited for Gene to answer the phone. Looking to the rear, he saw that Butch had rejoined Marie and Megan.

"Good morning, General," Jim said, as Gene answered.

"Good morning, Jim," Gene responded. "I didn't think I'd hear from you before you got home. What's so urgent?"

"First, Butch has some suggestions to modify the areas," Jim told him. "He and his commanders believe it will greatly enhance their ability to get to the farms the killer teams are targeting.

"I looked at the concept and it looks sound to me," Jim continued. "But Butch is reluctant to present his ideas to Debbie. What I'm asking you to do is have Debbie give Butch a call tomorrow and ask him if he has any suggestions now that he's had a chance to study the operation a little further.

"That will make Butch believe his suggestions are being requested instead of him just making them," Jim explained. "He's a little wary of countering Debbie, and I believe he'd be a little more forthcoming and confident of his plans if she's asking for his input."

"Not a problem," Gene said, laughing. "The lady can be a little, let's say, difficult to approach. I'll take care of it. Is there anything else?"

"Yes, sir," Jim answered. "Looking at the numbers of the people we believe involved with the killer teams, and the number of teams we're deploying, I'd like to suggest an additional method of eliminating those folks."

"If you're going to ask for more people, that's out of the question at this point," Gene interrupted. "And we're not trying to eliminate every member. Just enough for them to understand the game is over."

"I understand, sir," Jim replied. "What I'm thinking is, we're planning to remove the head of the snake, who we believe to be the Steer, with one of our sniper teams.

"What if we never get the shot?" Jim asked. "How long are we going to keep people deployed over there waiting for an opportunity that may never come?"

"What do you have in mind?" Gene asked, after a short pause.

"I'd like for Debbie to come up with a way to plant an explosive in a cell phone," Jim answered. "I'll bet there are people in the Navy Ordnance Department who can work with her to devise a small projectile, say about the size of a twenty-two-caliber bullet, that can be fired through the receiver end of the phone.

"It should be dormant until activated by a signal to that specific phone," he continued. "Maybe I'm being a little too cautious, but I don't want it to just randomly fire. Hell, someone's kid may be playing with the phone.

"I want the phone to be monitored, which it already is, and activated when we're positive it's the target we want," Jim explained. "Now, I want enough of these phones to include those people below the Steer we believe to be involved, as well as every member of the group who is behind the expropriation.

"I'd like to remove everyone at least down through the leaders of the killer teams," Jim said. "I'm sure Debbie can designate those people from the monitoring program she's currently running."

"How do you plan to get the phones in their hands?" Gene asked.

"We first have to acquire the phones we'll need," Jim answered. "Then get them modified. As that is being done, we need to determine who is providing them with phones.

"It's possible the phones are coming from more than one source, but I believe we can convince one of them to offer newer and improved phones at a bargain price, if they order in bulk," he continued. "We've got to get the phones modified, the dealer located and then start a program of disinformation which leads these people to believe their phones have been tapped and they are being monitored and tracked.

"If this comes on the heels of a couple of ambushes at the first farms by Butch's teams, it will convince them they *are* being monitored and hopefully pause their operations until they get new phones," Jim explained. "If we can pull this off, we can eliminate a lot of the enemy without firing a shot, except the ones that enter their brains from the phones."

"I'm not sure we have time to do that," Gene replied. "We have three days before your meeting with the Bull."

"This doesn't have to be coordinated with that meeting," Jim said. "We knew Butch's operation would take more than one day. Hell, it could take weeks.

"But this could possibly shorten it by half, if not more," he continued. "It just depends on how soon we can get those phones in their hands. And there are a lot of pieces that must be put together for this to work.

"I'd ask Debbie what time frame she thinks would be required for her, but the phones can be ordered before she comes up with a device," Jim explained. "The ordnance folks can be working on the firing system, and dealers can be found and offers presented.

"I'm not a techie person, but I'll bet Debbie can figure out the activation system in her sleep," he continued. "And it wouldn't surprise me if the bomb folks haven't been working on a miniaturized device such as this for years.

"Hell, they may be able to get together this afternoon, have a workable phone-gun, and be ready for mass production when the sun comes up tomorrow morning," Jim theorized. "If an order for, say, a thousand phones, is placed today, there are companies that promise overnight delivery.

"Then Debbie has the phones infected with her bugs by noon, they're rushed to the ordnance people who insert their miniature explosive projectile, and they are on the plane with us three days from now," Jim said.

"Being a little over optimistic, aren't you?" Gene asked. "And why do we need a thousand phones? What are you going to do with the phones we don't use in South Africa? What about the phones that are left lying around over there that don't get activated? Have you thought about all of that?"

"No, I haven't," Jim admitted. "But if we don't get our asses in gear immediately, the opportunity to shut down the genocide and ethnic cleansing is delayed. Not to mention the famine we know will occur if the farmers keep losing their land.

"What's the downside of enacting this program?" Jim asked. "A few dollars spent on something that could probably be used in the future if not for this operation.

"What's the upside?" he asked. "Possibly the only other option of removing the Steer if we can't get a shot. Possibly shortening the time to eradicate the threats to the Boers. Possibly even saving the lives of our people.

"I can't think of any reason not to pursue this," Jim finished. "But for it to be effective for this operation, it should have been started a year ago."

"Okay, I'll get people on it," Gene agreed. "Now, before I get started, are there any other miracles you wish for me to perform?"

"I'd say turn some water into wine," Jim answered, laughing. "Except I prefer Jack Daniel's and that may tax even your abilities."

Chapter 49

After landing at Love Field and while they were taxiing to the terminal, Jim asked Megan, "Do you need a ride back to Decatur? Butch lives in Aurora, just a few miles from there."

"No, I left a car at Love Field, and I need to make some stops before I head home," she answered. "And yes, I know Butch lives in Aurora. We had time to talk about stuff like that with Marie while you were on the phone."

"Just checking," Jim said. "Do you need a ride when we head to South Africa?"

"Butch already asked, but no," she answered. "I don't want to take a chance of getting stuck in Dallas if Butch needs to stay longer. I do appreciate you guys' concern, but I do pretty well on my own."

"I understand," Jim replied, as they parked, and the stairs were lowered. "If anything comes up and you need a ride, you can have Gene give me a call, or have Butch come get you since he's close."

"Butch already gave me his phone number, and Marie gave me hers," Megan said, as she got out of her seat and headed for the door. "I'll let you know if I need anything. Otherwise, I'll see you back here in a couple of days."

"If you guys want to head on down, we'll bring your bags," Buzz said, as he left the cockpit. "We're going to be staying overnight in case we're needed tomorrow."

"Thanks," Jim said, following Marie to the exit. "Hopefully, you brought a suitcase."

"I learned long ago to pack for three days," Buzz replied, handing a suitcase to the copilot. "And even then, I've had to buy a pair of jeans or something when my three days turned into five or six."

"Aviation, what a great life," Butch said, as Jim took the stairs to the ramp. "Worldwide travel with an opportunity to review every hotel chain that exists anywhere, even some of the most god-awful locations that barely have running water.

"But it beats the hell out of working for a living," he finished, descending to the ramp. "Enjoy your night in beautiful downtown Dallas."

"I'll see you in a couple of days," Jim told Butch, as he put his and Marie's suitcases in his truck. "Call if you need anything."

"Will do," Butch said, getting into his car. "Let me know if you hear anything."

"What do you think about Butch and Megan?" Marie asked, as they pulled out of the parking lot.

"I think Butch is a nice guy and Megan is a nice lady," Jim answered, as he headed north.

"I mean, what do you think about them as a possible couple?" Marie asked. "I know he gave her his number."

"And I know you gave her your number," countered Jim, as he merged onto the road heading east to join US 75. "I think he just did it as a favor since he lives a few miles from her. Maybe in case her car breaks down and she needs a lift to the airport when we return to Quantico.

"What are you going to do tomorrow?" Jim asked, trying to avoid the subject of Butch and Megan.

"Not sure yet," she answered. "The girls are coming down, so we'll probably hang out at the house, go for lunch somewhere, and to dinner with Mom and Dad. What about you?"

"Mow the grass, wash some clothes, check the mail," Jim answered, as they came to the intersection with US 75. "The neighborhood yard Nazi will raise holy hell if my yard doesn't adhere to his specifications.

"Then he'll put little post it notes on my door," he continued. "I don't think the guy has anything to do except walk his damn Chihuahua four or five times a day and bitch about everybody's yard."

"Speaking of mail, what do you do about it when you're gone?" Marie asked.

"There's an old guy who lives a couple of houses down," Jim answered. "I met him when Jennifer and I first moved there.

"Jennifer used to take him cookies and stuff occasionally," Jim continued. "Anyway, after she died, he volunteered to collect my mail since he knew I was gone for days at a time.

"He put a box on my front porch, and he just tosses it in there if he knows I'm gone," he finished.

"What happens if it rains?" she asked.

"The mail gets wet," Jim answered, as he shifted lanes to let the cars taking the next exit move to the right side of the road.

"What's his name?" she asked, as they crossed beneath the 635 Loop.

"Jerry something," Jim said. "Farmer, or Farwell, or something like that. We really don't talk much. More of a wave if we see each other.

"I believe he retired from General Motors or something," Jim continued. "I don't think I've ever seen him outside, except when he's checking his mail."

"I can't believe you know so little about a neighbor," Marie said. "I've only lived in my new house a couple of years, and I know just about everyone, their husbands, or wives, and their kids. And you can't even remember a guy who collects your mail's last name."

"Guys don't get involved as much as you ladies do regarding people's personal lives," Jim replied, as they arrived at Marie's house. "About all we need to know is what whiskey he drinks in case he drinks the same as you. Then we know to buy twice as much."

Getting out of the truck, Jim grabbed Marie's suitcases and followed her up the walk to her house as she continued, "It's a wonder you guys ever speak at all unless it's about something you have in common."

"Like whiskey?" Jim asked, as she opened the front door. "Otherwise, we really don't delve into each other's private lives. Private means exactly that … private.

"If a guy wants you to know something, he'll tell you," he continued, setting the suitcases on the floor. "Now, I've got to get home and see if Mr. Something put my mail in the box.

"I'll give you a call in the morning," Jim said, kissing her on the cheek. "If I get time, maybe I can join you and the twins for lunch."

Chapter 50

The following morning, after he had cut the grass and done his laundry, Jim was having lunch with Marie and her twins when his phone rang.

Stepping from the table, he answered, "Hello,"

"Hope I'm not interrupting anything," Gene said. "But I have some good news."

"I'm just having lunch with Marie and the kids," he answered. "What's the good news?"

"You were right about the Navy Ordnance having something that Debbie says she can use," Gene answered. "It seems that they had developed a small bullet, more like a steel ball, that fits in a twenty-two short casing.

"They had developed them to fill a section of a wall, or alley, with hundreds of these bullets embedded in the walls to disable a group of people trying to access some area they wanted to establish as a kill zone," Gene explained. "Debbie says she can install a single shell into the top of the phone, next to the speaker, and use the phone's power to detonate it."

"That's great," Jim replied. "What about getting the phones?"

"I've got a thousand on their way and they should arrive by noon today," Gene answered. "Debbie says she'll have them installed within an hour of when they get here."

"That is good news," Jim agreed. "And the distribution to the people with whom we need to communicate?"

"Done, as well," Gene confirmed. "Our dealer in Johannesburg is expecting them to be delivered when we get there. And that leads me to the not-so-good news."

"What's that?" Jim asked, dreading the answer.

"I need you to be at Love Field this afternoon by four o'clock," Gene answered. "And before you ask, Megan and Butch have already been notified."

"What then, a night at Quantico?" Jim asked, checking the time.

"You'll come here, and everyone will be put on two 757s we've leased to take you to Johannesburg," he answered. "You'll arrive there about noon the day before your meeting with the Bull. I took your idea about using the United Nations to our, call them sponsors, and they convinced the UN to lend a hand.

"They will provide you with your transportation needs, and they will send teams into the countryside to contact the farmers who are seeking refugee status as you suggested," he explained. "That actually frees up several of our teams to concentrate on taking out the killer teams. That was a good idea. I knew we hired you for something.

"Now, we've *contracted* with a tour group named Golden Diamond Safaris," he continued. "They are a *recently* old established tour group that Debbie managed to insert into the approved list of safaris, more or less through the back door.

"We've reserved rooms throughout Johannesburg, and you'll have transportation in the vehicles they use for the tours of the gold and diamond mines," he added. "There are vans, SUVs, and enough vehicles to move everyone to their locations in all the areas.

"You and Megan will still be picked up by whatever transportation the Bull has arranged," he explained. "You'll have no association with the tour group, other than the 757 going to Johannesburg.

"We've arranged for a United Nations car to pick you up at the airport and take you to the hotel," Gene continued. "You'll wait for the Bull to send his car and get you early enough to meet him in his house.

"From that point on, you're on your own," he finished.

"Is the FedEx package ready?" Jim asked.

"Yes, he'll make the pick up the night before the meeting," Gene assured him.

"You need to make sure the guy's wrists are wrapped in gauze before the zip ties are applied," Jim told him. "We don't need any marks that might indicate the man was a hostage before I shoot him."

"Got it," Gene agreed. "And we'll have him in place as soon as we know you've left the hotel with your driver. Anything else?"

"No, looks like the phone exchange is in place, or will be when we get there, and if Jewell has managed to get a gun into the Bull's pen, I think we're ready," Jim replied.

"The gun will be beneath the chair on the right as you face the desk," Gene told him. "It's taped behind the front of the chair, the part of the chair just below the cushion. There is a bullet in the chamber, so make sure Megan knows that. Anything else?"

"About a thousand things," Jim answered. "It's just that I don't know half of them, and nobody knows the other half."

"Okay, then," Gene said. "I'll see you here tomorrow evening. Enjoy your lunch."

Jim walked back to the table and said, "I'm sorry, but I've got to go home."

"Anything wrong?" Marie asked.

"No," he answered. "That was Gene, and I've got to return to Quantico this evening. I have to be at Love Field by four, and I need to go pack for the trip."

"Are you still going to South Africa?" Marie asked.

"Yes, we'll get on a plane tomorrow evening at Quantico so we can arrive the following morning," Jim answered, taking his credit card from his billfold.

"I thought you had another day," she told him. "What happened?"

"I don't know," Jim said, signaling for the waiter. "All I was told was that our plane to Johannesburg was leaving Quantico tomorrow night.

"Sorry, ladies," Jim said, handing his card to the waiter. "Maybe we can try this again when I get home."

Chapter 51

When Jim got back to his house, he finished the laundry so he would have sufficient clean clothes for what he figured would be at least a week and packed his suitcase.

With a final look around the house and checking to make sure the doors were locked, he tossed his suitcase in the rear seat of his pickup and headed for Love Field.

As he pulled into the parking lot for the General Aviation terminal, he saw Megan taking a suitcase from the trunk of her car. Walking over with his, he asked, "Can I take that for you, Megan?"

"No thanks," she answered, slamming the trunk lid closed. "But I appreciate the offer. I've been dragging my own bag for years now and was taught a person needs to carry their own weight."

"Did Gene tell you about some additional technology we'll be using against the teams trying to take over the farms?" Jim asked, as they approached the small terminal.

"No," she answered, stepping inside. "I haven't been involved in any discussions regarding that part of the operation. I'm only involved with the Presidential side."

"Anything new there?" Jim asked, spotting Buzz and his copilot standing at the counter.

"Just a lot of new photos and production data to present," she answered, following him to the door leading to the ramp.

"You know, it seems like a lot of effort when we could just put him on the list the same as the Steer," Jim said. "Especially since a bullet may be the result anyway."

"I've been trained to just follow my orders," she replied, as they headed for the plane. "So many times, I don't even know why a negotiation is taking place.

"A couple of times I've found out that it was just a cover for a meeting regarding something entirely different," she finished, as they set their bags beside the stairs.

"Did you ever read the old Mad magazine?" Jim asked, as they saw Buzz and the copilot coming toward them. "There were two spies, one black and one white. They were always trying to best each other.

"It was a comical look at the espionage of the Cold War era," Jim explained. "Often at the end of the comic strip, you were left wondering who the good guy was, and who was the bad guy.

"I'm sure it's the same today," he continued. "I guess someone could look at us and see us as the bad guys, and someone else sees us as the good guys."

"Good afternoon, folks," Buzz said, as they met at the bottom of the stairs. "I guess you're surprised to see us again."

"Sort of," Jim said, shaking his hand. "When you said you were remaining overnight, I had my suspicions. I've learned over the years that Black Water has a reason for just about every aspect of their operations.

"They probably figured yesterday we'd need to get back by tonight for the trip to South Africa," he finished. "Is it all right to take our bags up?"

"Certainly," Buzz answered. "I've finished the flight plan, and as soon as our other passenger gets here, we can head back to Quantico.

"There are some cheap ass inflight meals in the galley," he told them. "If you get hungry, just pop them in the microwave for a minute or so, whatever's on the package.

"The minifridge is full of drinks, unfortunately, none of them alcoholic," he continued. "It should be a smooth flight, and as before, let me know if there's anything I can do for you guys."

"Thanks, Buzz," Jim said, heading up the stairs with his suitcase. "We'll try to keep our rowdy behavior to a minimum. But seeing as how Butch is somewhat socially awkward, it can be difficult."

"Speaking of Butch, here he comes," Buzz said, looking toward the terminal. "I hope he didn't overhear your last comment."

"Hell, even if he heard it, he wouldn't understand it," Jim said, turning to watch Butch heading toward them with two suitcases. "Air Force, too many hours at high altitude without oxygen can damage the brain."

"At least I have a brain to damage, Marine," Butch said, shaking Buzz's hand. "We try to humor our special needs brothers, but sometimes it's impossible with those severely needy.

"Afternoon, Marine," Butch said, coming up the stairs. "I see you've mastered another skill set. Now they can remove the escalators from the airplanes."

Chapter 52

"You'll never guess what happened," Butch said, somewhere over Arkansas. "Don't even bother guessing, Debbie called me."

"That's not quite normal, but not unheard of," Jim replied. "What did she want? Updates to the expected target movements? Updates to the farms that have been abandoned?"

"No, she wanted to know if I had any suggestions regarding the division of our teams since I'd had an opportunity to study the areas and number of farms in each," Butch answered. "I gave her my suggestions, you know, what we had talked about, and she said she'd come up with a new proposal as soon as the computer applied the new parameters."

"That sounds great," Jim said, nodding. "At least it saved you lots of time trying to do it by yourself."

"Yeah, but it really surprised me," Butch continued. "That's so unlike what I've heard about her and what I've seen."

"Maybe she had just taken one of those pills that soften your mood, like *Damitall*," Jim told him. "I myself have never tried them, but I've heard good things from others."

"I've never heard of a drug named *Damitall*," Butch replied.

"I believe that's the chemical name, or scientific name," Jim continued, almost unable to keep from laughing. "I think I've seen it advertised as *Screwitall*, but that's probably a generic version."

"*Damitall? Screwitall?*" Butch said, shaking his head. "I think you're *screwing it all* with me."

Megan burst out laughing and said, "I wondered how long it would take you to catch on. My father always said, 'You have to shoot low when they're riding Shetlands'."

As Butch started laughing with them, he said, "You got me on that one, Marine. But this game isn't over. Not by a long shot. I may have been riding a Shetland this time, but I'll be mounted on a Belgian Draft next time I hear you start one of your bullshit stories."

Finally, as they all stopped laughing, Jim said, "Back to business. I talked to Gene, and he's made arrangements for all the hotel reservations, vehicles, and everything to be provided by a company called Golden Diamond Safaris.

"Even the 757s we're taking from Quantico to Johannesburg are leased under that company," he continued. "It wouldn't surprise me if every one of your people will be wearing a laminated picture on a chain denoting them as members of the tour group who contracted Golden Diamond Safaris.

"That will at least give us cover for such a large group of people showing up in South Africa," he explained. "I'm sure Debbie and her band of miscreants managed to have

Golden Diamond listed in some long-ago records as an officially recognized tour group.

"For all her less admirable qualities, of which there are a few, she's a wizard at computers or technology when it comes to attention to detail," Jim continued. "I'm glad she's on our side.

"I thought we were using the United Nations for our cover," Megan interrupted. "Is that out the window?"

"No, we still are, and I'll talk more about that in a second," Jim assured her. "This Golden Diamonds cover is just for the teams going to the farms where the killer teams are expected.

"The decision was made to add the Golden Diamonds since the UN buses and personnel would probably be under constant scrutiny," Jim continued. "Black Water believes the South African President will assign his people to watch them and report any defection of the farmers.

"While these buses and personnel are going to the farms where the families want to claim refugee status, the Golden Diamonds group will most likely be disregarded as they move about the country," Jim explained. "Hell, there are dozens of these safaris, or tour groups, traversing the country on any given day.

"Sort of like a magician, we keep their eyes on the right hand while the left hand is manipulating the disappearing coin. Our real operation is hidden in plain sight," he finished. "Now, we need to cover a specific issue regarding our meeting with the Bull.

"Before you move on," Butch interrupted. "Are these UN teams coming from my personnel? I'm damn short on people to start with, and I can't afford to have any of them acting as decoys."

"No, the people involved with the *decoys,* as you put it, will be arriving in the 767s we discussed at the beginning of the planning. And they will be people from the UN," Jim answered. "It was decided that if we are going to provide refugee status, we need a separate section devoted to that. We have no idea how many people that could entail, and we definitely don't want to impact your operation.

"Now, back to the meeting with the Bull, the gun will be beneath the chair on the right as we face the Bull," he continued, looking at Megan. "So, you need to take the chair to the left since I'll be following you into the room.

"It will be taped behind what's called the apron of the chair, the part just below the cushion," Jim explained. "And there is a round in the chamber, so be very careful you don't accidentally pull the trigger after I hand you the gun to hold on the President. The plan depends on that gun never being used.

"But my plan of getting us out of there alive is a little more flexible," he added. "I'll use any gun I can get my hands on if it means we walk out instead of being carried out."

Chapter 53

After landing at Quantico and parking on the ramp, Buzz said goodbye to everyone as they grabbed their suitcases and headed down the stairs to where Fabio was waiting.

"Good evening, everyone," Fabio said, as they reached the dark black Suburban. "How was the flight?"

"Same as always," Jim answered, putting his suitcase in the open rear compartment. "Four hours of sitting and trying to pass the time with small talk."

"You'll probably be pleased to know that you'll have almost twenty hours to finish what I'm assuming was a most interesting conversation," Fabio said, as he put Megan's suitcase in the car. "As soon as we get loaded, I'll take you to the headquarters where Gene and Debbie are waiting.

"I'll keep your bags, because I'll be taking you to where the airplanes are waiting for the flight to Johannesburg," he continued. "I think the other folks are already on the planes, and you're the last ones to arrive.

"Now, if you're ready, I'll get us to the Black Water headquarters for your meeting with Gene," Fabio said, as he finished tossing Butch's bags in. "I was told it would probably be less than half an hour, so I'll just stay with the car, and you don't need to worry about your bags."

"Thanks," Jim said, getting into the front passenger seat. "I'm almost looking forward to the flight. I could use a few hours of sleep."

"I'll probably be spending the flight going over whatever plans Debbie came up with," Butch said, as they pulled away from the terminal area. "And it's good to know that I've got a little more flexibility since the UN is manning the refugee crap."

"And I'll probably be spending my time looking at any updates on crop production, number of unproductive farms, forecast weather, and food shortages in the major cities," Megan told them. "And if that doesn't keep me busy for the entire flight, maybe I'll get a couple of hours of sleep."

"I don't envy any of you," Fabio said, as they reached the outer fence and security checkpoint. "I'll happily be at home in my own bed about the time you folks get out over the Atlantic Ocean.

"You can have that all night flying stuff to yourselves," he continued, as a guard approached the car. "If I can't get there in the daytime, I don't think I need to go."

After clearing the first point, the gate slid open to allow them to enter the holding area before they could continue into the main complex. Once cleared through the second checkpoint, the gate slid open, and Fabio headed for the entrance where they could see Gene waiting.

"Good evening," Gene said, as they exited the car. "I'll try to make this as quick as possible so you can get headed to Johannesburg."

Clearing the last security checkpoint upon entering the building, he continued, "We just have a couple of quick updates, mainly for Megan, but Debbie wants to do an explanation of the new areas to make sure that's how Butch wanted them.

"We'll meet her in one of the briefing rooms where we can look at the changes on a smaller screen than in the auditorium," Gene explained, as he led them down one of the many halls that led into the interior. "And all of the latest information for the negotiations is in a couple of files."

"Is there any new information on either the Bull or the Steer?" Jim asked, as Gene opened the door to where Debbie was waiting.

"Yes," Gene answered, as they entered. "The Steer has scheduled a couple of rallies, which may give us an opportunity to remove him from the ballot."

"What about the new phones?" Jim asked, as Gene handed Megan a folder containing the updates.

"They are in the country," Debbie answered. "I've begun a systematic assault on their current phones to disrupt their conversations, and I've used a voice-over in a couple of calls that mimics the Steer.

"We've heard numerous complaints and suggestions that someone other than their teams are using their phones," she continued. "And, less than an hour ago, one of the guys who work with the Steer called *our* dealer asking if he could supply the number of phones they were going to replace.

"Bottom line, we believe by the time you get in place, at least all of the folks involved with the expropriation and the leaders of the killer teams will be carrying our new, and improved, means of communication," she finished. "Then we'll just be waiting for the final call whenever the decision is made."

"Sounds good," Jim replied. "Now, who will make the decision?"

"Butch will," Gene answered. "The entire side of the operation involving the Steer and the killer teams are his. He's in the best position to know when the right time to activate the phones is, so I'm giving him the authority as of right now.

"How can I make all of the calls needed?" Butch asked, looking up from the laptop he was studying. "Unless I have a group call feature, I don't have time to call every phone."

"The calls will come from here," Gene reassured him. "But it's on your command. And, you can have them call any single number, group of numbers, or any combination, depending on what you decide is the optimum method of removing the players."

Chapter 54

"What are you doing to ensure that the person we want to receive the call is actually the person on the phone?" Butch asked.

"That part is easy," Debbie explained. "These phones are a generation above the phones they are currently using. As with the current phones, we can monitor their movement with GPS, hear their conversations or any conversation within twenty-five feet, mute their phones, and activate the cameras on the phones.

"With the new artificial intelligence, or AI, we've been able to record all of the voices of the key players, mainly the Steer, and we can mimic it perfectly," she continued. "So, we can intercept a call to him and provide any detail we want to share with the caller.

"Or we can place the call, and the person on the other end will never know it's not the Steer," Debbie said. "Now, another feature is we will know if the person using the phone is on speaker or not, and since the camera is on the back side of the phone, we'll see the view and know if it's the correct height to be against their ear.

"It's not perfect, but I'd say we're ninety-nine percent sure we'll know who is using the phone and if he has it against his ear," she finished. "Now, are there any other questions?"

"Can you give me a quick tutorial on the new areas?" Butch asked, looking at the screen on one of the laptops.

"Sure," Debbie said. "I've divided the areas into more of a numeric farm system. By that, I mean there are approximately the same number of farms in each area instead of just square miles.

"Now, I've assigned numbers to each farm," she continued, as she pointed to the screen. "That way, we don't have to mention any farmer's names. The screen is a touchscreen, so by placing your finger on a particular farm, it provides you with the name and coordinates.

"You can compress or expand the area on the screen using two fingers," she demonstrated. "That allows you to see more details of the farm or specific area you're interested in.

"You'll have three laptops, one for each area, and the commanders of each area will have one that matches their area," she continued. "Any of the areas on the computers can be expanded slightly in the event you need to send someone from area one to area two.

"Let's say we find that a killer team is headed for farm number one seventy-five," she explained, putting her finger on the screen. "First, the point on the screen will turn red, designating it as an active target. Then all of our teams in the area closest to the farm will begin blinking green.

"Let's say we can estimate the killer teams, shown in red, are seven hours from the farm," Debbie continued.

"Since the farm is in area one, a team from that area should respond.

"However, the closest team is nine hours away, but a team from area two is only four hours away," she said, touching the screen as she showed where each team was, and an estimated time to the farm appeared beside the team's designation.

"So, you can direct the area two commander to send his team," Debbie finished.

"What if the killer teams are two hours away and we don't have any teams that can get there until four hours later?" Butch asked, looking at the number of points representing the farms.

"We make a call to the farm and warn the family," Debbie answered. "We know we can't stop every killer team, but hopefully we can protect the families by giving them a chance to get off the farm and to somewhere safe.

"One other feature of the system we've put on the computers is if we hear a name as a potential target, such as De Vries, we highlight his farm in yellow," she explained. "Then, if we confirm it, we will highlight it in red. You can see potential targets before they become active and maybe be able to reposition your teams.

"I've explained it here," she said, handing Butch a folder. "I've given the same information to your area commanders, along with their laptops, and you guys can access them during the flight to South Africa.

"The main thing to remember is we'll be doing most of the manipulating of the data you'll see on your screen," Debbie added. "All you have to really understand is what it means and how to access it.

"Being a touch screen, you don't really need to make any keystrokes," she finished. "And we're monitoring each of you twenty-four hours a day. If you need help, just ask. Now, anything else?"

"I have one quick question," Jim said, as Butch started packing his laptops and the folder Debbie had provided. "You said the Steer had a couple of rallies planned. Do you know when and where?"

"Not yet," Gene answered. "Our friends over at the Central Intelligence Agency, the CIA, have had numerous assets on the ground for quite a while. They've been more or less assimilated into the local population at each of the three capital cities.

"They will be the first to see where any efforts are being made to secure an area for the rally," he continued. "I expect we'll have more information by the time you land. Possibly the exact location."

"Would it be possible to have those assets evaluate the most likely locations for our shooters?" Jim asked. "It would save considerable time to have some preplanned sites, so our guys don't have to start looking with only a day or two's notice.

"It doesn't have to be a perfect site but at least narrow it down to those with a clear view of the spot where the Steer will be," Jim continued. "Also, take a look at access and egress for our shooters."

"I'm sure our CIA friends can handle that," Gene answered. "This won't be their first involvement in an operation of this sort. I'll try to give you as much notice as possible."

"Not me," Jim said. "That's Butch's problem. Tell him. I'm just over there to keep our negotiator safe."

"And I'm sure you can handle that," Gene replied, handing Jim a folder. "Here are your and Megan's UN credentials. There's also a letter from the South African Ambassador to the UN stating you have an appointment with the President tomorrow. That should get you through Customs without any problems. There will also be a limousine from the US Ambassador's office to pick both of you up and take you to the hotel once you clear Customs."

"What if Customs wants to verify this?" Jim asked, taking a quick look at the folder.

"We've managed to tap into his phone and will verify everything," Gene answered. "The letter has the official seal of his office and his exact signature, with his contact information. Now, if there are no more questions, we need to get you to the plane. At least you'll have several hours to think up something else to ask."

Chapter 55

As the two 757s left for Johannesburg only minutes apart, Butch met with the commanders of the three newly developed areas and spent an hour or so discussing prepositioning their teams.

Then the commanders met with the team leaders and confirmed the tactical benefits of each location.

Jim was just relaxing in a window seat in the first-class section when Butch took the seat beside him, saying, "Well, I think we've got a reasonable plan now to guard the farms. But I'm still a little concerned about the snipers."

"What's your concern?" Jim asked.

"Gene said we may possibly have a location for the rallies," Butch replied. "I'd like to put my snipers in those cities as soon as we know which ones will be holding the rallies."

"Okay, do it," Jim told him. "That's part of your responsibility. I'd say the biggest part."

"What if the information I get isn't correct?" Butch worried. "What if I've sent the snipers to Pretoria and the rally gets moved to Cape Town?"

"I think you're seeing problems where there are none," Jim said, sitting up straight. "First, you'll never get perfect intelligence every time. You just do your best with what information you've been given.

"Gene knows that as well as anyone," Jim continued. "He'll be the first to tell you if the information he received and passed on was faulty. Could have been a last-minute change, or it could have been a misdirection due to possible threats he had received after the initial plan.

"Doesn't matter, you acted on the information you were given, and it proved wrong," Jim said. "Now, you have three areas, and each have a capital city in them. You have three snipers in each area, so you could logically place two of them in each of the capital cities and have one in reserve.

"Then you could put any of the three remaining snipers together at some location that new intelligence reveals as the best location," he finished. "You probably don't know, but six hundred and thirty-eight assassination attempts were made on Fidel Castro's life, and all of them failed. Sometimes things just don't work out."

"What do you think about asking Gene if he can arrange for me to put two of the snipers with the CIA's people where they think the rallies will be?" Butch asked. "I think that would be better than having my guys wandering around town not knowing the area."

"That's a good idea," Jim agreed, having already broached the idea with Gene. "Why don't you see if the pilots can patch you through to Black Water, and you ask him."

"How do I get my guys to find the CIA guys if he agrees to do it?" Butch asked.

"How the hell am I supposed to know?" Jim answered. "Maybe they'll meet up at Dingle Butt's Bar wearing pink shorts and using the password, 'Who's on first?', from the old Abbott and Costello baseball skit. You've got to quit worrying so much.

"Black Water and the CIA have been having clandestine meetings all over the world for years," Jim said. "Let them work out the details. Just tell Gene what you need in the way of support, suggest something like you ask me, and let them do their jobs.

"You can't possibly have the information, time, or experience to manage something like this all by yourself," Jim assured him. "Just do your best to think the problem through, see the possible holes in the plan, think of a way to resolve those issues, and let the big boys in the back room help.

"You were selected for this part of the operation because you have a unique ability to plan," Jim said, looking directly at him. "You think things through and come up with a plan.

"Just as you saw flaws in the original area plans," he continued. "You saw a solution and got it enacted. I believe you're letting the snowballs pile up into an insurmountable mound.

"Take one issue, the snipers for now, and figure out what you think is the best approach," Jim advised. "Ask for help with the things over which you have no control, just don't ever blame anyone else if mistakes are made. We all make mistakes. Especially, always own up if you make mistakes.

"There are too many unknowns and potential new developments for anyone to be correct one hundred percent of the time," Jim finished. "And since this is the first major operation with Black Water where you're in charge, it's normal to be a little apprehensive. You need to have as much faith in yourself as the rest of us have in you."

Chapter 56

Butch had barely left when Megan stepped beside Jim's seat and asked, "Got a minute for a quick question?"

"Probably more like one thousand, four hundred, and fifteen, or so, minutes," Jim answered, smiling. "Have a seat."

"I've just been thinking," Megan said, as she sat in the seat beside Jim, "what are the chances that we can convince the Bull to sign the agreement to stop taking the land from the Boers?

"And to at least publicly condemn the genocide and ethnic cleansing?" she continued.

"I'd say there's a zero chance of any of that happening," Jim answered, wondering what she was thinking. "I'd be as surprised as having Bigfoot and Yeti showing up at my next birthday party.

"Why are you worried about this now?" he asked. "I thought we both understood this was more of an extermination than a negotiation."

"I know," she replied. "But I was just wondering what would happen if he should agree. Maybe it's because I've always been asked to negotiate an agreement, and I've spent so much time looking at everything that needs to be done.

"Maybe I'm being naive, but I just thought a lot of this could be avoided if we could convince him to listen to us," she continued. "Otherwise, why am I working so hard to build a convincing case?"

"I understand that this is probably the first time you've been asked to build a convincing case which has a foregone conclusion," Jim told her. "I believe the only reason the Bull is even interested in hearing your argument is because he's interested in something besides a solution to a problem he doesn't recognize as a problem.

"If we hadn't sent him your picture with your resume, I doubt he'd have given you a second's consideration," Jim continued. "The man has an agenda that has nothing to do with the state of his country's future.

"He's sort of put himself in a corner," Jim explained. "He's running for another term against a man who espouses the elimination of the white farmer and an expropriation of the land.

"It appears that that policy has the support of the majority of the population, so he can't afford to be seen as opposing the people he expects to vote for him," Jim said. "Combine that with his backdoor support for his opponent, the Steer, and their agreements regarding the redistribution of the land, and he has no intention of any changes to the genocidal actions.

"You can present every solid piece of evidence showing the effect of the expropriation on the people as the crop production plummets, but that doesn't fit his agenda," Jim finished.

Pausing for a moment, he continued, "Now, the reason you're spending so much time building a convincing case is to provide the distraction I'll need to administer the drug. If you didn't know your shit, he'd see right through the charade and toss us out as soon as you opened your mouth.

"The fact that you are exactly the type of woman he desires wouldn't keep his attention," Jim explained. "If that was all we needed to do, we could have sent anyone who triggers his hormones. But his arrogance demands he show his grasp of the issue and can dispute any argument you can present.

"He not only wants you physically, but he wants to dominate you intellectually," Jim continued. "I guess you could consider it his method of foreplay. The more capable you are of countering his arguments, the more engrossed he will be in demonstrating his superiority.

"Does any of this make sense to you?" Jim asked, after a moment's pause.

"I guess so," Megan answered, lowering her head. "Maybe I don't understand why a country's leader would condemn the people of his country to certain disaster. I can foresee the impact of a famine on the children.

"How can any human do that to an entire country?" she asked.

"All you have to do is look back at the history of mankind," Jim answered. "We have constantly condemned an entire race or population to unimaginable suffering for a piece of land. Or a philosophy that differs from theirs.

"If there's one thing I think you need to fully believe, it's that removing that one man may possibly prevent the horror you see if the inevitable famine occurs," he continued. "Just as someone eliminating Hitler before he gained power, maybe the attempt to eliminate the Jewish population could have been prevented. As well as preventing the millions of deaths in the rest of the world.

"Trust me, this operation is what everyone believes is the only way to resolve the issue in South Africa," Jim finished. "I'm sure there have been numerous more peaceful solutions presented and rejected by the Bull. Sometimes the only solution is extermination of the problem…the head of the snake."

Chapter 57

After touchdown at O. R. Tambo International Airport, they taxied to a small parking apron that was not connected to the main terminals. As they waited for the mobile stairs to arrive, the Captain of the first plane stepped into the cabin area and approached Jim.

"I just got a message from Quantico asking for you to contact General Barker as soon as possible," the Captain said. "I've talked to the ground crew here, and the buses taking you to the hotel are waiting for all of you to clear customs."

"Good," Jim replied, as everyone on the plane stood and began taking their suitcases from the overhead compartments. "What are your plans? Are you and the crew of both planes going with us to the hotel?"

"Yes," the Captain answered. "We have no definite date to return. It's an open-ended trip. The only thing we were told was to be prepared for a minimum of one week before returning."

"Well, I'm sure there are plenty of things to do here while you're waiting," Jim replied, as the mobile stairs pulled into place just below the forward door on the left side of the plane. "I guess you'll be coming with us to the hotel after clearing customs."

"That's right," he answered, as the First Officer opened the door and four airport buses stopped at the bottom of the stairs. "Anyway, the crew and I will remain onboard until everyone gets off the plane and onto the buses.

"I'll probably see you when we get to the hotel," he finished, as people began descending the stairs. "It's been a pleasure, and don't forget to call the General."

"I'll make the call as soon as I get on the bus," Jim said, pulling his suitcase from the overhead storage. "Thanks for the flight."

Jim took his phone from his pocket as he descended the stairs and dialed the preset number for Black Water. Walking to where the buses sat idling, he stood to the side as the others boarded.

"General Barker, please," Jim said, as the phone was answered.

"How was the flight?" Gene said, answering the phone.

"Long, but uneventful," Jim answered. "Exactly why I don't like international trips. I'd rather be sitting in Podunk, Montana, having dinner and a beer at five o'clock, instead of midway across the Atlantic anticipating another hotel room in France where I barely have time for some sleep during my normal wake cycle back at home."

"I understand completely," Gene replied. "Now I get to sit here in a consistent time zone and let you young pups chase the sun across the sky.

"Anyway, I have some updates for Butch and his crew," Gene continued. "It appears activity is increasing all across the country. The number of killer teams has increased by about twenty-five percent, and savagery has seen a marked increase as well.

"It seems as if they are doing their best to demoralize the remaining farmers since the Bull was notified the UN would be arriving to help with the refugee program," he explained. "Now I'm glad we disassociated our operation from the refugee aspect. They are certainly focusing their attention on the UN.

"Any issues from your end?" Gene asked, after a slight pause.

"Some pre-mission jitters," Jim answered, as the last of the people came down to the buses. "Not unexpected, but I think I've managed to soothe their apprehensions.

"And I believe Butch will be calling you as soon as he gets a chance, and his nerve up," Jim continued, chuckling. "He's coming up with some good ideas, which is just why you wanted him to run that part of the operation.

"All he needs is a few days in the field, and I'm positive he'll be more aggressive when he sees an issue," Jim said. "Just don't let on I discussed this with you."

"What's the issue?" Gene asked.

"He wants some cooperation from the CIA on determining possible sniper positions as soon as they figure out the exact location and time for the Steer's rallies," Jim answered. "That shouldn't be too difficult since we cooperated with them on similar missions before, and they have the expertise."

"I'll make a call," Gene replied. "How's Megan holding up?"

"Same," Jim answered. "Last-minute jitters and some questioning of the mission.

"She'll do okay," Jim continued, as he followed the last person from the plane onto the bus. "I'll give you a call when I get settled. Just please confirm our appointment with the Bull and give him our contact information at the hotel."

"I'll take care of it," Gene said. "You know, once you get to the hotel, you and Megan have to avoid being seen with anyone from the *tour group*. And your rooms are listed under the contract with the UN."

"Got it," Jim said, putting his foot on the steps into the bus. "I'll make sure Megan knows. And Butch as well."

Chapter 58

Getting on the bus, Jim spotted Megan talking to Butch near the rear. Making his way to where they sat, he said, "Butch, I need to let you know that once we get off the bus, you don't know Megan or me.

"We'll split off as we get off the bus and stand by ourselves while we wait for the Customs folks," he continued. "If you need to contact me for any reason, do not use the hotel switchboard. Go through Black Water so we know the line is secure."

Turning to Megan, he asked, "Do you have your UN credentials and the letter from the Ambassador handy?"

"Right here," she answered, holding her purse out.

"Good," Jim replied. "Now, you are in charge the minute we step off the bus. I'm just your assistant, and I'll only respond to anyone if asked a direct question.

"Otherwise, you answer," he concluded. "I'll even look at you for your concurrence. If you've ever needed to make a convincing act, this is it. Any sign of me being anything but your assistant could tank the entire thing.

"Do you think you can convince everyone about our relationship?" he asked, looking at her face.

"Who do you think you are, to be asking me such a ridiculous question?" Megan answered sternly.

Jim looked at her for a second, smiled, and then replied contritely, "Sorry, ma'am. I didn't mean to make any assumptions. It will never happen again."

Moments later, the bus pulled up to the building where the Customs office screened everyone coming from an airplane that didn't use the main terminals.

"I'll see you on the plane home in a few days," Jim said, shaking Butch's hand. "Just remember, you have an army of experts a phone call away. And don't forget to call Gene about the CIA assistance."

Butch looked at Jim and Megan, saying, "You guys be careful. I want to buy the first round when we get back to Quantico. And I brought enough money for three."

Megan gave him a quick hug and said, "I'll buy the second round. And I brought enough for only three. And I know Jim would try to make me buy him a second if you're not there."

When the Customs agent finally motioned for Megan to step forward, she marched to the desk and waited for him to ask for her passport.

"Here's my passport and my United Nations identification, sir," she said, laying both documents on the top of the counter the moment he asked.

The agent looked at both, looked at her, and back at the passport and UN identification, before asking, "Purpose of your visit?"

"I have an appointment with the President of South Africa tomorrow," she answered quickly.

"Do you have any proof of this appointment?" the agent asked, pushing her passport and ID back.

Reaching into her purse, she extracted the envelope holding the letter from the South African Ambassador to the UN, handed it to the agent, and said, "I believe this should be sufficient to verify the purpose of my visit."

The agent pulled the letter from the envelope and took his time reading every word before saying, "Everything appears to be in order. You may go."

"Before I go, I want to make sure my assistant is allowed to enter the country as well," she said, turning to motion for Jim to step forward.

As Jim stopped beside her, the agent said, "Passport and ID."

Jim laid his passport and UN ID on the counter and took a step back.

The agent looked at the documents and at Jim, asking, "Do you have a letter from our Ambassador?"

Megan stepped back to the counter and said, "Sir, I've told you this is my assistant. And, if you'll look at the Ambassador's letter again, you will see that his name is also listed.

"Now, if you care to verify either of us, the Ambassador left his contact information, and we'll gladly wait for you to discuss our business here in your country," she said, with a hint of threat in her voice.

The agent tapped Jim's passport and ID on the counter a couple of times, looking at him, and then handed them to him, saying, "You may go now."

Jim followed Megan out of the room, carrying both of their suitcases, thinking, 'I believe she's developed the appropriate attitude. Damn sure didn't take long'.

Chapter 59

As soon as Butch got to his room, he called Black Water. As he waited, he set his three laptops on the small desk in his room. Connecting them to the satellite system, he opened the maps of the three areas.

"Hello," he said, as the phone was answered. "Is General Barker handy?"

Hearing he would be right with him, Butch looked at all the yellow dots representing those farms where potential threats had been made. Knowing it would take at least a day to get all his people in position, he thought about the phones and how many of the killer teams and support personnel he could remove without risking any of his people's lives.

"General," he said, as Gene answered. "I just wanted to check in and let you know I'll have most of my people in the field by noon tomorrow."

"That's good," Gene replied. "I'm guessing you've set up your initial operational location there at the hotel. Have you talked to anyone about the vehicles Golden Diamonds is supposed to provide?"

"The desk clerk gave me a message asking me to call once we're all here at the hotel," Butch answered. "I'll give them a call when I hear from the three area commanders.

"What I really need now is to see if you might be able to enlist some support from the CIA," Butch said. "If they could do some initial reconnaissance of the areas where we expect the Steer, it would save my guys a lot of time. Maybe give them a chance to be in place before the rally.

"It would make my life simpler if we could remove the target at his first location," Butch continued. "Then I could concentrate on the farms. And maybe with him out of the picture, the bottom echelon would fall apart."

"I'll make a call," Gene replied. "I should know something within a couple of hours. Don't expect much more than their agreement to assist you at this point, but once we get a network established, your men will be able to communicate directly with them.

"That should allow your shooters to be in position with a chance of getting a shot," Gene continued. "Have you cleared the shooters to take the shot or are you asking them to get your approval before shooting?"

"I haven't cleared them yet," Butch answered. "But I plan on giving them the authority to shoot if the opportunity presents itself. I just want to make sure we have a positive ID of the target and a clear shot.

"I'd hate to get this close and miss," Butch continued. "That would alert the target and may destroy any further chances of removing him."

"I understand," Gene replied. "I'm sure you realize any delay from getting the sights on the target to pulling the trigger could result in a missed opportunity.

"It's your mission and your choice as to the execution, but I'd hate to lose the possible only opportunity," he continued. "Maybe I can get the CIA to assign you a spotter. I know they already have men in the field, and I'm sure there are several qualified men in that group."

"That would be great, sir," Butch said. "Not to push it but having a spotter with each of the nine shooters would be fantastic. If that's not possible, I'll certainly be thankful for any one they can put with the team at the first rally location."

"I'll do what I can," Gene told him. "Now, while I go make a few calls, Debbie needs to give you a quick update. Hang on while I put her on."

"Butch, Debbie here," she said, taking the phone from Gene. "Have you got your computers set up?"

"Yes," Butch answered. "I got them connected to the satellite and see the mass of yellow farms. I'm sure you realize I can't have my men anywhere close for at least five or six hours.

"And that's for area two here around Johannesburg," he continued. "The other areas, south to Cape Town and north to Pretoria, will take more like eighteen hours or more."

"I realize that," Debbie responded. "If you'll look at the screens, I've put an ETA to each of the areas from the hotels where all your green dots, teams, will be located.

"What I'm trying to do is show you where your commanders may want to divert their teams when they leave the hotel," she explained. "Possibly have an area one team be prepared to change their route to pass closer to a potential target in area two that is between the hotel and the first farm in their area.

"I'm just suggesting that possibility since we know we can't cover all of the locations," Debbie continued. "If your team can take out a killer team enroute to a location in their area, I thought that might be an option you'd want to explore."

"That's a good suggestion," Butch replied. "I'll get my commanders to look at those options as they prepare to leave the hotel. The vans or whatever vehicles Golden Diamonds are providing should be here as soon as I hear from the commanders that they are ready to leave, and they can monitor the yellow farms as they go for any updates.

"Thanks, Debbie," Butch then said. "I appreciate all of your help. If you have any other suggestions, please don't hesitate to call. I'm willing to listen to any idea, regardless of who it comes from. Again, thanks."

Chapter 60

About thirty minutes later, Butch had briefed the three area commanders, and they had selected the routes each team would take to their areas. After the ten teams associated with each area left, Butch told his commanders to pay close attention to where each team was in relation to where any farms were located that had just been placed on the yellow alert.

Then he called Debbie to make sure they were getting the most recent and up-to-date information. As she answered, he began, "Debbie, as you've probably seen on your screen, my teams are heading toward their assigned areas and are watching for any reasonable opportunity to take out one of the killer teams along the way.

"The one thing I haven't seen on any of my screens is a red designation," he informed her. "Does that mean there are no firm threats against any of the farms?"

"As of now, that's true," Debbie answered. "There have been several attacks, but they are well past you being able to have any impact on the farm. I've intentionally left those off the screens so you could concentrate on getting your teams in place at their areas.

"If one of the yellow farms turns red now that you are on the move, I'll definitely update your screens," she continued. "Then your area commanders can reassign a team to a known threat instead of a potential one. The same logic applies, if an area one team is nearing the border going south from Johannesburg, and is the closest team to the threat, I would expect him to divert that team.

"However, you're the final decision as to the deployment of the teams," Debbie added. "Now, another factor is the time. It's just after ten o'clock at night over there, and we haven't seen any activity for almost six hours.

"That's probably another reason for no red farms on the screens," she explained. "You can expect little to no activity for the next ten or so hours. Using the potential threat locations, and the probable time delay before any activity against the farms, the area commanders can position their teams based on that factor.

"I'm going to add the red teams to the screens so your guys can see how long before they could reach the targeted farm," Debbie announced, as the red dots popped up on Butch's screens. "Now, I have no usable intelligence as to which of the yellow farms will be selected in the morning. My best guess from watching the killer teams while you were over the ocean is that a team will be sent to the closest farm.

"However, I've seen them bypass a farm for one several miles further away," she continued. "I realize there are a lot of moving parts and only unreliable data to act upon, but this is the best I can provide for now.

"You can expect some major changes after the sun comes up," she added. "And if you toss in the impact of the

UN folks roaming around the country, it gets even more complicated.”

“Well, I can’t just sit here waiting for a better picture of what’s going to happen in the morning,” Butch admitted. “So, I’ll direct the area commanders to continue as we’ve discussed until the sun comes up.

“At least we’ll have a hundred men out in each area instead of here in Johannesburg,” he finished. “Thanks for the information about the lack of activity during the dark hours. That gives me a little wiggle room to get my guys in place.”

“Just doing my job,” Debbie replied. “I’m going to activate a bell on your computers in the event you doze off and a red threat appears. Maybe you can get a little rest since I’m sure you didn’t get any on the plane.”

“Thanks,” Butch said. “I may try to catnap while I’m waiting for the teams to get in their areas. Not to change the subject, but how are Jim and Megan doing?”

“They are checked into the hotel and downstairs in the restaurant,” she answered. “I just got confirmation of his appointment for ten o’clock tomorrow morning with the Bull, and I’m notifying him as we speak. I’ll let him know how you’re doing, but I’m guessing he’ll be pretty busy working with Megan coordinating any last-minute changes to his operation.

“Speaking of that, I’ve got to get off here and make sure we have a FedEx delivery set up,” Debbie said. “I’ll get back with you when there are any changes to the status of the farms.”

Chapter 61

Jim was in the restaurant with Megan, and they had just finished placing their dinner orders when his phone rang. Recognizing the number, he answered, "Good evening, Debbie. I bet you know I just ordered Bobotie for dinner and a glass of Chocolate Block red wine."

"As a matter of fact, I didn't know that," she answered. "Whether or not you know it, I have more important things to do than spy on your culinary desires.

"First, I'm calling to let you know I've verified the FedEx delivery you requested," she continued. "I've also verified that there will only be one guard in the house when you arrive.

"Your appointment is for ten o'clock tomorrow morning," she said. "I'm guessing the limo picking you up will be downstairs by nine o'clock to allow for traffic issues.

"Your host does not tolerate tardiness very well," she continued. "And I'm sure your driver knows that and realizes he'll be to blame unless you aren't downstairs when he arrives.

"Just to ease any doubts about tomorrow," she said, "I'm monitoring every listening device and camera at the location.

I haven't seen anyone checking the location where your alternative method is, so I assume it's still there.

"It might be a good idea to scratch your calf, or something, to make sure it's there and you won't have to fumble around to find it, if necessary," she suggested. "Have you decided on a phrase to alert the FedEx driver to bring in the package?"

"Yes," Jim answered. "I'm going to ask Megan if we need to get fresh data FedExed. That will be the signal. Or any phrase with FedEx in it."

"Got it," Debbie said. "I'll make sure the driver understands. The last position we looked at for him to wait was two minutes from the front door of the house.

"Any place closer drew too much attention and only gave us a forty-second advantage," she explained. "We decided not to continue looking for a better location because it would become evident something wasn't normal about a FedEx truck being in the same vicinity so many times."

"That's not a big issue," Jim said, as their dinners arrived. "I think Megan and I can work with a two-minute delivery schedule. Have there been any changes to his schedule, other than our appointment?"

"No, not yet," Debbie answered. "It's possible that all the activity involving the UN could mean some adjustments to his schedule.

"And, when word of some other activity in certain areas of the country comes to light, that could impact his schedule," she continued. "That's something we won't know until tomorrow morning.

"Is there anything else?" she asked. "I've got a few more things to take care of regarding another part of this operation before the sun comes up over there."

"No, I guess not," Jim answered. "Megan and I are going to run over our plan one more time after dinner and then try to get some sleep before meeting our host."

"Fine," Debbie finished. "I'll give you a call in the morning before you go downstairs to meet the limo. By the way, that Potjiekos Megan is having looks delicious."

"Anything new?" Megan asked, taking a small forkful of her meal from the small cast-iron pot it was served in.

"No," Jim answered, looking at the camera lens on his phone and sticking his tongue out slightly. "You heard most of the conversation except for some details that aren't relevant.

"We'll do a quick review of what we expect after dinner back upstairs in your room," he told her. "I just want to be sure we're both satisfied with our roles and look at things which could go wrong."

"Sounds good to me," Megan replied. "I've prepared myself as much as I can for the possibility of having to shoot, but I'm not sure how steady my hand will be.

"And I know that doesn't fit with the optimum scenario, but I can do it," she finished. "At least sitting here right now, I feel sure I can."

"I hope it doesn't come to that," Jim replied, finishing his Bobotie. "The only thing that truly matters is that we get the mission accomplished and get away. Let the politicians sort out the rest.

"There are always going to be factors that arise during something like this," Jim explained, signaling for their check. "When people are involved, you can never be sure of their response. Even if you think you know them. Stress causes some erratic behavior sometimes."

Chapter 62

The following morning, while Jim and Megan were having breakfast, Jim said, "If he doesn't mention the frog after your first attempt at presenting your information, say something that will draw his attention away.

"If he's offered the wine, I'll take that opportunity to administer the remedy to our problem," Jim continued. "If he doesn't respond, or it's so slight I don't have a chance, we'll start planning on solution number two.

"At that point, I'll be ready to reach for the gun," he explained. "I'll need you to do something to draw his attention away. Maybe drop some papers and lean over to pick them up.

"Not trying to tell you how to handle him but having a button or two at the top of your blouse open would be a possible idea to grab his attention," Jim suggested. "Once I have the gun, all attempts at option one are over.

"I'll be using the FedEx phrase to get things in motion," he added. "I'll hand you the gun, and I'll demand he call his guard.

"I'll be standing by the door when the guard comes in and I'll demand his weapon," he continued. "At that point, we're committed to option two as we've discussed several times.

"Now, it's not supposed to take more than two minutes, according to Debbie, but those estimates were under simulated conditions," he said. "Just be prepared for longer.

"If things go to shit, the President does something stupid, the guard won't give up his gun, then you have to take a shot," Jim continued, "shoot for the chest. Put at least two in the center.

"That may not be fatal, but it will certainly stop him from being a threat," he said, looking at her. "But I hope that doesn't happen.

"If things go as I'm planning, I'll have the guard's gun," he explained. "Then I'll take the one you are holding and hand you the guard's gun.

"If any shooting happens before the FedEx arrives with the package, I'll do it with the gun Jewell left," Jim explained. "I'll probably shoot both of them, and hopefully the noise won't bring any response from whoever else is in the house.

"I'll figure out what to do if that happens," he continued. "Any questions or doubts about your role?"

"No," she answered. "It's just becoming so real. Never in my life would I have imagined I'd be involved in something like this."

"It'll be okay," Jim assured her, signaling for their check. "Once the package is delivered, shit is going to be a blur until I take the guard's gun from you.

"We'll have a few seconds to set the stage before we have to leave," he told her, as he signed the check. "Then we'll just follow the driver out as if nothing had happened. Now, we need to get to the lobby and wait for our transportation.

"If you have any questions, it's got to be now before we get into the car," he continued. "After that, you're my boss and I'm a mild-mannered assistant."

"I'm ready," Megan said, following Jim from the restaurant.

As they were waiting for the limo, Butch was watching red dots popping up all over the three screens in his room. Watching the green dots representing his teams heading for the red farm locations, he made a quick call to the area one commander, asking, "One, how many teams do you have in reserve?"

"Three," came the answer. "I've deployed seven who had a better than even chance of getting into place before their guests arrive.

"Things should get interesting in the next twenty minutes," he continued. "I just noticed another three yellow farms on the screen, but I don't have time to get to them."

"Keep me in the loop," Butch said, before switching to the area two commander.

"Two, looks like you've got folks racing across the pasture," he said, as the commander acknowledged the call. "I see five red farms. Are your folks going to make it in time for the reception?"

"Gonna be tight," came the response. "We may have to come from behind if the cars are empty when we get there. I've notified the residents, and they are leaving right now."

"Looks like you have two teams down by area one," Butch said. "Do you think you can send them south to lend a hand?"

"I can send one," the commander answered. "I've looked at the intercept time, and even that one will be close."

Butch looked closely at areas one and two's screens and said, "Send them. And notify One they are on the way."

Looking at area three, Butch called, "Three, are you there?"

"Here," came the reply. "Hold on a moment, I've got four teams who've almost made it to the farms. I'm also sending another one to a new red spot."

"Take your time," Butch said. "I don't see any other teams that can help you at this point. And remember, this is a black flag operation with a bonfire at the end."

Chapter 63

"Mr. President," Megan said, as they were ushered into his office. "It's so kind of you to take the time to meet with me."

The President looked up from some papers on his desk and said, "I agreed to meet with you. Just you."

"I'm sorry, sir," Megan replied. "But I specifically said my assistant would be accompanying me. I made that clear when I talked to your Ambassador to the United Nations."

"I don't care what you made clear, or who you made it clear to," he said, putting his elbows on the table while he leered at her and ran his eyes up and down her body. "You are the only one I'm interested in meeting with."

"Then I'm afraid I must leave," Megan said, starting to turn away. "I don't have any meetings without my assistant. He's here to take notes, handle the many papers I'll be referring to, and ensure our meetings are professional.

"If that's unacceptable to you, I'll kindly ask for your driver to return us to our hotel," she finished, as she stared at him. "Those are the only options … my assistant remains, or I return to the hotel."

The President sat silently for a moment, then waved the guard away, saying, "Very well. Please have a seat."

Megan took the seat to the left as they had discussed and said, "Thank you, Mr. President. Now, if you would like, I'll begin showing you the damage that's being done to your country by losing the farmers who have been providing the food for your people for many generations."

"First, let me apologize for my earlier demand," the President said, reaching to the corner of his desk where a bottle of wine and two glasses sat. "I also apologize for only having two glasses, as I only planned on one guest."

"That's perfectly fine, sir," Megan replied. "My assistant doesn't drink. At least not when he's working with me."

"Never trust a man who doesn't drink," the President said, handing Megan a glass of wine. "A man who doesn't drink knows he has a weak will and is afraid he'll succumb to the addiction of alcohol. I, myself, have no such problem. I am the master of my body and my spirit. But then, neither am I just an assistant to anyone.

"I am the President of one of the most important countries in the world," he continued. "Our gold and diamonds are sought by every nation on earth. They are our nation's treasure, and it is greater than the treasure of all the other nations put together."

Pouring another, he raised his glass, smiled seductively at her, and said, "To an interesting and productive discussion."

Megan slightly raised hers, gave a slight nod, and said, "And to your health, sir."

Nodding to Jim, she said, "First, I'd like to show you the amount of farm products your farmers brought to market over the last five years."

Jim set the briefcase he was carrying on the floor, opened it, and handed her a folder marked 'Farm Production'. As Megan accepted the folder, she rose and stepped toward the desk, saying, "I hope you don't mind if I get a little closer so I can point to the information on these sheets."

"That's no problem," he answered, looking down the top of her blouse. "You can come around to this side if it would make it any easier."

"I better stay on this side," she replied, with a slight, suggestive smile. "I need to be able to reach the papers my assistant will be handing me."

Stepping to the desk and slightly to her right, she placed the folder on his desk and leaned over as she opened it.

As she was blocking the President's view of Jim, he reached down and found the pistol just where he had been told it would be. Giving it a slight tug, he knew it would come loose with very little pressure.

"Now here are the production figures we're looking at," Megan continued. "You can plainly see that the numbers were steady, within two percent from lowest production, to highest, up until last year.

"Now, looking at last year's production, it has fallen over forty percent," she explained.

"That was because of the lack of rain," the President countered. "The other years were some of the wettest years in our history."

Turning back to Jim, she merely said, "Climatology."

Jim bent over his briefcase once again and handed her another folder.

Megan once again bent over the desk and placed the new folder beside the farm production folder, saying, "Here are the annual rain amounts. These numbers are taken at various locations across the country by the World Meteorological Organization, the WMO, which is the United Nations system of monitoring the weather around the world.

"As you can see, the average rainfall during the four years preceding the year when the crop production fell dramatically was almost a half of an inch less than the year in question," she explained. "There was actually more rain that year, yet production declined."

"Maybe that's what the so-called experts say," the President said. "But I was here each of those years and I know the difference between when it's raining or when someone is pissing on my boots. And I'm telling you ..."

Just then, the guard opened the door and said, "Mr. President. There is a very important call for you."

"I told you to never disturb me while I have guests," the President almost shouted. "Now, close the door and don't come back unless I send for you."

"Sir, excuse me, but the person on the phone, a man you know and trust, says he must speak to you ... immediately," the guard said, bowing and waiting before leaving.

The President stared at the guard before finally picking up the phone, saying, "This better be damned important. Who the hell is this, and what do you want?"

Listening, his face began to scowl, and he finally said, "I'll look into it when I have a moment."

Listening for another minute, he finally said, "Fine. I'll do it now."

Slamming the phone down, he looked at Megan and said, "This meeting is over. My guard will escort you to the car, and my driver will take you back to your hotel. I'll let you know if there's to be another meeting. Now, get out."

Jim stood and asked Megan, "Would you like for me to get the folders so we can bring them back whenever the President wants to see you again?"

"No, leave them," Megan said, turning to leave. "He can take a good look at them before we return."

Chapter 64

While Jim and Megan were with the Bull, Butch was watching the red dots of the killer teams as they moved toward where the teams were waiting for their arrival.

"One, looks like you're about to get some action," Butch said, as he saw seven red dots merging on the farm where the green teams were. "Did you get the information from two that he was sending a team to the north part of your area?"

"Yes, and they are there waiting," he answered. "Looks like we're going to eliminate eight of their teams this morning. It would be nice to know how many teams they have in reserve."

Butch was taking a closer look at the screen for area two when the phone rang. "Hello," he answered, as red dots were less than ten minutes from the five farms where his teams were waiting.

"Good morning, Butch," Debbie said. "I know you're busy, but I just got word from our CIA friends that we have a time and location for the Steer."

"Great," Butch replied, as two of the red dots merged with the green ones at the farms. "Where and when?"

"A large city in the south," Debbie answered. "And you have three hours to get your men in place."

"I believe there are three there now, if I'm correct about the corral," Butch said, looking at area one where Cape Town was located.

"I see your men there," Debbie confirmed. "Now, expand the screen until you see two black circles with a red X in the middle. It will be close to the center of the city."

"Got it," Butch said. "Is that the location of the rally?"

"No, that's where two of our friends are waiting to meet your friends," Debbie explained. "They will take your friends to a good viewing location if they want to take pictures.

"When your men get there, they will see two men wearing gray slacks, one wearing a white knit shirt, and the other a light green shirt," she continued. "The man in green will have a green wristband on his left arm.

"If you want, we'll be watching your men as they get closer and tell them when they are at the location," she offered.

"That would be great," Butch said. "Is there any special password my guys need to know?"

"Yes, tell them the two CIA friends are Bert and Ernie," Debbie answered. "Your friends are Amos and Andy."

"I'll have my guy down there get things moving," Butch said. "If you have time, please give me a heads up when everyone is in position. I may be a little distracted with another group of problems."

"I'll call when the cameras are set up," Debbie replied. "Looks like you made some wise choices with the current locations."

"I had some inside information," Butch said. "Now, I'll get my guys moving. And thanks again, Debbie. You're making my job simple."

"Technology is making both of our jobs much easier," she answered. "And this new AI stuff is changing the way we'll be operating for years in the future."

Hanging up, Butch looked at the screen for area one and called, "One, time to move your shooters."

"Ready," came the answer. "Give me the location and I'll have two of them on the way."

Butch led him through the process of locating the two black circles and gave him the description he had received from Debbie, as well as the code names.

"You have slightly less than three hours to have everyone in place," Butch informed him. "If we can pull this off this morning, maybe we can go home much sooner.

"Give me a quick call when you get things wrapped up out in the field," Butch continued. "I'm going to be watching the *Photo shoot* very closely.

"What do you plan on doing with the teams in the field once they've burned the trash?" he asked, waiting to see the green dots representing the snipers start moving toward the black circles.

"For now, I'll leave them in place," the commander replied. "But I already see a few more yellow farms, and I'll send the last three teams I have here in that direction.

"I've got a pretty wide-open area, but I can't see any other locations for the teams until something changes," he finished.

"Sounds reasonable," Butch replied as he saw the two snipers moving. "I'll try to keep an eye on them, but my main priority now is the Steer."

Chapter 65

As the two snipers merged with the black circles, Butch got a call from the commander of area three saying, "I've destroyed five killer teams, I have two more teams en route to a farm that recently turned red, and it looks like I have a twenty-minute lead on the killer teams headed for that farm.

"I've got three teams unassigned, and if area two needs any assistance, I'll send them as long as it's no more than thirty minutes from my area," he offered.

"I don't see any need for that right now," Butch said, looking at the area two screen. "They sent a team south to lend a hand, and area one just sent their last three teams to cover some farms which recently turned yellow.

"And, I don't see any new red movement, or changes in the farms," he continued. "It's quite possible that they deployed all of their assets this morning and were waiting for them to finish with the first farm before reassigning them to the next one."

"I noticed there haven't been any new red teams," the commander agreed. "Has Black Water heard anything that supports your theory that all of the teams are already in the field?"

"No, but I haven't asked them," Butch replied. "I'll check with two, but looking at his area, I see a definite lack of red movement. Damn, it would be great if we'd wiped out most of them on the first day.

"I'll get back to you and the rest of the guys after I talk to Quantico," Butch said, before hanging up.

He spent a few minutes studying the screen of each area and noted that even where the red farms had been located, the red dots signifying members of a killer team, were not moving.

Trying to determine why that was happening, he dialed Black Water and asked for Debbie when the call was answered.

"Quick question, Debbie," he said, seeing more red dots stationary. "I know several of the killer teams are destroyed. And it appears as if my guys have taken their phones before burning them, as I directed. Can you tell me why there aren't any new red teams moving?"

"We're looking into that right now," Debbie answered. "We had several red teams located, but they've dropped off the map. We did hear some chatter regarding the issue of our bugging their phones.

"Now it appears that someone is having teams who haven't deployed to destroy their phones," she surmised. "It's possible the ambush of the teams this morning has made them realize their movements are being monitored.

"Hang on a minute, Butch," she suddenly said. "I may have the answer in a second."

A minute later, she was back, saying, "I was right. Word of your operation destroying the red teams got the notice of one of the Steer's lieutenants, and they know they are being monitored.

"The lieutenant just ordered all of the phones destroyed, and he contacted our dealer demanding replacements no later than midnight tonight," she continued. "It looks like you may have a lull in operations for a few hours.

"Oh, and it looks like they are blaming the Boers," she said, laughing. "They believe the farmers are banding together to ambush their teams. This couldn't be going any better.

"You can tell your area commanders that we don't think there will be any more attacks today," she continued. "But it could also mean they are not using phones to communicate.

"If that happens, we probably won't be able to identify their targets unless someone didn't destroy his phone and we overhear a conversation," she explained. "If we hear anything, we'll try to put it on the screen, but I'd bet if there's a phone or two still active, the next fiasco at any farm will cost someone their head.

"Looks like you've only got a few minutes before the Steer makes his appearance," she said, a second later. "Is everyone in position? Do you need anything from us?"

"I think we're ready," Butch answered, switching his focus to screen one. "The circles and the green dots have split and haven't moved in the last ten or so minutes.

"I'm getting ready to send a message to both shooters, reminding them that they are cleared to shoot, and to try to coordinate their shots so both bullets hit at roughly the same time," he explained. "The difference in the distance for each will make a slight difference in when the bullets hit, but it will be so minuscule, it won't make any difference."

"Okay," Debbie said. "Since you don't have much to occupy you with the guys in the field, I'll let you go. I don't need to tell you they are in position now since you already know."

Chapter 66

Butch was watching closely as he waited for his men to take the shot, when suddenly he saw both green dots representing the shooters begin moving. Thinking they had successfully made the shot, he reached for the phone to call the area one commander to congratulate him.

Just as his hand touched the phone, it rang. "Yes?" Butch answered.

"The target left the stage before my guys could get a shot," the commander of area one said. "The son-of-a-bitch had just stepped on the stage when someone grabbed him and said something that made him turn and leave.

"Then, someone stepped up to the podium and announced that the rally had to be cancelled due to an emergency," he continued. "I'm bringing my guys back here. Let me know if anything changes."

Butch quickly called Black Water and asked Debbie when she answered, "What the hell happened with the Steer?"

"We listened to the guy who spoke to him via the phone the Steer had, and he told him about the number of failed attempts on the farms," she said. "Then the Steer made a couple of calls to some of his men before calling the President.

"We know that Jim and Megan are just now leaving the President's office in Johannesburg, and I expect to hear from him as soon as they get to the hotel," she continued. "It appears that our success on the farms this morning is turning our other operations into an unmitigated disaster.

"I'm not sure what's going to happen with the Bull, nor do I have any idea about whether or not the Steer will make another attempt at a rally, or where that may be if he does," she added. "All I can tell you for now is to just sit tight until the new phones are issued.

"We may have something more in the morning," she finished. "Now, it looks like Jim is calling."

"Yes, Jim," Debbie said, answering.

"I guess you know how our meeting went," Jim said. "Do you know why it was ended so abruptly?"

"Yes, matter of fact I just got off the phone with Butch and told him why he didn't get his shot at the Steer," Debbie answered. "That reason was because the Steer left the stage to call the Bull.

"He then proceeded to tell the Bull about the disasters in the field and how many men were lost to the ambushes," she continued. "That's when the Bull ordered you to leave."

"So, we wait?" Jim asked.

"I don't know what else to tell you," Debbie answered. "Once the folks figured out we were using their phones, they destroyed them and are waiting for the new ones.

"It appears that our effort to get them to toss the old phones so we could supply them with our small caliber phones was a great success," she continued. "But it's put a small delay in our field operations, and possibly our only chance with the Bull.

"We'll just have to wait and see if you get invited back," she finished.

"If I'd have known we were going to be tossed out, I'd have taken a shot," Jim said remorsefully. "I had my hand on the gun and could have pulled it out before the guard came in.

"Even then, I could have taken both of them out," he continued.

"Hang on, Jim," Debbie said. "General Barker has been listening on the speaker and wants to talk to you."

"Jim, Gene here," General Barker said. "You did the right thing not taking the shot.

"First of all, such an impromptu move could have jeopardized your or Megan's life," he continued. "If you'd shot before the guard came in, he'd have heard it and been ready to shoot as he came in.

"If you'd tried to pull the gun from beneath the chair with the guard in the room, he probably would have had his gun out before you got yours out, and we know how that would have ended," Gene explained. "Now, had you been extremely lucky and shot both of them, there would have been nobody to leave behind to shift the blame to the Steer.

"Even if the FedEx delivery was made after the fact, the bullets in all three people would have been from the same gun," he continued. "Let's say you took the guard's gun before the FedEx came. The time delay would have given any number of people in the house a reason to come in.

"No, walking away was the best option," Gene informed him. "Now, I'm going to make a few calls and see if we can't arrange another meeting within the next few days.

"You guys just hang out at the hotel or go sightseeing," Gene recommended. "Just stay clear of the Golden Diamond tour group. I'll get back to you as soon as we know more about a new meeting, the action in the field, and possibly a new rally.

"Lots of scurrying around going on here at headquarters to put this operation back on track," he finished.

Chapter 67

Jim called Megan's room and told her he was headed down to the restaurant if she wanted to join him for lunch.

Just as the elevator door began to close, he heard her asking to hold the elevator. Stepping in, she said, "Thanks. After the way the meeting went, my nerves are about as frazzled as they could be.

"I'm going to have to have something stronger than iced tea for lunch," she continued. "I'm not sure if I want to go back, even if he asks us to.

"I still can't believe how scared I was," she continued. "Now, I'm so tired, I almost said no to the lunch offer. I feel as if I could lie down and sleep for two days."

"That's just the post-adrenaline rush," Jim said, as the doors opened at the ground level. "Don't be too alarmed if you start getting a headache or get jittery. That's normal.

"I can't tell you how to fight it, just give your body time to readjust," he continued. "It's sort of like running the one-hundred-yard dash. You're out of breath and gasping for air.

"Then your oxygen level returns to normal," he explained, as they headed for the restaurant. "If it's any help, you did a great job today. Nobody would have ever thought you were the least bit nervous.”

“When do you think he’ll let us come back?” she asked, as a waitress led them to a table.

“Hell if I know,” Jim said, pulling a chair out for her. “Gene’s working on it. And I’m sure he wants this to wind up as soon as possible.

“Things are moving more rapidly than we imagined regarding the farms,” he continued, as he took the chair across from her. “And Butch almost got his number one priority this morning.

“Matter of fact, that’s what led to the phone call that got us kicked out,” he finished, as a waitress arrived with a tray bearing two glasses of water.

“Do you need a couple more minutes or are you ready to order?” she asked, setting the water on the table.

“I’d like a bourbon on ice, please,” Jim said, picking up a menu.

“Same, but a double,” Megan said.

“I’m not going to lecture you, but alcohol may increase your fatigue,” Jim said, looking at her over his menu. “Either way, I think you should get something to eat.”

“Okay,” Megan said, picking up her menu. “I’m not really hungry, but maybe something spicy would be good.”

“Weren’t you nervous?” she asked, looking at Jim.

“Of course,” he replied. “But I just try to concentrate on the task, constantly looking at the situation, and deciding if I need to do something.

“Perhaps I’ve become somewhat immune to it, but honestly, that was pretty tame,” he told her.

"I don't want to see something that's not tame," she said, as their drinks arrived. "I don't think I'd make a good field operative."

"Are you ready to order now, or do you still need a couple of minutes?" the waitress asked.

"I'd like the Boerewors and some Mealie Bread," Jim answered, looking at Megan.

"I don't know," she said, looking at her menu again. "What would you recommend, Jim?"

"I think you'd like the Bunny Chow," he answered.

"Is it rabbit?" she asked, frowning.

"No," Jim answered. "It's a beef curry with chickpeas and potatoes in a hollowed-out loaf of bread.

"If you're not a fan of curry, I'd try the Chakalaka," he recommended. "It's mainly a vegetable dish. And, I'd be glad to share my Boerewors, a sausage, and the Mealie Bread, a type of cornbread."

"I'll try the Chaka-whatever," she answered, setting her menu on the table. "I've never really liked most Indian dishes. Too much curry."

"Should I have said something about the frog?" Megan asked, taking a sip of her bourbon as the waitress walked away.

"No," Jim answered. "I don't think he'd pull that little stunt with me there."

"Is that option out?" she asked, holding her glass against her cheek.

"No, but I'm leaning more to the other option," Jim answered, sipping his bourbon. "I've thought about it, and I think I'd have to put a little of the ingredient on the frog's back in case they swabbed it after determining that's what killed him.

"And I don't know if it would kill the frog," Jim continued. "That would also double the chance of getting the stuff on me. And I damn sure know I don't want that.

"But let's not worry about what might be," he said, as he saw the waitress coming with their lunch. "We'll take it one step at a time and see what happens, if we even get another meeting."

***

Jim had fallen asleep on his bed when the ringing of his phone woke him. Glancing at the number, he answered, "What are you doing up this early? It's only what, seven o'clock there?"

"I'm not up early," Gene replied. "I'm up late, very late. Matter of fact, I haven't been to bed in over twenty-four hours.

"But somebody has to make all the arrangements for your little vacation," he continued. "First, you have an appointment tomorrow morning, same ten o'clock, but the President refuses to provide transportation. "I've arranged for a car to pick you up at nine o'clock and drop you off at the President's home. I believe we have an asset in the area who will take you out of there when you're ready to leave.

"Also, in case you're wondering, the cancelled rally is rescheduled, same place, same time," he said. "I've already talked to Butch, and he's letting his people know."

"I'll let Megan know," Jim replied. "She's a little shaken up from today's meeting. But I'm sure she'll be just fine in the morning."

"Not a surprise," Gene said, nodding. "If you have any doubts, let me know tomorrow before you leave, and maybe we can reschedule the appointment for the next day."

"I'll do that," Jim said. "But, if things keep going as well out in the field as it appears to have been today, he may start wondering about the coincidence of us and the other UN people running around the country."

"I agree," Gene replied. "But if Butch gets his shot, and you take care of your issue, I think we can depart the country tomorrow afternoon, and let ET make his call, or more likely, calls home."

"What's new with Deputy Dawg?" Jim asked. "Is he still the de facto incumbent?"

"That's the plan," Gene confirmed. "He's on a sort of sabbatical at the moment. Somewhere up in Botswana, visiting some distant relative. That gives him a more or less rock-solid alibi for any accidents that may befall other interested parties."

"Good," Jim replied. "It's great when a well-thought-out plan comes together. Now, I'll see if Megan is still awake and let her start mentally preparing for another round with the round man."

"Have a good evening, Jim," Gene said, before hanging up. "I'm hoping for a safe return for you guys tomorrow."

"Me, too," Jim replied, as he hung up. "Me, too."

Chapter 68

The following morning, as Jim and Megan were having breakfast, Jim asked, "How do you feel about the meeting today?"

"Still a little nervous," she admitted. "And I have to admit, knowing I may have to shoot someone just makes it worse."

"I understand," Jim replied, breaking off a piece of bacon. "That's why I've decided to make a slight revision."

"What's that?" Megan asked, slicing a small piece of sausage.

"I'm going to be the only one handling the guns," he told her. "After yesterday, I don't want to put any additional stress on you.

"If we don't get a chance to use the poison, it's going to be the gun," Jim explained, as he took a forkful of baked beans from his plate. "And it's got to be split second with three individuals being shot in rapid succession.

"You'll be in the left chair, just as yesterday," he continued. "And when you move to block his view of me,

I'll remove the gun and place it between my right thigh and the arm of the chair.

"If he hasn't mentioned the golden frog in the first fifteen minutes, I don't believe he will," Jim said. "Then I'll stand and step to your right side. When he notices me, I'll have the gun pointed at his face.

"You need to step away from the desk and get behind your chair," Jim added. "I'll make sure he understands that if he doesn't follow my orders exactly, I will put a bullet through his face.

"As soon as I tell him to call his guard, I'll call for the FedEx guy to get there," Jim continued. "The door to the President's office swings inward, hinged on the left. When the guard enters, his left hand will be on the doorknob, and his gun will be on his right hip.

"I'll be to the guard's right, a foot or so from the door, and against the wall so he won't initially see me," he said. "With his focus on the President, I'll step beside him and put the gun barrel against his head.

"Then, I'll take his gun and have him move to the front of the President's desk," Jim explained. "That's why I want you out of the way and behind your chair.

"I'll hold the guard's gun in my left hand, and when the FedEx guy enters with our package, I'll have them walk about half way from the door to where the guard is standing, and I'll step beside the driver and shoot the package in the chest with my left hand, the guard's gun," Jim continued. "Then, I'll shoot the guard once with the gun I got from beneath the chair, also in the chest.

"Next, I'll shoot the President, hopefully in the heart," Jim said. "Now, all three are down. The package will be in front of where the guard falls. The President either in his chair or on the floor behind his desk. That's irrelevant because I won't need to shoot him again.

"Next, I'll wipe down the guard's gun, put it in his hand, and shoot the package in the chest again," he continued. "Then I'll wipe down the first gun, the one from beneath the chair, put it in the package's hand, and shoot the guard in the chest again.

"As I'm doing that, with the help of the FedEx driver, you need to gather any papers from the desk, put them in the briefcase, and bring it with you as we leave," Jim finished. "Do you understand what I'm planning and why?"

"Yeah," she said, with a slight look of relief on her face. "Makes it look like the package shot the President and the guard. And the guard shot the package. But why do you need to make the second shots?"

"There needs to be gunshot residue on their hands," Jim explained. "That's the only way to get their prints on the guns and the residue on their hands."

"So, the only thing I have to do is block his view of you, step behind the chair when you get up, and gather all of the papers and briefcase before we leave," she said, looking at Jim. "Anything else we need to do?"

"Not that I know of, right now," Jim answered. "But you know the saying about the best laid plans. However, make sure you don't touch any glasses or anything on his desk that might leave a print."

"But I've already left prints everywhere," Megan countered.

"I know," Jim said, nodding. "That can be explained because we were there yesterday. "If I can get everything right, there will be no record of us ever returning to his office.

"Since the driver today will be one of our guys, there won't be anyone who can positively say we ever returned," Jim explained. "And, since we're leaving with the FedEx guy, he damn sure doesn't want anyone to know he was there. Therefore, no record of going. No record of leaving.

"Of course, once we leave the area, we cease to exist," Jim finished. "I'll ask Black Water to scrub any electronic records the President, or his staff may have. And the same for the hotel records.

"There will be no records of you or me ever being in the country," he finished, signaling for their check. "Now it's time to go meet our driver. This is your last chance to let me know if you have any problems with any part of the plan."

"No," Megan said, following Jim to the exit. "I'm just so relieved that I don't have to handle one of the guns or shoot anyone. Thanks."

Chapter 69

Jim was still in the shower that morning when Butch's phone rang. "Hello," he answered, groggily.

"Time to get to work," Debbie said. "They have their phones, and they are on the move."

Giving him a couple of minutes to wake up, she continued, "I've got four red farms and three yellow ones in area one. Area two has five red and four yellow ones. Area three has three red and two yellow ones.

"You need to make sure your commanders are up and monitoring the situation," Debbie advised. "We've only been monitoring the new phones for less than an hour, and the teams are just now moving.

"I've put all the information I just told you on all of your screens, but I don't have firm estimates on arrival times yet since they are just now leaving where they spent the night," she continued. "I'll have that data in the next twenty minutes. But I know it's going to be close in a couple of instances, based on where the green teams are."

"How many of the phones are with the killer teams right now?" Butch asked, now fully awake.

"Only one for each team," Debbie answered. "There were a few issues with the dealer last night regarding the number of phones required and how much the bill was.

"Bottom line, the leaders of the Red Teams couldn't pay for all the ones they wanted, and the dealer wouldn't accept an IOU. Especially after all the people they lost yesterday," she explained. "What are you thinking?"

"I'm thinking about using the phones to remove the red teams we can't beat to the farms," Butch answered. "I wish everyone in the cars or vans had a phone, but there are negative issues with that also, such as every phone ringing at once."

"You know, once you start using the phones to eliminate the targets, that will soon be known, and they will toss them," Debbie told him.

"I know," Butch answered. "That's not much different than them tossing their phones because they realized we had bugged them, is it?"

"What do you want me to do?" Debbie asked. "I can fire the shell in each phone, regardless of whether or not it's in someone's hand. I can even fire the ones still in boxes at the dealer's place. Or I can take out the leader of the teams, you can't get to soon enough. What's your choice?"

"I'll have to get back to you on that," Butch said, as he started seeing green teams headed for the farms showing red on the screen. "Right now, I've got to make sure my snipers are awake and prepared for another shot."

"Do you want me to ask the CIA folks to meet you?" Debbie asked.

"That would be helpful," Butch answered. "I'm sure my guys can find their way back to the original locations, but it would be nice if the CIA got there first and cleared the area."

"I'll see what I can do," Debbie replied. "Anything else?"

"How accurate of a head count can you get on the number of red folks going to the farms?" Butch asked, watching the red dots racing the green dots to the designated farms.

"I'll guess at maybe fifty to sixty percent," Debbie answered. "I can distinguish between voices in any car. But someone may not have said anything. Then, if there is a second car, I have no idea how many people are in it.

"If you want me to make a guess, I'd say the same number you were looking at yesterday," she continued. "That makes my guess about as good as yours.

"Now, if whoever's funding this operation can come up with the balance for the rest of the phones before the next groups go out, I can be as accurate as yesterday," she finished.

"Understand," Butch said, trying to locate his snipers on the area one screen. "I'll get back to you on shooting with the phones when I give it a little more thought."

"Hey, One," Butch said, as the phone was answered. "Have you talked to your shooters today?"

"Just about ten minutes ago," the commander answered. "They were still at the hotel, but they had their cases packed and were leaving as soon as they paid their breakfast bill.

"You should see them pretty close to where they met Bert and Ernie yesterday any time now," he finished.

"Okay, I see them now," Butch said. "How's it going with the teams headed to the farms?"

"I've got five teams headed out to the red ones," the commander said. "That gives me five in reserve."

"Why five?" Butch asked. "There are only four red farms."

"If you look at the yellow ones, there is one of them between where the red teams are and a red farm," he explained. "Since they are going right by a yellow farm, I decided to park one of my teams there in case they decide to drop in."

"Hell of an idea," Butch concurred. "Let me know if you need any help later. And let me know if a red team did stop by for a quick visit at the yellow farm."

Chapter 70

After being dropped off at the President's house, the same guard as before escorted Jim and Megan to the office.

After knocking and hearing permission to enter, the guard opened the door and stepped inside, saying, "Sir, the people from the UN are here. Do you wish to see them?"

"Send them in," the President answered, barely looking up.

"You may go in now," the guard said, stepping aside for them to enter before closing the door as he left.

Approaching the desk, Megan said, "Good morning, Mr. President. Thank you for seeing me again so quickly."

The President merely glanced up, saying, "Please, sit down. I'll be with you in a second."

As Megan took the left chair, Jim sat the briefcase on the floor by his feet and opened it.

A few moments later, the President looked at Megan and said, "Is there anything else you want to tell me? I thought we covered everything yesterday. And everything you told me then was Western propaganda.

"We don't have a production problem," he continued, becoming belligerent. "We have an interference problem."

"Sir," Megan began. "We aren't here to interfere. My job is to merely present the facts of what the United Nations believes to be an impending food shortage in your country.

"I'm not here to dictate policy, or tell you how to run your country," she continued. "But, since you are a member of the UN, we want to make sure you are aware of the situation."

"I'll tell you what I'm aware of," the President said, raising his voice. "Someone is killing people within my country, who have not threatened anyone or broken any laws, and then burned their bodies.

"Now, I don't have proof it's the United Nations," he continued. "But your damn cars and vans are seen all over the countryside where these atrocities are being committed. Don't you find that to be a strange coincidence?"

"Sir, it is my understanding that the people from the UN are only in your country to provide assistance if the farmers whose land is being expropriated want to claim refugee status in order to apply for a visa to leave your country for another country.

"If you have an issue with that, I suggest you contact your Ambassador to the UN and let him become involved," Megan argued. "My sole purpose is to determine if the United Nations World Food Programme needs to become involved."

Megan paused, then said, "Jim, please hand me the folder showing the gross sales of farm products in the major cities."

Taking the folder from him, Megan rose and placed the folder on the President's desk, saying, "Sir, here are the total sales for farm produce across the country. They cover the same five-year period as the production and climatology we looked at yesterday."

Stepping closer and to her right, she continued, "Sales in your grocery stores are down almost thirty percent. If there is no production problem, why are the shelves empty?"

Jim leaned slightly forward as if to get another folder and slipped the pistol from beneath the chair. Placing it beside his leg, he waited to see what response the President would have to Megan's statement.

"I've been to the grocery stores," he almost shouted. "The shelves are not empty. They are stocked with anything the people want to purchase.

"My chefs have no problems getting whatever they need," he continued, getting more irate. "This data you brought here is a fabrication. I'm constantly visiting the farms. Crops are more abundant than ever before.

"The stores are fully stocked, from canned goods to fresh produce," he exclaimed. "Unless you have more than fabricated numbers, I remain unconvinced of any impending famine."

"Satellite photos," Megan said, turning slightly to look at Jim.

Jim pulled another folder from his briefcase, handed it to her with a slight nod, saying, "Here they are, ma'am."

Megan placed the folder on the desk and pulled out a series of overhead shots of vacant fields and obvious overgrown areas, saying, "Here are the most recent satellite photos taken only a week ago.

"Here are photos of the same areas taken a year ago," she continued. "How do you explain this?"

The President pushed the photos aside and said, "I can photoshop pictures of my dog and make it look like a lion. I've had enough of your bullshit. Guard!"

Chapter 71

As Jim and Megan were dealing with their problems, Butch was watching the two snipers move into position.

"Just a reminder, guys," he said, as he monitored their phones. "You have clearance to fire when you have a clear shot.

"If either of you has a shot and the other doesn't, don't wait more than a second or two," Butch said. "Take the shot."

Listening to their coordination, he heard the first shooter saying, "I'm in position and I have a perfect view of where he should be standing when he begins his speech."

"I'll be ready in a minute," the second shooter said. "There are a couple of people making some adjustments to the microphone or something."

"Looks like the crowd is a little larger than yesterday," shooter one said. "At least fifty percent bigger. But thankfully, no one is fifty percent taller. That could spoil my shot."

"How much longer, Debbie?" Butch asked. "I don't have him on my screen."

"He's probably fifteen minutes away," she answered. "The police escort is having a little problem clearing the traffic."

Butch switched screens and saw that the killer teams at two of the red farms in area three were less than five minutes from making contact with the green teams, who were already positioned. The third farm was still ten minutes from the red dot heading there.

Area two showed three red dots still twenty minutes from the farms and his teams were waiting. The two other farms still didn't have any red dots heading for them.

Expanding the screen of area one, Butch saw that the situation was roughly the same. It looked as if his teams were ready at all the red farms, and one in position at the yellow farm the commander had said he would cover.

"Looks like shit's going to hit the fan everywhere about the same time," Butch said to the snipers. "The guys in the field are going to be shooting about the same time as you. Hopefully, they will be using a lot more bullets than you."

"I only plan on one," shooter one said. "If I miss, I don't think I'll get a chance of a second shot."

"I think I'm ready," the second shooter said. "The guys have left the podium where they were working, and everything looks clear."

"Ten minutes," Debbie told Butch. "Looks like he's moving a little faster now."

"How many people with him in his car?" Butch asked.

"Three," she answered. "The driver and two guards."

Butch expanded the screen of area one and told the shooters, "You can expect the two guards with the Steer to stay beside him until he steps up to the microphone.

"It's possible they may stand on both sides of him, a couple of feet away, watching the crowd," he continued. "Since he knows about the shootings across the country, he may have tightened his security."

Butch took the opportunity to look at area three, where he could see the single red dot at one farm was stationary while the ten green dots were moving toward it.

"Three," Butch said. "How many red folks at the farm where it looks like the fight is over?"

"Seven," the commander of area three answered. "We were expecting a couple more, but maybe they are running out of people."

"Let's hope so," Butch replied. "Try to get a good count at the other farms. If they are getting shorthanded, maybe we can wrap this up today."

"Five minutes," Debbie told Butch. "Looks like everyone is in position. Do you need me to keep you informed about his arrival time at the rally?"

Butch expanded the screen for area one and saw the moving target saying, "Nope, I've got him on my screen now. I can follow him myself. Thanks."

"Still clear?" Butch asked shooter one.

"Clear," came the answer.

"How about you, shooter two?" he asked, as he watched the target stop mere feet from the podium where he would be speaking.

"Clear," came the same answer. "I've got him getting out of the car."

"I can't see him yet," shooter one said. "I should pick him up as he steps up on the stage.

"Got him now," shooter one said. "Any time now. Let me know when you've got a clear shot, and I'll start the countdown. We'll shoot when I say 'one'."

"Got it," shooter two said. "I'm clear. He should stop at the podium in five or six more steps."

Butch watched the screen as the Steer's dot stopped moving, and he heard, 'Three, Two, One' as the shots were fired.

"He's down," shooter one said, breaking his rifle down and putting it in the case. "I'm gone."

"See you at the bar," shooter two said, doing the same. "You're buying."

Chapter 72

"FedEx," Jim quietly said as he turned to see the door opening.

"Yes, sir?" the guard asked as he entered the room.

"Escort these people away from my sight," the President ordered, as Jim stood holding the pistol beside his leg.

Jim pushed Megan to the left as he turned and pointed the pistol at the guard, saying, "Keep your hands away from your body. Do not try to reach for your gun.

"Any movement toward it with your right hand, I'll take your head off," he continued, as he moved toward the guard.

"Now, turn around and face the door," Jim ordered, as he approached his right side. "And keep your hands up."

Taking the guard's pistol with his left hand, he said, "Now, walk over to the desk and face me."

"What is the meaning of this?" the President demanded, starting to rise.

"It means you need to sit back down and keep your mouth shut," Jim answered, pointing the gun at him. "If both of you will remain calm, Megan and I will be out of here shortly.

"If you don't stay calm and do as I ask, I will shoot you," he continued. "Do we understand each other?"

The President sat back down and asked, "What is it you want?"

"I want you to stay in your chair and keep your mouth shut," Jim answered. "Isn't that what I've already told you to do?

"Megan, please gather your material and get the briefcase," Jim told her. "It looks as if we need to be ready to leave here in a couple of minutes.

"Then go stand by the door on the side away from the door," he continued. "We'll be leaving as soon as our driver gets here."

Megan was just getting to the door when the FedEx driver walked in with his prisoner walking in front of him with his hands behind his back. Stopping a couple of feet from where Jim was standing, he asked, "Where do you want me to leave him?"

Jim moved to his right so the prisoner was clear of the driver and said, "Right there should be fine."

Taking two steps toward him, Jim raised his left hand and placed one shot in the center of his chest.

Turning back to face the guard as the prisoner fell forward, he raised his right hand and shot him in the chest.

As the guard fell, Jim pointed the gun at the President and said, "You've stolen the land from families that have provided your country with food and produce for generations. They produced the very food that allowed the ships from around the world to stop for resupply as they connected the East to the West.

"You've committed genocide against the very people who made this country what it is, or was," Jim continued, stepping closer. "Your ethnic cleansing is destroying a great country.

"For what?" he asked, looking directly into the President's eyes. "For some perceived injustice from centuries ago? I'm sorry you're such a sorry, worthless, arrogant, pompous ass, and your country, as well as the rest of the world, will be a much better place without you.

"Ironic, isn't it? A mere assistant is going to assist you into the afterlife. Say goodbye, Bull," Jim said, shaking his head as he pulled the trigger, placing a bullet squarely between the President's eyes.

"Now, let's get to work," Jim said, as he pulled a washcloth he had brought from his hotel room from his pocket. "Driver, please get those Zip ties off your friend while I wipe these guns down.

"Megan, take a quick look around and make sure we've got everything we brought today," Jim continued, as he wiped down the guard's pistol.

"Now, hold him up by the shoulders," Jim said, placing the pistol in the guard's limp hand. "And stay to his side."

Jim raised the guard's arm, aimed the pistol at the limp body the driver was trying to stay as far as possible from, and pulled the trigger.

"Now, lift the guard," Jim said, as he laid the guard's arm down.

Wiping the other pistol, he knelt beside the still body of the first man he had shot, and put it in his hand, saying, "Lift him a little more, the shot has to be perpendicular to his chest."

Lifting the dead man's arm, he pointed the pistol at the guard, and fired a single shot, saying, "Lay him back gently, and let's get the hell out of here before someone comes to see what all the shooting was about.

"Megan, are you all right?" Jim asked, taking a final look around.

"I think so," she replied, looking at the people who had been alive only moments ago.

"Good, now stop looking at these guys and just follow the driver," Jim said, stepping to her side. "Just put one foot in front of the other. This will all be over with soon."

As Jim closed the door behind them, he asked, "Debbie, are you there?"

"I am," she answered. "And I see you're headed out. Do you need anything from us?"

"Not unless you hear any signs that some police or anybody is headed our way," Jim answered, following the driver and Megan out of the house. "I plan on getting our stuff out of the hotel and having the FedEx guy take us to the airport.

"I believe Megan wants to go home now," he continued, as he shut the front door to the house and walked to the waiting FedEx van.

Chapter 73

As Jim and Megan were leaving the President's home, Butch was watching the two snipers leaving the scene of the assassination. As they were almost back to where they had first met their CIA friends, Butch's phone rang.

"Are you seeing what's going on in my area?" the commander of area three asked as soon as Butch answered.

"Not really," Butch answered, looking at the screen covering area three. "What are you referring to?"

"Look at those red dots up on the northern section," the commander said. "You may not have noticed, but two of them had almost reached the farms when they suddenly stopped. Do you know what the hell is happening?"

"Not a clue," Butch admitted. "I've been a little involved with the operation down in area one. I'll make a quick call and see if I can get you an answer."

As Debbie answered, Butch asked, "Have you seen what's happening in area three? Are the killer teams stopping before they reach their targets?"

"Yes, they are," Debbie replied. "And there were two red teams who had just left their base heading for the yellow farms, who stopped before they got there also.

"We believe they heard about the Steer being assassinated and were ordered to stop by someone down in area one," Debbie started, as she looked at the other screens.

"Hang on a second," Debbie said. "I've got some reports going to the other teams in areas one and two.

"Yes, all of the red teams are being recalled," she continued. "We're not sure who's running that operation right now, or if it's just a momentary pause, but it's evident they know something has gone dramatically wrong and someone is recalling everyone."

"Don't you know who it is?" Butch asked as he looked at the other screens, where the red dots had either stopped or were reversing their routes. "I thought you had voice recognition of all of the players."

"Not if we hadn't heard the voice before, or not enough to establish a pattern," Debbie admitted. "We're running that voice through every recording we have to try to identify it. Maybe it's in the background of one of the other known voices.

"We'll find him, eventually," she assured Butch. "But for now, let's not assume anything other than the red teams appear to be going into a defensive posture. I'll let you know more when I do.

"Before I forget it, good job with the Steer," she said. "If what I think is happening, it was because of that. Now, I have to figure out who is in charge and what his agenda is.

"It would be nice if he were in opposition to the former regime, but I'm not holding my breath," she finished. "And

Jim completed his mission and is getting ready to head home."

"Lucky bastard," Butch replied. "Of course, he only had one target. I've got hundreds."

"And he'll probably say that he had only one target and one shot," Debbie countered. "And you had hundreds of people to manage yours."

"Don't get me wrong," Butch quickly replied. "I'd much rather be sitting here in air-conditioned comfort watching the drama on TV than staring into the eyes of my victims.

"How's he going to get home?" Butch asked, as he watched every red dot heading for some spot in the major city in their areas.

"Gene's working on that," she answered. "But, if what's happening is any indication of how the regime is changing, there's a chance all of you may be heading home later tonight.

"Okay," she suddenly continued. "There has been a complete recall of the red teams and orders for them to return to their homes after leaving all the weapons and phones at their bases of operation.

"It looks like you can call all of your teams and get them headed back to Johannesburg," Debbie announced. "Gene has just recalled the pilots from the hotel and told them to prepare their flight plans for a return to Quantico. I'll let you start bringing your guys back while I try to get more information about how this ended so suddenly."

Chapter 74

Jim and Megan had barely reached their rooms to collect their belongings when Jim's phone rang.

Looking at the number, Jim answered, "Good evening, General. You caught me just as I was about to leave the house."

"What if I hadn't called until you had left the house?" Gene asked. "You'd still have your phone, so what difference does it make whether you're in the house or in some sleazy dive bar in downtown Johannesburg?"

"You have a point," Jim said, stuffing everything he had brought into his suitcase. "But I'm sure that's not the point of the call, is it now?"

"No," Gene answered. "First, congratulations on a job well done. So far, we've had no fingers being pointed at anyone, especially us.

"Second, I don't know if you've heard, but the farming operation is being shut down," he continued. "All of the troops are being recalled over there, and I just received word that Deputy Dawg, as you put it, is minutes from taking the oath of office.

"If you think you need to know, and I think you have a right to, he's the reason this is over," Gene told him. "The agreement we have in place demanded a cease to all of the expropriation, and any other activities associated with it would either cease, or we would release some tapes revealing him as the man behind both assassinations."

"Do you really have such tapes?" Jim asked, setting his suitcase on the bed and sitting beside it.

"Of course we do," Gene answered. "I believe Debbie told you about our voice-mimicking ability with this new AI stuff.

"So, we have the man on tape discussing the entire operation with a gentleman who will soon be discovered lying on the floor of the President's house," he continued. "And since that man can no longer testify, and the match with the Dawg's voice is a one-hundred-percent match, he's made a very wise choice.

"I've got a car coming to pick up the pilots," Gene said. "You and Megan can ride with them to the airport and wait for the rest of the folks, if you so desire.

"Or, you can sit around your hotel rooms watching reruns of Little House on the Prairie, if they have that there, waiting for everyone else to get back," he finished.

"We'll head downstairs as soon as I can grab Megan and catch an elevator," Jim said, getting up and picking up his suitcase. "I know she wants to get hell out of here as soon as she can. Probably wishes she'd never come."

"Any problems?" Gene asked, as Jim headed for the door, leaving his key on the desk in his room.

"Not really," Jim answered, as he shut the door behind him. "Just seeing a trio of bloody corpses was a little more than she had imagined. Especially watching a face shot at close range for the first time.

"But having said all that, I admire how she handled herself when we were actually negotiating," Jim said, heading down the hall to Megan's room. "She's either a hell of an actress … or a hell of an actress.

"I damn near laughed every time she played the part of a tyrannical female boss," Jim told him, laughing softly. "Hell, if I didn't know better, I would have thought she'd neutered her assistant and wouldn't hesitate to do the same to anyone who questioned her authority.

"It's going to be an interesting flight back tonight," Jim said, as he knocked on Megan's door. "How much of what you've told me is open for dissemination?"

"None of it," Gene answered. "Nothing about our discussions with the Dawg, or any hints as to our AI capabilities. You may tell everyone that the reason for stopping the entire operation was due to his orders.

"Anything else is to go no further," Gene finished. "Now, I see on Debbie's screen that you're waiting for Megan to open her door, so I'll tell the pilots to wait for you downstairs for your ride to the airport."

"Ready to go?" Jim asked, as she opened the door.

"Just a couple of more things from the bathroom," Megan answered, turning away. "I'll be ready in ten seconds."

"I'll take your suitcase," Jim said, as she shut it. "Just toss you room key on the desk and we'll get the hell out of Dodge, or Johannesburg in this case."

Chapter 75

Several hours later, after everyone had boarded the 757s, they could see the reflection of the moon and stars on the black ocean below them as they headed west across the Atlantic.

Most of the people had gone to sleep or were talking quietly. Butch and Jim were sitting together in the front row of the plane when Butch asked, "How much do you know about what caused this to end?"

"Gene called me right after I got back to the hotel with Megan," Jim said. "And I asked him the very same question."

"What did he say?" Butch asked, turning to look at Jim.

"That the newly sworn-in President, the former Deputy President, had demanded the actions against the Boers cease immediately," Jim answered.

"That's it?" Butch asked, incredulously. "One single phone call?"

"I didn't say it was a single phone call," Jim countered. "I just said he gave the order.

"Now this is supposition on my part," Jim continued. "But I'd bet a dozen donuts that he had been planning this for some time.

"I could be wrong, but I'd also bet a dozen apple fritters that someone at some level way above my loftiest ambitions had made some backroom deal with the man," Jim confided. "I certainly don't have any proof, but why would we have been assigned to do what we were assigned to do if that weren't the case.

"I mean, I don't trust our government, especially the dark side, any more than I'd trust a hill of fire ants to let me use their mound as a pillow," he continued. "After what I saw in Viet Nam with some of the CIA operations over there, and some of the previous assignments I've had over the years with Black Water, not much of what our government does under the radar surprises me anymore."

Butch nodded knowingly and then asked, "How'd Megan hold up? Debbie told me there was a lot of noise, which I took to mean blood, after negotiations failed."

"I'd say she's a bit frazzled," Jim said, glancing across the aisle at her sleeping. "And now she's just hit the post adrenaline rush wall. Two days in a row. It'll take three days and ten chilidogs before she recovers this time.

"But she did her job," he finished. "I also heard you managed to juggle some cats on your end."

"Sometimes I thought there were twelve cats, seven mice, and a Doberman pinscher I was trying to keep in the air all at once," Butch admitted. "If it hadn't been for the great systems Black Water provided, I'd have been as lost in the first hour as the guitar player at the end of the song with the banjo player in the movie Deliverance was."

"Technology," Jim replied, as he eased his backrest down. "Makes me wonder just who is watching me, recording it, and will transform it into an admission of harboring a coven of witches.

"Now, if you don't mind, or even if you do, I'm going to try to get a couple of hours of sleep before we hit Quantico," Jim said. "I believe Gene has planned a short debrief at Black Water headquarters, but knows everyone wants to get home.

"Not to be giving advice," Jim said, laying his head on the seat headrest. "But I'd advise you to do the same since I know we'll be on the same plane with Megan heading for Love Field. And you'll still have an hour of driving to get home."

Twenty-some-odd hours later, after the debrief and the flight back to Love Field, Jim called Marie as they taxied to the terminal and asked if she wanted to come to his house for dinner that night. Hearing that she would stop by Siciliano's for something, he got in his pickup and headed home.

After putting his dirty clothes in the hamper and taking a shower, Jim turned on the news and watched as the newly elected President of South Africa promised every displaced farmer he could have his land back if he would come back.

He also promised to rebuild any destruction that occurred during the previous administration's policy of expropriation. Then he agreed to pay double the value of the farms where the former farmers lived if they didn't want to return.

He then promised to hunt down everyone who had committed any criminal acts against those who had been harmed and assured the country that his administration would take care of all the citizens of their wonderful nation.

'Of course you will,' Jim thought as the doorbell rang, and he went to open the door for Marie. 'Of course, you will take your ten percent before you take care of the citizens.'

Chapter 76

"It's good to see your face," Jim said, opening the door. "It's been too long."

"It's only been a day or so longer than your normal schedule flying for American," Marie said, kissing him on the cheek.

"Maybe so," Jim told her, following her into the kitchen. "But this seemed like weeks. Must have been the damn time zones that kept me wondering if it was dark but supposed to be light, or if it was dark when it was supposed to be dark.

"I never knew if I was supposed to be tired or just middle of the day needing a catnap," he continued, as he took plates from the cabinet. "Exactly why I don't bid international trips."

"So, how'd the negotiations go?" Marie asked, setting two servings of lasagna on the table.

"I'm sure you've seen the news about someone assassinating the President," Jim replied, getting two bottles of Zeigen Bock from the refrigerator. "Well, we were having our negotiations the previous day.

"We hadn't been in the room more than thirty minutes when the President got a call and threw us out," Jim continued, getting two frozen mugs from the freezer. "Then we hear he's been shot before we can make another appointment."

"What about the other guy who was shot?" Marie asked, sitting down across the table from Jim's usual seat.

"I don't know," Jim answered, pouring the bottle of Zeigen Bock into Marie's mug. "I've heard from some of the United Nations people that the President had him killed because of the upcoming election.

"I also heard he was behind the assassination of the President," Jim continued, as he poured his beer into his mug. "Then, there's the other rumor that the new President, the former Deputy President, had both of them killed."

"And you had nothing to do with either of the shootings," Marie said, watching Jim's eyes.

Jim looked directly at her and replied, "I was in the President's office with Megan for probably less than half an hour before we were kicked out. All I can tell you is that he was still breathing and mad as hell when the guard escorted us out of his office.

"Then we're on a plane home the next day," he finished, as he got a fork of the steaming lasagna from the ceramic boat tray. "Maybe the South African police, or their version of the FBI, will discover what really happened over there. That's a mystery for them to solve.

"Now, the only mystery I want to solve is, are you wearing those red bikini panties with the fluffy white fringe I bought you for Christmas last year?" Jim asked, with a mischievous smile on his face.